WOLF'S
REVENGE

Also by Lachlan Smith

WOLF'S REVENGE

A
LEO MAXWELL
MYSTERY

LACHLAN SMITH

The Mysterious Press
New York

First Grove Atlantic hardcover edition: October 2017
First Grove Atlantic paperback edition: October 2018

Published simultaneously in Canada
Printed in the United States of America

ISBN 978-0-8021-2872-0
eISBN 978-0-8021-8929-5

Library of Congress Cataloging-in-Publication data is available for this title.

The Mysterious Press
an imprint of Grove Atlantic
154 West 14th Street
New York, NY 10011

Distributed by Publishers Group West

groveatlantic.com

18 19 20 21 10 9 8 7 6 5 4 3 2 1

To Sarah

CHAPTER 1

"Where's Carly?"

"Didn't she go with you?"

"Did we *say* she was going with us?" Jeanie asked.

My brother Teddy and I stood up and began looking in every direction. We were in the cheap seats high in the Coliseum, watching the A's trounce the Devil Rays. Only five years old, my niece wouldn't have wandered away by herself. She must have tagged along behind Tamara and Jeanie when they'd gone for food.

My mind went to the guy about my age who'd been sitting two rows behind us. I'd noted him because he had the look of someone who'd recently been in prison. The popping muscles of his upper body, clearly the result of many hours spent pushing weights, weren't typical for a civilian, nor were the tattoos visible on his arms and neck, the faded colors and gothic lettering of prison art.

How easy for him to have noticed the child following her absentminded mother, and, at the same time, the distraction of my brother Teddy and me.

I high-stepped over the seatback. Behind me, Jeanie, my brother's ex-wife, like an aunt to Carly, was on the phone, while Tamara, Carly's mother, scanned the crowd. "I'm calling security," Jeanie said.

"We've lost our little girl," I shouted to the nearest usher as I entered the cavern-like concourse. I paused briefly to give the man a description of Carly, which he dutifully repeated into his walkie-talkie: tall for her age at four-four, light-skinned but visibly African-American, with a narrow face and wide eyes beneath cornrows and beads her mother had painstakingly woven.

One thought simultaneously heartened and chilled me. If the man I'd noticed earlier had taken her, this likely was no random abduction. Far more probable was that Carly had been targeted by a man named Bo Wilder. If Wilder had ordered this, it was to send a message, one to my brother Teddy or to me. Wilder had no reason to hurt Carly.

Not unless one of us had given him one.

Whenever I passed an usher or a security guard I shouted my alarm about a lost girl. I'd run a near-complete circle of the stadium before my phone vibrated. It was Teddy. "We found her," he said. "A guy brought her back."

I slowed to a walk, but only for a moment. Then I began to jog again. My brother, his instincts dulled by the massive brain injury he'd suffered nine years before, was unlikely to have noticed the stranger who'd been sitting behind us, and even more unlikely, now, to think back and suspect him. As for Jeanie, I was unsure how much she knew or guessed.

I arrived at our section and slowed, trying to look casual as I came down the stairs, my hard breathing reminding me how long it'd been since I'd ridden my bike. The man with the prison muscles was there, talking to Jeanie. Carly stood looking down at a little mascot doll he must have bought for her. I came down the steps behind them and grabbed the guy's arm.

He turned, his smile betraying no sign of the pressure I was exerting just above his massive triceps, his arm as thick around as the leg of a sedentary man, his head shaved bald. I pulled out my cell phone and suggested that Carly pose for a picture with the man.

His expression didn't fade as I snapped a series of shots. His hand remained on Carly's shoulder, but his eyes never left my face.

He'd already explained to the others what had happened. Now he told me. "I walked up right behind the ladies and the girl," he said. "When I come out of the washroom, I saw her standing there, looking like she was gonna start crying any minute. I figured her mom was in the head, but she was too little to be waiting by herself. When I was coming back from getting a hot dog she hadn't moved. I bought her the doll to cheer her up, then right away I escorted her back here."

Teddy shook hands with the man. "Thank you," he said with relief.

"Don't mention it," the guy told him. "Call me Jack." But even as he addressed Teddy, his eyes returned to me, communicating a wordless message none the less brutal for being indecipherable. I shot Jeanie a look. She frowned, her warning instinct aroused, but she seemed not to know what to do. None of us did. Carly was fine. Nothing, it seemed, had happened.

So "Jack" reclaimed his seat behind us, and we all sat down and resumed watching the game. After two innings, Tamara was still restlessly stroking her daughter's hair. Like his wife, Teddy was silent beside me, often reaching up to touch the child's arm or shoulder as if reassuring himself she was still there.

Don't blame yourselves, I wanted to tell them. *It wasn't your fault.* I knew, however, that any reassurance I could offer would be hollow. It's an objective truth that no parent can watch his or her child every minute. Kids need freedom, at least within certain boundaries, and most parents' attention occasionally lapses. The thing is, 99 percent of the time nothing terrible happens to the kid.

Teddy and Tamara weren't "most parents," however. They'd met when both were residents in the same brain injury rehabilitation clinic. There, they'd been tasked with relearning how to live on their own, how to dress and feed themselves. Teddy had been shot in the head, and, though he'd already made a recovery beyond all reasonable medical expectations, his chances of ever being able to live on his own still had seemed slim. Tamara's brain had been ravaged by a virus, leaving her without the ability to form new short-term memories. At a time when they were each scoured shells of their former selves, they'd fallen in love.

Defying their doctors' prognoses, the couple had achieved a remarkable, shared self-sufficiency. Teddy, whom we'd once feared would remain bed-bound and speechless, had even regained his law license, though he would never again try a case in San Francisco's criminal courtrooms. Tamara now made a modest living as a children's book illustrator and graphic designer. They owned a small cottage in Berkeley, purchased with settlement funds from a case I'd filed for Tamara in 2003. Though they'd learned to care for themselves, that didn't mean they were qualified to raise a child. But who was?

They'd proved excellent, if occasionally forgetful, parents, rising to their newfound responsibility. Still, there were lapses that gave us pause. Even now, if I was honest with myself, a nagging doubt remained in the back of my mind. When Carly became older, a teenager, maybe it wouldn't matter that her dad couldn't navigate the Bay Area's freeway system, or that her mom had little ability to recall events she hadn't written down. Yet the simple fact was that their impairments weren't going to improve much more, if at all. I kept expecting the old Teddy to step out of the new Teddy's shell, but that person was gone forever.

Among the four of us, I was the only one who suspected that this incident almost certainly wasn't their fault. The stranger—"Jack"—had cut Carly away from her mother and Jeanie with the skill of a wolf working the herd. That's all we were to these people, in the end: sheep good for shearing while the season lasted. When the time came, we'd be led to the slaughter without a second thought.

After the sixth inning I rose with the excuse of getting another beer. Normally my brother would've joined me, but now he had no interest in leaving Carly's side. She was bent over watching a movie on Jeanie's phone while the rest of us stared down at the field, pretending to follow the game that in the space of an hour had lost much of its meaning.

When I reached the top of the steps I glanced back and saw that the man who'd called himself Jack also had risen. I waited at the top of the stairs, but he passed me without a glance. He was about five-nine, wearing a Giants windbreaker and a pair of cargo pants, and on his feet, Vans. I fell in step behind him, drawing from him a quick disparaging over-the-shoulder look. We walked together until we came to an area where there were no people around, a part of the stadium in which all the concession stands were closed and shuttered, adjoining one of the deserted sections of stands.

As soon as there was no one around he grabbed my arm and slammed me against the concrete wall. He pushed his face close to mine, and I felt his hand crush my balls. "You want to squeeze my arm now, motherfucker?"

I was in too much pain to reply, my guts churning. Such men, having burned my office a year ago, had already proved they'd use any means at their disposal to intimidate and control me.

He let go, and I sagged against the wall, coughing and gasping. "My niece is off-limits," I managed to say. "You have a problem, take it up with me."

"Somebody's under the impression you're not getting the message."

"Then maybe someone had better spell it out."

"Okay, how about that deal you made for that kid last week? He snitches on some year-old murder, gets two years? What the hell?"

I'd broken a sweat. "It wasn't connected with Wilder's business."

"How would you even know that?"

"Because if it had been Bo whom the kid agreed to testify against, I'd be dead, instead of playing this bullshit game with you." I pushed myself off the wall and, as well as I was able to, stood facing my assailant. But I had no illusions about my chances against him in a fight, fair or otherwise.

He studied me for a moment, then gave a laugh. "Fucking lawyers."

"That's right. I'm a lawyer. And these people your boss sends me are my clients, and I'm going to do right by them. Someday he might appreciate that, when a person he actually cares about gets jacked. You, for instance."

"Don't worry, he doesn't give a shit about me."

"Be that as it may, if Bo's got so little trust, maybe he ought to just fire me and find some other lawyer."

"He's *got* other lawyers. You think you're special? I heard he fired one once. It wasn't pretty. They found him a week later in his office, hanging from a light fixture. His suicide note mentioned a problem with booze."

Might suicide have taken the life of this nameless, and, I hoped, imaginary lawyer? I doubted it. "Threats don't impress me," I said. "I couldn't *make* any of Bo's people talk about his business if I wanted to. Believe me, none of us has any interest in telling stories to the DA. My clients want to live. *I* want to live. That goes for my family, too. So if you or Bo messes with my niece again . . ."

"You'll do what?" He was entertained, seeming interested in how far I'd go. "You're in a position to make threats?"

"Never mind. I'll tell him myself."

This seemed to get his attention. "You stay the fuck away from that prison. He don't need you on his visitor list. Your value is that you maintain a legitimate law practice, with no obvious connections to the other side of the business. Staying legit is the only way you're any good to Bo."

"I'd say my client list makes it pretty obvious whom I work for."

"Who you gonna represent, the Boy Scouts? Bo and I did five years together. Otherwise, I'd just have come to the office, made myself at home."

"Don't bullshit me. Bo sent you to grab Carly, just to prove he could. You know what? Now there's a police report on file. There's video evidence putting you two rows behind us. Those people in the stands are going to remember your face. What was Bo thinking, pulling a stunt like that?"

A flicker of alarm in his eyes tipped me off. "*Bo* wasn't thinking," I said, pressing what I saw as an advantage. "This was you. All you. Acting alone, getting smart. Thinking how a thug thinks. Only, the way I understand Bo's business these days, thugs are the last kind of people he needs. He's trying to go legit, because he's in prison for life. Meanwhile, you clowns out here are running around doing whatever comes into your head, making it up as you go along."

He stared at me with continued hostility, but didn't interrupt.

"Someone really ought to explain to him how a stunt like this can blow back on you in ways you can't predict. Imagine if the cops had been a little quicker on the draw, or if we'd freaked out when you brought her back with that doll you bought her. It's messes like this that can bring down an organization." I was aware of saying too much, the way I always did when I felt I was in danger.

He waited as if to make sure I was finished. "Listen, Bo sent me to deliver a message, I delivered it. And you heard me, right? The message is, no snitches unless you clear it first. This guy last week,

Bo would have said okay—if you'd checked with him. But you know how he is. He gets word one of his guys has cut a deal, and the first thing he imagines is there must be some secret angle, that his lawyer's trying to fuck him."

"If that's the case, I don't see how he ever gets a decent night's sleep."

He shook his head. "I already said, we were cellies for five long years. I had his back inside, now I've got it outside. And he's got mine. I'm the one who's got to keep the troops in line." He paused. "The last thing Bo needs is for him and me to get sideways." He stared hard at me. "But if you tell him what I did . . ."

"Why shouldn't I?" I wanted an apology, as well as future assurances.

"If you tell Bo about this . . ." he said, stepping close.

His face was an inch from mine. I stood my ground, not daring to move or inhale. At last he released a cigarette-stale breath.

"I think you got the message now."

CHAPTER 2

When I returned, the others were standing, ready to leave. Carly's face now was tear-streaked. Tamara was trying to comfort her, but she kept pushing her mother's hands away. Then as I came down the steps she broke from her mother and wrapped her arms around my legs.

We rode the Bay Area Rapid Transit train from the stadium back to the stop nearest Teddy and Tamara's place in Berkeley, where Jeanie and I had left our cars. I now lived in the city—San Francisco, that is. Rents were cheaper in Oakland, where I'd been based during my first stint in private practice, but I'd been born and raised in Potrero Hill, a formerly working-class neighborhood above the old Navy Yard. After leaving the Public Defender's Office last year, I'd decided to open my new office near the intersection of Seventh and Mission, not far from the Hall of Justice courthouse.

Still, I spent a great deal of time in Berkeley with Teddy and Tamara. I was there for dinner at least once per week, often even spending weekends with them, helping ferry Carly to her various activities—T-ball, ballet practice, preschool birthday parties. Soon, life was to become even busier, with Carly set to enter pre-K.

We said goodbye to Jeanie, who was heading back to Walnut Creek. Even an hour after my encounter with Bo's foot soldier, my hands were still shaking as I strapped Carly into the back of my aging Saab. I'd picked it up used and recently added the car seat. Lately I'd been leaving the thing permanently installed. I figured being an uncle was the closest I was ever likely to come to fatherhood. Each time I got in my car for the lonely drive across the bridge after a visit like this, I felt as if an elastic band still connected me to the place I'd come to think of as a second home. Now, as we approached their house on Gilman Street, I felt a familiar tightening between my shoulder blades.

"Want to come in?" my brother asked, as he always did.

"Yes, come in," Tamara said. But only after a pause.

On a normal day I'd have taken my cue from her tone and departed. Today had been anything but normal, however. The three of us needed to talk.

Carly was overtired, resisting her bath. Teddy, who'd begun to help her, was forced to turn her over to her mother, the only one who could reason with her at such moments. After reviewing the available options in the kitchen, I shuffled through a pile of delivery menus and settled on Chinese.

There'd been a time when I might have said what I needed to say to Teddy in the privacy of the kitchen, leaving it up to him how much to share with Tamara. But, in my mind, Teddy was a main part of the reason we were in this situation. And so I waited until after we'd eaten, enjoying Carly holding forth as usual, the goofy center of attention.

She wanted me to read her a bedtime story, so I did, then yielded my place to her mother, who spent a quiet fifteen minutes lying down with her. Then, when she came out, the three of us sat in the kitchen, Tam working on a glass of wine, Teddy and I nursing after-dinner beers.

They each seemed to anticipate that I had something to say, Tamara looking at me with open defiance, as if expecting me to blame her for losing Carly this afternoon—an event she'd no doubt memorialized in the notebook she carried everywhere with her for this purpose—and readying her response. Teddy looked sheepish and ashamed, unable to meet either his wife's eyes or mine.

I showed them the picture on my phone, the dude calling himself Jack standing with his hand on Carly's shoulder, Carly holding the mascot doll he'd bought. Even now, in bed, she still had the doll clutched against her chest. Jack's eyes were fixed on the camera with their secret message just for me.

"This man kidnapped Carly this afternoon," I said.

Tamara gazed at the phone as if she were seeing the picture for the first time, then looked up at me in apparent confusion. "He brought her back. That's what I wrote down. She got lost and a man bought her a doll and brought her back."

"Why?" Teddy, having already accepted the truth, looked braced for the worst.

"Because last week I pleaded one of Wilder's guys to a deal that involved him giving testimony in a murder he happened to have been a witness to. Today's scare was Wilder's way of reminding me who's in charge."

Tamara had risen from her chair like someone obeying an inaudible command. Without a word she walked past me, through the dining room, and into Carly's room, leaving the door ajar. I heard the creak of bedsprings, then a pair of gasplike sobs. Carly's incredibly deep, slow breathing continued without pause.

Teddy and I spoke in lower tones. "Did he tell you this when you left us?" he wanted to know.

Instead of answering his question, I brought up a topic I'd waited far too long to mention, a failing I was resolved to remedy now. "You and I, we never talked about why I left the Public Defender's Office."

"You always spoke about going back to private practice. I figured you were ready, that it was just a matter of time."

"It must be obvious to you that I've been repping Wilder's crew. You think I'm doing that by choice?"

"What're you saying?"

"I'm saying I left because Bo threatened Carly. About six months ago, he sent a guy from jail to take the place of one of my clients. The one who showed up did a number for me on Carly. Where she goes, what she does, her weekly routine. They even knew what books she had on her shelf beside her bed, as if they'd been in her room. The message was clear—go back to private practice and work for Bo, otherwise she gets hurt."

Teddy looked at me sadly. "You never told me this."

"I didn't want you to feel responsible for my choices."

But I did hold him responsible, as he must have known. Until four years ago, our father, Lawrence Maxwell, had been serving a life sentence in San Quentin for murdering our mother when I was just a kid. I was the one who'd found her body when I came home from school one day, and I'd spent most of my life believing him guilty of this crime that had irreparably tainted my life.

It turned out, however, that he was, instead, the victim of misconduct by a prosecutor who'd sent more than one innocent man to jail. Although Lawrence's conviction had been vacated, he was required to stand trial again for her murder, twenty-one years after the fact. At that point, a jailhouse snitch had come forward claiming our dad had confessed to him on the inside that he actually had killed his wife, making a return to prison look likely. Next, however, this snitch, an ex-con named Russell Bell, turned up dead. Without his testimony, the present-day jury voted for acquittal.

The party responsible for the witness's murder, as it turned out, was an inmate named Bo Wilder. He'd protected Lawrence on the inside while the two of them were serving their life sentences. Now, because of this "favor," Wilder expected our father to dedicate his freedom to working for him on the outside, serving as a check on greedy associates Wilder couldn't afford to trust.

Lawrence proved an able and willing consigliere. But Wilder also needed legal representation, ostensibly to handle the legitimate side of his business, which he hoped to expand. Over the years, he'd invested the money he made off drugs, guns, and prostitution in real estate, with the result that he now owned half a dozen apartment complexes badly in need of a steady managing hand. Lawrence, in turn, had recruited Teddy, who, deskbound by his impairments—a far distance from the courtroom force he'd once been—was struggling to make ends meet. Seduced by the promise of making easy money while keeping his hands clean, my brother allowed himself to be recruited. Probably Bo had intended to rely on Teddy in the same way Teddy's former client Ricky Santorez once had done. But he'd soon discovered that, since the shooting, Teddy's legal abilities were limited to serving wrongful detainer suits. Given the situation, Bo had turned his sights on me.

"We need to call Dad," Teddy said. "I think he's meeting with some people in the city tonight."

I heard the bedsprings creak again, then Tamara appeared in the doorway. She wiped tears from her eyes.

"No," she said forcefully. "We need to call the police."

"I don't disagree with you, in principle," I told her. "I've been wondering all day if the time has come for that. Here's the problem: Bo had Russell Bell killed. Lawrence is the one who benefited from that murder, and the police suspect he was involved. Going to the cops now means coming clean about the role the three of us have been playing in Bo's organization. They'll naturally assume this relationship was in place before Bell's murder, that we were in on the conspiracy to murder Russell Bell to prevent him from testifying, but that since then, we've had a falling-out—not an uncommon event in a syndicate like Bo's—and that's why he grabbed Carly. We'll be charged with murder. Bo's already in prison for life. *He's* got nothing to lose."

Tamara took out her little book and jotted a quick note. When she closed it and looked up again, it was with the shocked expression of someone waking from a bad dream into a reality that was somehow even worse.

"I'd better call Dad," Teddy said, repeating what he'd said a moment ago, as if he thought our father could make everything better with the wave of a hand.

"No." I agreed with Tamara. "Not until we've talked this through. We can't ever have a repeat of today, and threats are the only kind of power Bo knows. We first need to agree on our next step. Then we'll tell Dad what we've decided."

Teddy now turned his anger on me. "When something comes up, Dad's the one you always look to blame. Even after you've been proved wrong about him time and again, you still don't trust that he's got our best interests at heart."

"If I blame him, it's because he deserves some of the blame," I replied. "You would never have gotten this deep in bed with Wilder if Lawrence hadn't been leading the way. I'll always blame him for that."

Teddy's face showed his outrage at my defection. Tamara had never been eager to accept Lawrence into their life.

"You're talking as though you're the ones who get to decide," she said from the doorway.

She was right, of course. Out of all of us, she and Carly were the only ones who hadn't done anything to deserve the mess we were in. They were the innocent victims. At all costs, we needed to protect them.

Of course, that was precisely the thinking Bo had used to lure me this far.

Tamara went on. "When things turned bad last time, after your office burned, Lawrence left the country. He stayed away until he thought it was safe to come back." She held up her little notebook. "I've got boxes and boxes of these, filled with the most horrible memories of waking up in a panic every time the neighbor's cat jumped off the fence. All through the worst of that time, your dad was on *vacation*."

After our father's acquittal, Bo Wilder had sent me a message I'd refused to accept. I'd had no intention of becoming an enabler of organized crime, a role in which my brother had seemingly thrived before paying a near-ultimate price when he took a bullet in the head. As a consequence of my turning down Wilder's "proposal," he'd ordered my office burned. No one had been hurt, but the message was clear: I could choose to make my living through him or not at all.

Caught between the two dangers of the police, who wanted to arrest him for Russell Bell's murder, and Wilder's rougher sense of justice, my father, just as Tamara had said, had fled to Europe with his wife, Dot. There they'd quickly run through the proceeds from his wrongful conviction settlement. Meanwhile, I'd gone for a time to work in the San Francisco Public Defender's Office.

Slow learners, Wilder's crew eventually had seized on a more effective means of intimidating me than arson: threatening Carly in the manner just described.

Teddy rose from the table and took his wife in his arms. They held each other for a moment, and then she pushed him gently away.

"Tell me what you're going to do to end this," she said.

When her husband couldn't answer, she turned and walked across the dining area into the master bedroom. I heard a closet door bang open and the thump of a suitcase hitting the floor.

"Tam!" Teddy called, and went after her, tugging the bedroom door closed behind him. Still, I heard their murmured voices, Teddy's pleading, Tam's alternately accusing and agitated. Not knowing whether to stay or leave, I went into Carly's room, leaving the door open, and lay on the rug beside her bed.

There, in the dark, I marveled at the great drinks of air she sucked in, as if the motive force came not from within herself but from something outside. I could make out the sound of her parents' discussion, two rooms away, but not what they said. Presumably Tam wanted to leave, and Teddy was talking her out of it. Because where would she go? To her mother in East Oakland, where Wilder's thugs could get at her even more easily than they could here?

I must have fallen asleep, because I awakened with a start, momentarily fearful and disoriented, to find the house still and cold, darkness showing beneath Carly's closed door, the night sounds beyond the window telling me no one was awake. Someone had thrown a light blanket over me and shut the door. In the bed, Carly slept on.

I kept telling myself that I'd rise in a moment and let myself out of the house, then drive back to the city. But before I could carry out this intention I slipped again into a deep and dreamless sleep.

When I woke the second time the window had just started to brighten. On the bed a few inches above me, Carly lay on her stomach, staring into my face. She smiled as I opened my eyes. Then she gathered her knees underneath her and launched herself off the bed onto me, like a wrestler leaping from the ropes. I threw my arms up to protect my vital parts. Then, with a laugh, she was up again, running through the door to the washroom.

I closed the door to Teddy and Tamara's room to let them sleep. She wanted oatmeal, so I made it for her. After an exhaustive search I found the brown sugar in the fridge. I figured this was another of Teddy's mix-ups, but Carly set me straight, informing me that they kept the sugar there because of the ants.

Just yesterday, it seemed, she'd been eating her meals strapped into a high chair, scooping mush with both hands. Now she ate daintily, using her spoon to perfect effect. Despite what ought to have been a restless night sleeping on the floor, I hadn't dreamed of pursuit and blood. Watching her now, I was grateful.

After she finished her breakfast we took the dog for a walk. We didn't go far, just around the block—that was all the asthmatic yellow Lab could manage. All its life this duplicitous animal had seized on the couple's memory lapses to beg for extra feedings, resulting in an immovable bulk that he used to maximize his opportunities for contact with his humans, typically positioning himself across doorways or on top of discarded clothes.

We returned just as the sun was breaking through the fog. When we came in, we found Tam in the kitchen with her coffee cup at her lips, staring at the front door with a spaced-out look that suggested she'd been steadily gazing at it for minutes, willing us to appear. Teddy emerged from the washroom a moment later. It was obvious neither of them had slept well. My brother, in his mid-forties, suddenly seemed aged by the restless night he must have passed.

I'd overstayed my welcome already, I knew, especially after the news I'd delivered yesterday evening. Seven hours later, none of us had the answers Tam had demanded; none of us knew how we were going to free ourselves from Bo Wilder's grip. I kissed Carly, hugged my sister-in-law, looked with concern at Teddy, and hit the road.

CHAPTER 3

After a shower and a change of clothes I headed to my office, on the fifth floor of a building between the Civic Center and the Hall of Justice. Working for Bo hadn't changed my routine of spending Sunday afternoons at my desk.

My clientele was standard for any solo criminal defense practitioner—DUIs, gun charges, car thefts, assaults, child porn and molestation. My clients mostly paid with credit. Charging a retainer onto a client's already overloaded card was far more palatable to me than playing bill collector. I wanted my clients to answer my calls. Let MasterCard worry about its pound of flesh.

Sundays, I'd learned, were good for reaching clients by phone. Five had court dates next week, a small fraction of the number I'd have had if I still worked for the Public Defender's Office. I went down my list, covering with each one I talked to what would happen in court, with reminders to dress professionally, preparing one for the possibility that he'd be taken away in handcuffs for no-showing at a drug test. Through all of it, not surprisingly,

Bo Wilder and what had happened with Carly were never far from my mind.

After I'd finished with these, I tried to focus on the files in front of me, but my thoughts swirled around the brief kidnapping. Finally I went to the window, took out my cell phone, and called my father. Not wanting to speak on the phone about the Wilder business, I arranged to meet him for a beer at a nearby watering hole.

Lawrence had returned from his self-imposed European exile last year after I'd informed him that Bo had begun placing late-night recruitment calls to Teddy from prison. At the time, Lawrence had come in the guise of our would-be rescuer. He and Dot lived in San Rafael, but he was often in the city on Wilder's business.

"Teddy told me what happened," he said when we were seated. "I intend to take it up with Bo personally the next time we talk."

Of the three of us, Lawrence was the only one in direct contact with Wilder. Because he was a former prisoner, Lawrence was prohibited from visiting anyone at San Quentin—and he'd never have set foot back in that hated place even if he'd been allowed. However, the two of them spoke regularly, with Bo utilizing an ever-changing series of contraband cell phones and SIM cards.

"You shouldn't be having contact with him," I said. But we'd been through this so many times before that I knew my advice was falling on deaf ears.

"Teddy couldn't give me a very good description. What'd the guy at the game look like?"

I told him that I could do better than a description, that I had a picture. I took out my phone and showed it to him.

He studied the picture. His face tightened. "Jack Sims."

"Evidently he's one of Bo's main guys now, or so he says."

"This asshole? No way. He's on the periphery, a hanger-on. I'm sure he'd like to be in on the main action." He stopped and thought a few moments. "But Bo'll never trust him."

"Why not?"

"No skills. Only muscle, and second-rate muscle at that. Punks like him, they lack the ability to thrive in today's more complex environment. You've seen it. They're hammers, and to them, the world's full of nails. The trouble is, these days the business side of the enterprise requires a bit more finesse."

Briefly, I explained to Lawrence the message Sims had delivered. And I offered my theory that he'd been acting on his own initiative. "Or maybe Bo was behind it," I told him, acknowledging the alternative possibility. "They've threatened Carly before."

My father reacted with shock and anger. "You never told me that."

"I'm telling you now."

I explained about the incident that had precipitated my sudden departure from the Public Defender's Office, when Bo's stooge had turned up instead of my client during a meeting at the county jail, forced me to listen to private details about Carly's life, and urged me to return to private practice.

"You didn't flinch when they burned your office."

"Yeah. But that wasn't the same as threatening Carly," I said. "I had no choice."

Lawrence nodded. He seemed to expect me to say something more—maybe even ask him for help in extricating us from this increasingly dangerous situation. I understood I'd need his help eventually, since he'd done everything in his power to make himself indispensable to Bo.

"How's Bo do it, anyway?" I asked.

My father looked uneasy. "Do what?"

"Run the shop while serving a life term."

"You're asking me about something that isn't any of my business. Or yours. Our role is strictly on the legitimate side of whatever's going on."

"Right," I said quickly, with more than a hint of sarcasm. "One hundred percent aboveboard. You're pulling, what, five grand a week keeping the books on his rental business?"

"Now you're asking questions about *my* business."

"I know I'm not worth three hundred an hour, but that's what he pays me to defend his crew of dealers, pimps, and whores. Don't tell me that's not going to come back on me someday."

"What do you want me to say? I thought offering my services would be a way of protecting my family. I was wrong."

"I didn't need protecting. I still don't."

"Carly does," he told me. "I'll make sure that what happened this weekend won't occur again. I plan to pay a visit to Sims. That way he and I can reach a little understanding."

"The kind Wilder reached with Russell Bell?"

My father glanced around quickly as if to make sure nobody had heard, then leaned closer to me. He gripped my arm, tightly. His whispered voice was urgent. "You must have had a few drinks before you came over here, otherwise you wouldn't say something so reckless in a public place like this."

I wasn't drunk but didn't care if he thought so. "You'd prefer I say it in private?"

He let go of my arm.

I exhaled. "Look, I figure part of staying on top of an organization like this is being responsive. That means not only maintaining regular contact, but also being reachable when split-second calls need to be made. That side of the problem isn't insurmountable. The prisons are filled with cell phones these days."

My father just stared straight ahead, his face set in a look of endurance.

"Just as important, he needs to be able to control his people," I went on. "Hand out punishments, deliver rewards. For this, he needs a lieutenant feared and respected by the rank and file. Someone ruthless, but under Bo's control. This lieutenant's in a dangerous spot. If anyone's going to make a move on the organization, he'll be the first one hit. At the same time, Bo can't trust him too far, out of fear he'll wake up one morning and realize he doesn't need to answer to a boss who's never getting out of prison. So there's got to be *another* guy whose job it is to keep tabs on the lieutenant. You follow me?" But even I knew it wasn't rocket science.

Lawrence couldn't contain his discomfort. "Why're you talking to me about this stuff?"

"I'm only trying to figure out what we've gotten ourselves into."

"Well, don't. You're not paid to figure anything out. People find out you're talking like this, even just to me, then we'll have real problems. If he thinks any of us might run to the feds . . ."

His voice trailed off. His meaning was clear.

I nodded, sipping my beer. Beside me, my father shifted on his stool.

"It's not going to be like this forever," he finally said. "I've got an exit strategy for all of us. Just give me time."

I nodded again. Yet his words meant very little to me. As far as I was concerned, they lacked even a semblance of conviction. If he'd wanted a way out, he'd never have gotten us in.

He watched me for a moment as if trying to read my thoughts, then drained his Manhattan's watery dregs. Taking out his wallet, he slapped a twenty onto the bar. "This is the last time we talk about any of this in public. I'll deal with Sims."

CHAPTER 4

From the moment I heard the girl's voice-mail message I knew it was no ordinary case. She'd left it on the office line Sunday evening, a no-nonsense, five-second communication consisting only of her inmate number and the prearranged code: "My friend gave me your name."

Even as I listened to it, I received the email telling me that ten thousand bucks had been wired to my trust account.

As simply as that, I was hired.

It didn't take me long to learn that my new client had a jail number but no name, having refused to give one when arrested. So, for now, she was Jane Doe. I'd never come across a woman on the operational side of Wilder's organization, though I'd represented plenty of prostitutes in his employ. Jane Doe was charged not with prostitution, however, but rather with a sensational murder, gunning down a man in San Francisco's Tenderloin district.

My private investigator, Car, filled me in with a few details. "The victim's name was Randolph Edwards," he said. "An ex-con, out of prison a little under a year. From what I hear, he was a member of the Aryan Brotherhood inside, which means he was still in the AB after he got out. He'd done six for armed robbery, with the last three spent in the Q. San Quentin. So he'd have crossed paths with Bo Wilder, your dad, and Russell Bell—the whole crew."

"How'd it happen?"

"He was standing outside that Motel 6 on Larkin Street, smoking a cigarette, when your client ran out of the alley full tilt, dashed through traffic, and shot him in the head."

Dressed in jailhouse orange, Jane Doe was five-two and light-skinned, looking smaller than she actually was because the T-shirt they'd given her was several sizes too large, the sleeves hanging down past her bony elbows. She sat in the corner of the courtroom holding cell, her head against the wall. When I saw her, I had the sense her body might be uninhabited, her spirit having absented itself, leaving this hollow shell behind.

I introduced myself, getting no name in response, and asked how old she was.

She spoke without lifting her head. "Old enough to blow out a man's brains."

"There must be better definitions of maturity," I said. But she was also right. California's criminal justice system decreed that a child ceased to be a child the day she committed first-degree premeditated murder.

"Why won't you give anyone your name?" I asked.

"Guess you'll have to figure that one out for yourself."

"Tell me why Wilder's paying for me to defend your case and maybe I'll understand."

Her manner remained flat. "Wilder? I don't even know who that is."

It was the same answer any of my other clients would have given, except that she seemed unconcerned at being asked the question, almost as if she truly *didn't* know the name and what it represented in California's criminal underworld. It was, in fact, a serious lapse to speak his name aloud in this context, and my other clients would have reacted badly. I'd wanted to see the look on her face.

I watched her for a moment, trying to gauge if her ignorance was sincere. It was possible she'd been given my name and number by someone far beneath Bo in the hierarchy of the organization.

"Bo Wilder's a white supremacist, doing life in San Quentin," I finally said. "He still owns a good cross section of the street action between here and Stockton. But, last I checked, he doesn't typically use young African-American females to carry out hits on his associates."

"I don't want any white supremacist lawyer."

"You don't have one." I took out my pad, along with a folder containing blank forms. I selected one and directed her attention to it.

"This is a conflict waiver form. You need to sign it because the money to pay for your defense is coming from a third party. I won't let that affect my representation of you in any way, just as it says here. Nor will I disclose information about your case to anyone else. I'm your lawyer, and nothing you tell me ever passes these lips. If someone put you up to this, then I want to help you. But for me to do that, you'll have to tell me about it. Sign if you acknowledge that."

I watched to see how she'd sign her name. Without hesitating, she wrote in a neat cursive script, *Jane Doe*. When I reached for the paper, she suddenly snatched it from my hand and crumpled it. Then she sank back against the wall, her foot beginning to tap, her chin nodding forcefully as if in answer to some question only she could hear, her eyes boring into mine.

I picked the form up, smoothing the paper as best I could. I'd represented murderers before. Usually, they didn't scare me, especially when they were behind bars. But Jane Doe's involvement was outwardly senseless, and it was becoming clear to me that my client was a bomb still primed to explode.

"You don't have to let Bo Wilder pick your lawyer for you," I told her. "You don't want me, all you have to do is walk out there alone. When they call your name, tell them you want a PD."

Nonetheless, I knew that if she elected to go with the PD, we'd both have to answer for it.

Whether she understood this or not, she now said, "I shot the guy, so we might as well get on with it."

"I can always say I talked to you and found out I have a conflict of interest. All I have to tell them is I've learned that one of my former clients may have been a witness to the shooting. Given that it went down in the Tenderloin on a Saturday night, I'd even say that's a safe bet. That would let us both off the hook."

Jane Doe only shook her head. So I explained briefly what would happen in a few minutes, then knocked on the door for the deputy to let me out into the courtroom. As I left, I reminded her that I'd see her when her case was called.

The judge, meanwhile, was working at a steady pace through the felony arraignments calendar. He read charges to those defendants who didn't waive this formality, finding probable cause for those arrested without warrants, appointing counsel, hearing bail arguments, and even occasionally allowing himself to be swayed to depart in one direction or the other from the bail schedule posted on the wall.

Finally, when the courtroom was cleared of defense lawyers, with only me, the DA, and the few spectators and reporters in the gallery remaining, the bailiff brought in Jane Doe and walked her to the lectern. She was shackled now. He backed up a few steps but remained within reach. I took my place by her side.

On the bench, the judge studied the documents, flipping through the affidavits in the court file, copies of which I'd just been handed by the DA. He made the required probable cause finding in a monotone intelligible only to his court reporter, then took off his glasses and leaned forward to squint down at my client.

"What's your name, young lady?"

She looked up at him, obviously ready to accept the consequences of her stubbornness. The judge turned his gaze to me. Then, accepting as a given that my client hadn't opened up to her lawyer, he nodded toward the DA's table.

"I take it from the 'Jane Doe' pleadings that the state hasn't managed to trace her fingerprints."

The Assistant DA, Jillian Sloane, stood behind the prosecutor's table and spoke with evident reluctance. "She hasn't been arrested in San Francisco or anywhere else in California. We're still searching national databases. Next step is to get her picture out to state and local departments, check the missing person reports. But for now, it looks as though Jane Doe has her wish."

"Mr. Maxwell, I hope you don't plan on making a bail presentation for a client who won't reveal her identity."

I shrugged, then shook my head, a gesture of acquiescence that wouldn't show up in the transcript, should anyone ever have reason to check. All I'd accomplish in asking for bail would be to lose credibility. I couldn't think of a client in recent memory more likely to flee if released than the one beside me now.

"Will your client waive the reading of the complaint?"

"Yes, Judge. And she'll enter a plea of not guilty."

The judge set the case for a preliminary hearing, then adjourned. I spoke a few words of empty encouragement into my client's ear, at which juncture the deputy took her back into the holding cell, agreeing to keep her there for a few minutes so that we could chat in private after I'd talked to the DA.

"I wish we didn't always have to meet under these circumstances," I said to Sloane.

She was packing a rolling file box. "They don't get any more clean than this. The gun was still smoking when the first officers arrived, and we have eyewitnesses half a block away who saw her pull the trigger. If I could ask for anything more, it'd be video footage. You can't have everything, I guess."

Thirty-five years old, Jillian Sloane had been mentioned a few years ago as a likely candidate for an open judgeship. But she'd let the opportunity pass. She was rumored to have her eye on political office, perhaps the DA's job. What this meant was that any high-profile case could be the one to make—or derail—her career.

"She can't be older than sixteen. Girls that age don't just find themselves in the Tenderloin with murder in their hearts."

"Well, she did," Sloane shot back. "And that means she's going to big-girl prison."

I tried again to humanize my client. "When we figure out who she is and why she did this, my guess is we're going to be dealing with one of the saddest backstories any of us has ever heard."

Alicia Dunham, the detective on the case in court with Sloane, wasn't buying what I was selling. "If Wilder's had the bright idea of blaming this murder on a rival, think again. If your client wants to deal, she's got to come forward with something more substantial than a story her lawyer hasn't had time to cook up."

I have a short fuse for self-righteous cops. "I don't see why. The unsupported word of a snitch has always been good currency in this courthouse."

Sloane now offered the voice of reason. "Let's hear him out, Detective. If his client can point the finger at someone in Wilder's crew—say, Jack Sims—then the DA's office would be inclined to hear him out."

I kept my voice level. "Who's Jack Sims?"

Sloane continued packing her things before completing her thought, though she didn't answer my question. "Given the victim's AB connections and your being on the case, I'd be skeptical of any information that points away from Wilder's crew."

I had to make some response. "I'll keep that in mind. I don't think my client's interested in turning snitch, though."

"Because we all know what happens to snitches," Dunham said, putting in her two cents, deliberately echoing words once thrown in my father's face.

I turned and started to walk away.

"Leo," Sloane said in a voice that made me turn back. In it, pity and kindness were both detectable. Yet it seemed for an instant as if she'd felt she'd made a mistake in speaking. Then she stepped forward and actually put a hand on my arm. The courtroom was empty except for the three of us and the bailiff yawning in her chair with a Linda Fairstein novel.

Sloane spoke in a low, careful voice, looking into my eyes. "I'm only going to say this once. If this girl committed this murder because, for whatever reason, she was forced to do it, then she needs to step up. There can't be any gamesmanship. You have to put everything on the table. If you do, I'll help her. If you screw me, on the other hand, there are a thousand ways I can get you back."

A held breath escaped me, a nervous germ of laughter that died as soon as it was born. I couldn't remember the last time I'd felt this uncomfortable in a courtroom. I was spellbound by her candor, so unusual in the world of bullshit we both swam in.

Finally I forced myself to nod. "Let me talk to her."

She nodded, holding my eyes before turning away. "You do that."

I waited for the deputy to unlock the door. Once in a great while a criminal defense attorney has the opportunity, literally, to save a life. The depleted young woman I'd faced across the table would have a very hard time surviving in prison.

Suddenly the deputy screamed an oath and ran forward. I was steps behind her, but Detective Dunham reached the holding cell door first. "We need paramedics!" the deputy shouted, kneeling in the blood next to my client.

Jane Doe's eyes were glassy, staring at the ceiling.

"Prisoner down!" The deputy's hands hovered uselessly over my client's body, which now had begun to jerk and twitch. Her lips moved, but the roaring in my ears kept me from hearing what she said. Dark blood fountained from her neck. With a horrified shudder I realized she'd stabbed himself with a ballpoint pen.

Mine. It stuck out beneath her jaw.

Dunham, kneeling, pressed her thumbs on either side of the shaft, the blood staining her sleeves.

Taking a step backward, I bumped into Sloane, who was on her phone screaming something. As Dunham and the deputy worked to keep my client alive, I found that my legs would no longer support me. I sat in the jury box. I was still sitting there a few minutes later when the paramedics hustled in.

They were the ones who saved Jane Doe's life that day.

CHAPTER 5

You might wonder how a person stabs herself in the neck. I saw the holding cell footage a few months later when it was produced by the government in response to our pretrial discovery requests. I'd left my pen on the table, and Jane Doe had quickly covered it with her hand. After I'd gone out, she'd squeezed it in her fist and pressed the point against her throat, then with horrifying deliberateness measured her blow and slammed her face against the bench. The ballpoint was driven through her jugular and into her trachea.

Once she'd finally stabilized, they kept her shackled to a bed in the locked jail ward at San Francisco General, with a round-the-clock suicide watch, a deputy at her side. For the first twenty-four hours she'd remained sedated and couldn't have talked to me if she'd wanted to.

After that, she didn't want to talk. While she lay silent, the clock hands traced their silent arcs.

The next day, Wednesday, I had to wait outside while the doctors made their rounds, then an intern explained the situation. There was nothing wrong with her vocal cords. They didn't want to let me in, but they couldn't very well deny my client access to her lawyer, and, after a hurried phone call, the sheriff's deputy nodded me through. When the doctors had filed out, I sat beside the hospital bed, the deputy having agreed to remain just outside the door. In the room, there was something wrong with the TV, or maybe they'd unplugged the cable, because the TV monitor high in the corner showed only crackling fuzz.

"My father did twenty-one years in San Quentin," I said, trying to draw her out. "I think if he had to choose between dying out here and going back, he'd choose death. But he's an old man."

This earned me a glance, then her gaze went back to the static on the TV screen, as if those cascading patterns held some secret meaning for her.

"He was in prison for murdering my mother. He didn't do it, but I never believed that he hadn't. I was the one who found her, you see. For the next two decades I held to my belief. And because of this experience I learned to doubt the easy answers, even the obvious ones. No one ever knows the whole story, is what I also learned. When everyone agrees, the majority's probably wrong. That's all I came up here today to tell you."

My real purpose, though, was to make her realize that the world beyond her room here was still turning. Therefore, like it or not, she was alive and had to go on living.

But she said nothing. I sat there, listening to the silence.

"I'm going to find out who you are," I announced finally, standing up. "Next time you and I see each other, I'm going to call you by your name, and you and I are going to talk about real things, important things. Like what you're doing here and how to get you out."

The handcuff rattled on the bedrail. Because of the restraints and the thick bandage around her neck she couldn't roll away from me. I checked to make sure my pen was in my pocket.

Too little, too late.

I went out and nodded to the deputy to resume his post.

~ ~ ~

I was living that year in a studio apartment in a newly remodeled high-rise in the Tenderloin, which made me a harbinger of gentrification in one of the last neighborhoods that still resembled the city in which I'd grown up. In another five years, San Francisco as I'd known it—as a regular place where working people lived—would be a collection of nostalgic images to marvel at in movies set in the past. What had once been a place was fast becoming a museum of itself, an urban playground for the rich, home only to the 1 percent and an ever-decreasing wedge of ordinary wage earners. Most of my clients couldn't afford the price of entry, and the rest of the city was anxious to push them out.

The year before, I'd at last given up the SRO room where I'd lived after my attempt at solo practice in Oakland had gone up in smoke. Living in a hotel, even a long-term residence like the Seward, had given me a feeling of temporariness I liked. Often I'd imagined climbing into my car and driving until I reached a place where Bo Wilder couldn't touch me. But I couldn't bear the thought of leaving my family behind.

The evening of that Wednesday after my client's suicide attempt I met my investigator at my office.

Car was tall and lean, between forty and fifty years of age, though younger in appearance, with a shaved head and elaborate tattoo sleeves like jungle foliage. His accent was vaguely Eastern European. He'd worked cases for me on and off over the last eight years, and in the ten years before that he'd worked almost exclusively for my brother, back when Teddy had been the city's go-to trial lawyer. The details of Car's past remained obscure, but no prosecutor had ever succeeded in digging up dirt on him. Maybe that meant there was no dirt to dig, or else maybe Car had somehow succeeded in burying an equivocal history. In any event, he was the best investigator I'd ever worked with, even if it meant tolerating his frequent unfavorable comparisons between me and the lawyer Teddy once had been.

"So you've got a client who prefers to remain anonymous," Car said, sipping his take-out coffee. "You think maybe you ought to respect her wish?"

"Respect's got nothing to do with it. It's my job to defend her. I guarantee you, the ADA's going to learn her name sooner or later. I'd like to know before she does."

"Your father can't help you there?"

Normally Car preferred pretending our San Quentin connection didn't exist. This was the closest allusion I'd heard him make to my new role in Wilder's organization.

"Putting his past as a jailhouse lawyer aside, my father isn't much help with legal work."

Car looked at me with faint condescension before throwing a curve. "You didn't notice you were down a pen when you walked out of that holding cell the other day?"

"Fuck you."

The Teddy he'd once worked for, we both knew, would never have found himself gazing down at a client lying in a pool of arterial blood because of his own carelessness.

"You want me to find out who she is, okay. I can try; one-forty-five an hour plus expenses buys a lot of 'try.' But I can't just fill in a blank. She didn't give you anything solid?"

"Only the deed itself," I said. "We'll have to start there and work our way backward."

"I've already started, thank you very much. Beginning with the victim, Randolph Edwards. Let's assume she knew him from somewhere, that the motive was personal. By tracing his life back, we should be able to find where it intersects hers."

"She's got to connect with him somewhere," I agreed. "I suppose it's possible she never met the vic in her life, that someone hired her to do the job. Still, she hardly strikes me as a pro."

"And if it was a contract of some kind, you'd think she'd have tried to get away." Car said this as he made a note on his pad. "So what's on the agenda tonight?" he asked, looking up.

"I've got a guy coming by. A former PD client. Name Carl Menendez. He deals when he's holding, and spends the rest of his time hustling to get high."

"I think I know the guy you're talking about," Car said, but clearly he didn't. It probably made him uneasy that my year at the PD's office had put me ahead of him in my familiarity with the characters who filled the streets of the Tenderloin after dark, bit players in a self-renewing, self-consuming theater of illicit commerce.

Car asked: "What do you even want me for, then, if you've got this guy?"

"You're the interviewer, not me. These people'll think Menendez might be holding, so they'll talk to him first. He'll vouch for you. I can't go out on the street and butt into people's business. That's your line."

"Then let me handle it my way."

"Trust me about this guy."

My phone buzzed before he could express any further misgivings. I parted the blinds and saw, standing below on the sidewalk facing the street, Menendez, the angle giving me a clear view of his lantern jaw, his skeleton arms, and a round bald patch in his gray-black hair. I'd met him before without ever realizing he was bald on top. Then again, he was six-foot-four.

We three sat at a table in my small conference room with its view up Mission Street, which at this hour was starting to host its own nighttime stream of commerce. He snatched a chocolate glazed from the box I'd had the foresight to pick up, biting off half.

"There had to have been fifty people within a two-block radius before she shot Edwards," I said, explaining. "Our Jane Doe didn't come out of nowhere. I need to trace back her movements, find out what else she was doing that night."

"I already talked to a few people who say they saw Edwards go down," Menendez now offered. "They were probably lying, though. A thing like that, everyone tries to say they saw it."

Car's boredom had morphed into a look of skeptical interest.

Menendez bit off another chunk of doughnut. "You want my help, you got to make it worth my while. Two hundred bucks. I'll use that to get the word out, so people'll come to me."

I held up a hand, keeping him from telling me any more about his intended method. I pulled ten twenties from my wallet. Car rose and went to the mini-fridge for a bottle of water, his disgust apparent.

"I don't care what you do with this," I told Menendez. "Consider the two hundred an advance on a long night's work. It's your fee to spend however you want. For every genuine witness you bring to me, you'll get twenty more. But I'm not paying you to haul in a bunch of liars. Meaning, it's your job to exercise quality control."

I could feel Menendez weighing the immediate reward of cash in his pocket against the possibilities for profit I'd sketched. Nothing stopped him from keeping the dough, buying a package of drugs, and slinging it free and clear of any obligation to me. He could double his money if all went well, but dealing was a risky business, and he had no great talent for it. Plus, he knew I had more, and he didn't have to risk being robbed or arrested to get it. All he had to do was talk to people—an activity he was much better at than at selling drugs.

"Take me an hour to connect with my hookup and get started," he said, decision made. "After that, piece of cake. If I were you, I'd be paying a visit to the nearest cash machine right now."

"No," I said, shaking my head. "I don't want people who *saw* the shooting, *or* the aftermath. I know exactly *what* she did. I don't need to waste time hearing about that. I want to know what she was doing *before*."

"Then let's talk price. Fifty per head, not twenty."

"Fine," I agreed. "And keep in mind, if this works out, I may have other jobs."

Once Menendez was gone, Car rose. I watched him move around the room, moodily examining the shelf of law books, the view of the whores and other nighttime denizens moving through the shadows and streetlights down Mission Street.

"You want to go and keep an eye on him, feel free," I said.

"He'll do better on his own. I just don't like waiting around."

I'd given Menendez Car's number. When he had a subject, he'd text Car, who'd meet the two at a prearranged spot and conduct his interview.

"Admit it," I told Car. "You were at a dead end."

He shrugged. "I spent most of today going around to all the businesses in a three-block radius from the shooting, looking at security camera footage from the hour before it happened. What I found amounts to about thirty seconds of footage of her running through the Tenderloin. I can't place her anywhere else before she pulled the trigger."

"There must be videos you haven't seen."

"Sure. Some owners wouldn't talk, told me to come back with a subpoena or not at all. Others don't have cameras, or their systems weren't working that night—or so they claim. Others, the footage had already been erased."

"So let's assume for now that we don't find a recording of her walking to the scene. What's that tell us?"

"Someone dropped her off." Car shrugged again.

Car was a superb investigator. But like all investigators, he was only as good as the attorney holding the strings. I'd let him treat me like Teddy's little brother for most of my career; now, those days were over. In the trouble I feared was coming, I needed to be the one who called the shots.

"So who gets dropped off in the Tenderloin?" I asked, to keep the conversation going.

"Hookers. That the obvious answer you're looking for? Does Jane seem like a hooker to you?"

"I don't know." I shook my head. "It's possible."

"She's female. Great deduction. But if she was a prostitute, it's about ninety-nine percent certain she'd have been arrested before, I don't care how young she is."

We were saved from rehashing the obvious by the chime of a message arriving on his cell phone. "Menendez speaks," Car said, not bothering to conceal his relief as he headed toward the door. "Let's see what kind of bullshit he's selling."

With Car gone, I eased gratefully into the familiar stillness of my office at night. In my hours I was beginning to resemble my brother, whose natural talents had been complemented by obsessive work habits. I was one of four tenants on the fifth floor. Only after I signed the lease had it occurred to me how much this office was like the one Teddy had rented before he was shot. The door from the windowless entrance hall opened onto a reception area, but having no staff, I'd slid the reception desk against the wall, where it supported a flat-screen TV.

My private office, located directly off the conference room through a door to the right, was my sanctuary, lined with bookshelves on two sides. There was also a couch with nice firm cushions on which I slept at least one night per week. This left little floor space, making the office seem like a cockpit from which, after twelve or fourteen hours in my desk chair, I seemed to be hurtling through the city lights.

I turned on the desk lamp and slid the thumb drive Car had left me into my computer's USB slot. It held half a dozen files, all the surveillance video footage he'd located during his afternoon tour of local businesses. I watched each clip, confirming Car's assessment that each showed her running, just as witnesses had claimed. But none of the videos showed what had made her run. It was as if she'd materialized out of thin air to gun Edwards down, then had been unable to repeat the trick and disappear.

Or maybe getting caught was part of the job. But in that case, why the suicide attempt? And if she was going to kill herself, why not simply turn the gun around and eat the bullet after completing the execution?

The answer wasn't in any of the video clips Car had obtained, and I finally forced myself to stop studying them. Whatever her secret was, it was safe from me for now.

CHAPTER 6

It was late when Car finally reported in—just after 2:45 A.M. I was dozing on the sofa, my laptop warm as a cat on my chest. His voice was tense, low. "I've found someone worth talking to," he said.

Following his suggestion, I went to meet Car and the witness at the all-night Wendy's off Market Street. Still blinking away sleep as I arrived, I found him crammed into a booth near the back with Menendez and another man. As I approached, Menendez slid out, nodded to me, and left the premises. I took his spot.

The guy was about forty-five, dressed in jeans and a T-shirt, with clear, intelligent eyes that held a mixture of guardedness, despair, and longing, framed by a pair of wire-rimmed glasses with a bent stem that caused them to tilt up on one side.

"No names," he said. "I'm not a junkie. I just, you know . . ."

"I understand," I told him. "There's no need to explain."

But he needed to make clear he wasn't one of the lowlifes I was used to dealing with. "I've got a good job, driving a delivery truck for a company in the South Bay. If they find out where I was that night, they might start asking questions, make me submit to a drug test. I can't have that."

"This is off the record," I reassured him. I glanced at Car, who gave me a nod, which I interpreted as meaning he could ID the guy in case we needed to subpoena him. If this guy turned out to offer valuable testimony, I wouldn't hesitate to call him to the stand. At the same time, I wasn't recording every word he said.

"You were in the Tenderloin last Friday night?" I asked.

He nodded. "I had this knee injury, and I got hooked on oxy. When the prescription ran out I tried so hard to quit, but I couldn't. Now the only thing that keeps me going . . ."

"Is heroin." I finished the sentence for him. "I used to hear that story every day. Or a version of it. In my opinion, what the medical industry's doing with these narcotic painkillers is a crime. Big Pharma convinces the docs to prescribe them, but, at the end of the day, the patients are left holding the bag. And it's they, not the docs or the drug companies, who end up taking the blame."

He licked his lips. It wasn't hard to perceive his craving for a high.

"Just like what I told Mr. Car here, I wasn't anywhere near the shooting. I was over in the TL, trying to scope out some action quick so I could get out of there, get back home, and have my fix. Soon as I heard the pop, all the people yelling, I took off in the opposite direction. I've been in way too much shit in my life."

"It's what you might have seen before the shooting that interests me."

"I saw the girl, if that's what you're getting at. Later on, when they showed her mug shot on the news, I remembered. She looked so young, is why she stuck out in my mind. And she didn't have the same expression on her face that everyone else down there has got. They're either jonesing or selling. I had to step out of her way, and she didn't even look at me as she went past. Like she was on some kind of mission."

"Was she walking or running?"

"Walking," the witness said.

"What was she wearing?"

He easily rattled off the correct details: black hooded sweatshirt and jeans.

"She had a nose stud," he added after a moment's thought. "I remember noticing that. Just a little metal sphere on the outside, like a ball bearing. It surprised me, because I usually think of that as more of a white-girl thing."

I had a copy of her property inventory in my email, and was able to call it up on my phone. Sure enough, one nose stud was listed among the belongings that had been confiscated from her at the jail. I tucked the phone away again and nodded for him to go on. I figured there must be something more. Car hadn't called me out here in the middle of the night just to meet someone who'd seen Jane Doe before the murder.

"Tell him what you told me," Car said.

"Okay," the guy said. He swallowed. "There was someone with her when she walked past me. A white guy. He had his arm around her and was talking to her as they went. Then before they parted he gave her a little pat on the back, and he turned and came back the way they'd come. Walking faster now."

"Can you describe him?"

"About five-eight, stocky. Maybe thirty, thirty-five years old, with a lot of muscles up top. The kind you only get with free weights and steroids."

I looked into his face, the wheels turning in my brain. I was all too aware of the corrupting role suggestion plays in any investigation. For that reason, I was exceedingly cautious when it came to the possibility of tampering with the unsullied memory of any witness, especially one whose story might later come back to bite my client in the ass. The worst thing I could do now would be to plant an idea in the man's head that hadn't been there when I sat down.

But, on the other hand, I had my suspicions, and I had to know if they were true.

Taking out my phone, I thumbed through the pictures until I found the ones from our Saturday afternoon at the Coliseum, just a few hours before Edwards's murder. I pinched it in on the man's face and upper body, framing Carly out of the picture, then turned the screen to show him.

"Did the man you saw look anything like this guy?" I asked.

My witness frowned, squinting nearsightedly. He reached up and pushed my hands back, leaning away at the same time to get a better view of the screen through his bifocals. Then he nodded. "That's him," he said. "That's the guy."

"You're sure," I said.

"You don't forget a guy like that. Where is that, the Coliseum?"

"He's no one," I said, darkening the screen of the phone with a feigned sigh of disappointment. "That's just a generic picture I've been using to test people who claim to have seen the girl before the shooting. It couldn't possibly be the guy she was with—if there even *was* a guy. I'm not calling you a liar, but I don't think your information's any good."

"Hey, come on." He half-rose, then paused, looking down at me nervously. "It *is* him, isn't it? Is this some kind of a trap? Am I going to walk out of here and get a bullet in my back because of what I saw? I won't tell anyone, I swear."

He was shaking, his bent legs giving little inward jigs as if he were doing a dance, only his feet weren't moving. It made him look like a kid who had to go to the toilet, his fingers braced on the edge of the table.

"You heard the man," Car said to him. "Get the fuck out of here. I told you at the beginning, I got no patience for junkies who waste my time."

The guy went with stiff-legged steps. Car and I both watched him until he was out of sight, me feeling a pang of regret at the way we'd treated him but hoping, at the same time, that we'd seen the last of him. I gave him enough time to get a block away at a swift walk. As I started to move toward the door, Car half-rose from the booth and grabbed my arm in a firm grip.

"Hold on a minute," he said, using my weight as leverage to bring his face close to mine. "What else have you been holding back?"

"I'm not holding back anything. I gave you a job to do and you did it. Now let me go."

He eased back down into his chair, his continued grip making it clear that neither of us was going anywhere until we'd had it out. Finally, I slid in across from him, feeling with distaste the way my jeans caught on the greasy molded plastic seat.

"I'm wasted," I told him. "I just want to get home and fall into bed."

He nodded toward my phone. "Who's that in the picture? And why didn't I have that before you sent me out here tonight? Jesus, I could have just been showing it on the street. Save me a hell of a lot of time. We both might have been home in bed hours ago."

"You know that's not how it works. If I had the answers, I wouldn't need your help. Just now, we both learned something we didn't know before."

"You had the fucking picture on your phone." His voice was like a hiss of pressure escaping. "Now, you either tell me the truth, or go find yourself a new investigator. From the look on your face, we just stepped in some shit. How am I supposed to keep that from happening if I don't know what you know?"

The look on his face was knowing, expectant, as if even now his thoughts were one step ahead of mine. I looked away. A tired-looking employee wandered near, sweeping under the tables. Nearby, a homeless guy dozed with his head on his arms.

I looked back at Car.

"You must have known Teddy was dirty all those years you worked for him."

"You've got this obsession about your brother's bathing habits. Long as I knew him, he took a hot shower every day."

"There's some dirt you can't wash off."

"What do you want me to say? This obsession of yours . . . Jesus."

"I'm sure it wasn't all black-and-white," I said. "I figure the jobs he gave you were always straight. Or almost always. I'm sure the two of you never said a word about the alibi witnesses who kept magically turning up, the eyewitnesses who suddenly forgot what they saw. I don't for a second believe that you ever paid anyone, or that you ever held a gun to a witness's head. Santorez had other people for that."

"Santorez," he repeated, as if the name was foreign to him. Except I knew Car had played a starring role in Teddy's most famous case, coming up with the witness who swore the police hadn't announced themselves before they burst into Santorez's crib and found him waiting with his AK ready.

Good cops died that day, men with families and the future ahead of them. Now, years after my brother won his acquittal, Santorez, too, had no future. This was because he'd been murdered in prison on the orders of Bo Wilder. Who, as a result, had concluded that every criminal asset of Santorez's now belonged by right of inheritance to him. This included my brother, and, by natural extension, me.

As if sensing the direction of my thoughts, Car looked away. "It does no good to talk about it." His eyes remained on the door as if presaging the appearance, a moment later, of two of San Francisco's finest.

During my time at the PD's office, I'd probably cross-examined one or both of these two uniformed officers. Most likely they came in here for a mid-shift break every night at this time; it was only that right now I couldn't place their faces. They ordered coffees, then lingered at a table on the other side of the restaurant, keeping a casual eye on the sleeping homeless guy whom it would probably be their business to roust on their way out. They also kept an eye on Car and me.

"I'm not my brother," I told him in a lower voice. "I didn't get myself into this situation. And, one way or another, I'm going to get myself out of it."

I had his attention now, and his interest. "So I take it this guy in the picture from the game is part of the 'situation,' as you call it."

"That's what I'm trying to figure out."

"And here I thought I was working a legit case."

"You *are* working a case. That's exactly my problem."

"So don't you think you have a little conflict of interest?"

"Maybe. But on the other hand, I'm the only lawyer in town who can possibly understand my client's predicament. Because I'm in it, too. You think she'd open up to the PD if I bowed out? We're talking about a girl who stabbed herself in the neck with a ballpoint pen."

Car looked aggrieved. For the first time since I'd sat down, I could see his fatigue. A few minutes ago I'd been ready to drop, but as 4 A.M. neared, I felt the irrational energy of our all-nighter beginning to gather in me for the rebound. I'd given up on the idea of sleeping anymore tonight.

Car, too, was in no hurry, "So what's his name and who's he work for?"

"Jack Sims, according to my father. They were in the Q together. He works for Wilder."

"I figured as much."

For reasons I didn't fully understand, I wasn't ready to tell Car about Sims's abduction of Carly at the baseball game. I suppose it must have had to do with my sense that, in the wake of what ought to have been an intolerable trespass, we'd gone on as if nothing had changed. My father had promised to deal with Sims, but what did his promise really mean?

"They think they have me by the balls," I told Car, omitting that, in fact, this was true. "This case, the girl—I don't know yet what it's about. But I do know that I'm not supposed to find out the truth. It's been made crystal clear to me that she's not to enter into any plea that involves her cooperating with the police. My role is to make sure she keeps her mouth shut. My first task is to get her to trust me. My second is to convince her to tell me what I need to know to defend her."

Car glanced behind him. I was reminded of my father's reaction to being questioned over beers about his role in Wilder's organization. The cops, having finished their coffees, now had risen and were headed for the door without so much as a glance at the homeless guy, who remained slumped over his table, deeply asleep, enjoying a warmth and safety that must have been rare.

Car brought my attention back to the subject at hand. "Why should she trust you? It sounds to me that you've got some idea of using her case as a means of getting yourself out from under Wilder's thumb. Only I wonder how carefully you've thought *that* plan through. Maybe this client isn't interested in putting herself in the line of fire."

He seemed to expect me to begin explaining or justifying myself. However, I kept my mouth shut, meeting his gaze, waiting for him to be finished. He was right, and we both knew it, but it didn't help me to hear it from him.

"I get it," Car went on. "Your plans are none of my business. Thus far you've made clear I'm on a need-to-know basis. But don't also forget, there may be some things I don't *want* to know."

"That's exactly what I was thinking."

Car gave me a pained, exasperated look. "In answer to your first question—your brother didn't start out intending to work for guys like Santorez. No one jumps into quicksand on purpose. He got blackmailed. Same as you. You see, once a guy like Santorez or Bo Wilder knows your biggest weakness, the one thing in your life you won't risk losing, it's impossible to beat him. That's because you're civilized and he's not, and he'll always have the capacity to be more ruthless than you. You know what Teddy's weakness was, don't you?"

Car was right: There were some things we were better off not knowing. Unfortunately, I'd already guessed the answer. "I have a feeling you're going to tell me."

"I don't need to say it, because you know. I see it in your eyes. You learned it the day they asked you where your big brother was going to be living after he got out of the rehab facility. Just the way they must have asked Teddy who was going to take care of you, when they put the screws to him. It was the question Santorez must have asked him: 'Who'll look after little Leo if Teddy Maxwell suddenly needs to disappear?'"

I had to hand it to Car for turning the tables on me, making it seem my fault that my brother had crossed the line that separated ethical criminal defense lawyers from the criminals they defended. After our parents died, Teddy had barely seemed to notice my existence. I was like a piece of furniture he was used to walking around. He showed no curiosity about me, and similarly shared no details with me about his personal or professional life. My teenage angst might have existed in another dimension, a layer of reality he wasn't capable of perceiving.

Yet in Car's version, all the most important decisions Teddy had made, the ones that had shaped his life and, perhaps, even sealed his fate, had turned out as they had because he'd shouldered the burden of raising me.

I didn't fully buy it, and told Car so. "I think it was a thrill for Teddy to work for a guy like Santorez. He was a true anarchist. He loved nothing better than to stick a thumb in the eye of authority, to see a guilty man get off. Tell me this—once he realized the mess he was in, did he ever try to get out of it?"

Car shrugged. "He was smart enough to understand that you only leave one way."

We were at an impasse, it seemed. I changed the subject by asking him something I'd always wanted to know—how he'd ended up working for my brother in the first place. At first, he seemed not to want to talk about it. Then he changed his mind, as if it'd occurred to him that hearing the story might do me good.

"Teddy and I knew each other from when we were kids," he said. "I was in the cops for a few years, and I got out right about the time he was starting as a lawyer. I guess you could say I had a bad experience."

"What happened?"

"Nothing unusual, in retrospect. A bad shooting that got made to look good." His voice caught, but only for an instant. "Here's how it went down. Dude was crouched beside a car and we pulled up right beside him. Suddenly he takes off running. I jumped out and chased him while my partner called it in.

"We round a corner, running uphill. He stops, and I fly smack into him. The gun's in my hand and as I'm falling onto my ass I squeeze off a round. The bullet blasts away the top of his skull. Dude's dead before he hits the concrete. My partner shows up a minute later, following us in the car. He takes a look at the guy, then a long look at me, and shakes his head. He goes back to the trunk and pulls out a rag. Inside's a .38 with the serial number filed off. He lifts the guy with his toe, finds his hand, and puts the gun in it. Never says one word."

Car had never before spoken to me about his past, or even told me anything meaningful about himself. I'd talked about wanting to gain trust with my client, Jane Doe. Now I was stunned to realize that Car was trying to do the same with me.

He went on. "I never went back on the street after that night. I kept reliving it. Telling myself the gun just went off, that it must have misfired, but I knew it wasn't the case. Truth is, I was scared, and I reacted, squeezed the trigger. Lack of training, failure of nerve, cold-blooded murder, call it what you will. I went along with it at first. But I had enough sense eventually to realize that if I was able to go back out there after what I'd done, after letting my partner cover for me, then I was the worst kind of cop, and I'd never be able to look myself in the mirror again.

"As I said, your brother was just getting started as a lawyer around this time. Shortly after I turned in my badge, I got a call. Teddy was thinking about representing the dead guy's family in connection with a possible civil suit over the shooting. He asked me if I'd be willing to talk to him. Seemed like fate, and so I told him yes, even though I knew I wasn't supposed to be talking to any plaintiff's lawyers.

"We met at his office and I described exactly how it'd gone down—what I'd done, how my partner covered it up. I wasn't going to lie again. What I wanted was to own up to what I'd done, get it off my chest. Your brother listened without interruption, without making a single note on his pad. I expected him to get angry, make me feel like a killer, the way most lawyers do when they've got you in a tough spot, even if they secretly know they can't make it stick. But he didn't do that. He listened, and at the end, he thanked me. He said that he believed every word I'd said, and that he was sure it'd happened just the way I'd described.

"It made me feel human again to have told it, and for him to give me the respect of listening and thanking me for being honest. I figured it meant I was going to be a defendant in a lawsuit, have my name all over the papers. From now on, every cop and ex-cop in the city would cross to the other side of the street when they saw me, because I'd broken the code, betrayed my partner. I thought I'd come out of my apartment in the morning and find my tires slashed, that kind of thing. I was ready to accept the consequences.

"So finally I got the nerve up to ask him, 'What happens next? Will I need to testify?' I thought I might even end up in jail, that's how green I was. He must've heard the fear in my voice, because he gave me this sad smile. You know the one I mean. The smile that said he'd done everything right but he wasn't going to get paid for his time and he knew it. The look that made you understand that for some secret reason, it had all been worth it anyway. That if he had to go back and do it over again he'd still take the case."

Car glanced at me, and I nodded. I knew exactly the look he meant, a look that was gone forever, obliterated by the bullet that had nearly killed Teddy, a look that seemed to express perfectly my brother's tragic brilliance in service of a profession and clientele that continually disappointed his expectations and betrayed his faith.

He went on: "'Nothing happens,' was your brother's answer. 'I'm not filing the case. I'd have to prove that you killed him intentionally; mere negligence doesn't suffice. I don't think any jurors in the world would return a plaintiff's verdict if they heard you tell them the story you've told me today. You're not a murderer, and the most brilliant lawyer in the world couldn't make eight upstanding citizens think so.'

"It was like he'd handed me back my life. I don't remember what I said next. I know I thanked him. Probably asked if there was anything I could do for the family to make amends. But Teddy waved that away. 'I'll talk to them,' he told me. 'The only thing you'd be doing is exposing yourself to more punishment. If that's your kick, have at it, but I've got a better idea. I need a good investigator. Come work for me.'

"And so I did," Car said. "Told him yes on the spot. I worked under the table until I got my PI license, and then I set up shop for myself. I took other jobs, but most of my work was for your brother. He trusted me, and I always gave it to him straight. He knew I'd tell the absolute truth on the stand, and that's exactly what I did. Case after case. He never asked me to do anything that wasn't legitimate. After how I'd felt when my partner put that throw-down gun in the hand of the guy whose head I'd blown half off, I wasn't going to cut another corner. Not again, not ever.

That's why your brother trusted me the way he trusted no one else. Maybe he was dirty, like they say. But if he was, he was damn careful not to involve me in the dirt."

"He's told me himself that he was dirty, Car."

"I don't put much stock in that. The thing about your brother is that he was always his own biggest critic. You ever talk to him right after he'd won a trial? Most lawyers would be looking forward to a drink, patting themselves on the back. Teddy did his share of celebratory drinking, don't get me wrong, but all he wanted to talk about after a win was what he'd done wrong, the things he could have done better. Just because he told you he was dirty doesn't make it so."

I made a sound that was neither agreement nor disagreement, more like appreciation. Car's faith in my brother was absolute, a faith consecrated by the loss of the qualities he'd respected most in Teddy. And, to be fair, Car had known him longer and better than I had, at least prior to the shooting. He'd ridden along in the passenger seat of Teddy's brilliant career, while I'd always had the feeling of standing on the sidewalk, watching his taillights speed away.

"Do you get it now?" Car said, jarring me from my thoughts. "Do I have to spell it out for you?"

I wanted to ask him where he'd been since Teddy'd been shot, but I knew the answer. I'd been witness to his acute discomfort during his increasingly rare visits to Teddy's hospital bed, and then to his room at the rehab center. The trouble was that he didn't know how to behave, and unlike me, he wasn't willing to accept the readjustment of roles Teddy's diminished capacity required.

Car's loyalty wasn't the kind that could find an outlet now that Teddy no longer captained the ship. This didn't mean, however, that it was dead.

"You said Teddy never involved you in any illegitimate business. There were things you didn't want to know."

"Fuck that," Car said. "You're going to need help. I owe Teddy. He protected you—that means you and his family are my responsibility. That's how I see it. Don't start with me, kid," he said as I began to interrupt. "Teddy couldn't keep himself from getting shot, and he was a thousand times more street-smart than you. You need someone on your side as ruthless as the people who'll be coming after you if you're going to have any hope of cutting loose from them."

Hearing him say this made the danger real in a way it hadn't been before. I felt a chill, understanding that he was right. If I did what I intended—though I didn't yet know how I was going to do it—there was no question Bo's people would come after me, and probably after Teddy and his family as well.

"Okay," I agreed. "I admit it. We're going to need your help."

"You're goddamn right you will. Now let's get out of this dump."

On the street Car gave me a nod and we went our separate ways, promising to touch base after I'd had a chance to speak with my father about Sims's evident involvement with Jane Doe in Edwards's murder.

Overhead, the sky was beginning to brighten.

CHAPTER 7

I went home to my outpost of gentrification high above the Tenderloin and showered as the sun came up. Wrapped in a towel, I eyed my bed speculatively, then thought better of it and dressed in slacks, a button-down, and the navy jacket I'd bought because it fitted me off the rack.

I drank my coffee black, standing at the floor-to-ceiling window that made up one entire wall of my studio apartment, with a view of the Marin headlands across the Bay between the stiletto towers of downtown. Having put in what passed for a good night's work, I was in no hurry to get to the office. I didn't need to be in court again this week, and most of the work I needed to do was the kind that could be done while I watched the sunrise spread across the headlands. I had half a dozen relatively new cases that required the big-picture treatment: strategy decisions about what motions to file and what arguments to pursue, and whether or not to press for an early plea deal.

My most urgent task, however, was deciding how much of what I'd learned could safely be shared with my father. After some thought, I decided that before I talked to him I needed to know everything I could find out on my own about Sims. With this resolution, I poured the rest of the coffee into an insulated flask and made the fifteen-minute walk to the office, picking up a breakfast burrito on the way.

From public databases I confirmed that Sims had done six years for armed robbery and gotten out two years ago, a few months after my father's release. It didn't escape me that he'd been on the street in time to have pulled the trigger of the gun that killed Russell Bell, the snitch the DA had planned to use in my father's retrial, a man whose own spell in prison had overlapped with Lawrence's, Wilder's, and Sims's. That gun had later come into my possession in hard-to-explain fashion, planted on me by one of Wilder's goons and later discovered in a search of my apartment by the police.

My father had promised that he'd deal with Sims, but it seemed to me that if Sims had been involved in Bell's murder, he'd been overly dismissive of the man. Excessive humility had never been my father's weakness, however.

Armed with these speculations, I called my father's cell phone and left a message. It was before nine, and still early for him, so I wasn't surprised that he didn't pick up. Next, just to be sure, I tried him at the property management office in Oakland, but the call went straight to the answering service. Again, not a surprise. Lawrence spent as little time at the office as possible, and my brother, when there, never picked up the phone, preferring instead to screen out calls from tenants.

Failing to reach Lawrence, I settled in to other work, sending polite emails to prosecutors that would never be answered, but which could later be filed with the judge to show that I'd asked for the discovery I wasn't given.

I tried my father again three more times that morning, and again after lunch, the calls ringing half a dozen times before connecting to voice mail each time. I included no details in my repeated messages but simply asked, with greater urgency in each, that he call me as soon as he could. Though I'd meant to leave work early after my sleepless night, I wound up at my desk past six. I picked up a Vietnamese sandwich on the way back to my apartment and fell asleep in front of the TV.

Still my father hadn't returned my calls.

Friday morning I forced myself to wait until nine, eating breakfast at my desk, then repeated my earlier exercise, this time calling Lawrence's home number as well as his cell and the rental office. Finally, with no more success than I'd had the day before, I resorted to trying Dot's number, which was in my phone for emergencies. When even this attempt at contact proved unsuccessful, I'd become sufficiently concerned to call the hospital in San Rafael where she worked as a trauma nurse.

I asked for the nurses' station, and the person who picked up told me that Dot had been scheduled to work the overnight shift but hadn't showed up, nor had she shown up for her previous shifts that week. "We rang and rang, but she didn't answer her phone."

That settled it. It was Friday now. I'd last spoken to my father Sunday night. I closed up the office and ran down the steps, lacking the patience to wait for the balky elevator. I jogged the eight blocks to the garage near the freeway where I kept my car because downtown parking was beyond my budget. Thankfully, the engine started on the first try. Ten minutes later, I was driving across the Golden Gate Bridge to San Rafael.

It was a blustery morning, and I kept both hands on the wheel as gusts of wind lashed the windshield. It wasn't raining, exactly, but a light mist kept materializing on the glass, hardly more substantial than the fog my breath made on the inside surface. I was sweating despite the chill, my bowels tightening with fear. Maybe they'd gone out of town on a bender and would return in a few days from Vegas or Mexico, hungover and annoyed with me for worrying about them.

I'd been to the condo only a few times. The place had been Dot's before she'd married my father, and I'd sensed he still didn't feel at home there, preferring to spend his days at a handful of favorite bars in Oakland and San Francisco, where, presumably, he managed the real business Wilder had charged him with. Though he'd resisted my inquiries, I suspected he was responsible for far more than collecting rents and putting in maintenance calls.

I had no spare key, but Dot's next-door neighbor did. She was a woman past retirement age, with a bichon that she kept tucked under her arm. Initially suspicious, she grew alarmed when I told her I was Lawrence's son. She hadn't seen my father or Dot all week, and she'd thought they'd been away. I pointed out that Dot's car and both motorcycles were in their parking spaces. Though Dot's entrance was mere feet away, the neighbor made sure her own door was locked before trudging down from the stoop.

She rang Dot's bell and knocked repeatedly on her door, though she'd been standing on her front porch for the last five minutes watching me do exactly that. Conceding there was no one home, she at last turned the spare key Dot had entrusted to her in the lock, and we stepped inside.

"Oh, no," she said, drawing back. I smelled it, too, like meat left out on the counter for several days. For a moment I could go no farther. The dog let out a whine and thrashed its paws in the neighbor woman's arms, trying to scramble down.

I took a step, then another, my head turning left, then right, searching out the telltale signs of the violence I already knew had been done in these rooms. It seemed to me that this had happened before, that I was only retracing my steps or someone else's. Dirty dishes filled the sink, food crusted on the plates, and flies buzzed in the garbage can.

I took the stairs slowly—both a man of thirty-six and a child of ten coming home with my backpack heavy on my shoulders— reached the top, then turned down a hall that in my vision seemed to stretch and meld to become the hallway of my worst memory, my vision narrowing to the point where my mother's blood pooled on the floorboards, set off by the whites of her eyes and the shat- tered bones that had pierced her cheeks. Her empty stare suddenly snapped into focus to become the death gaze not of my mother, but of Dot Cooper, with two bullet holes in her chest.

I came back to myself and found I was standing in the doorway of the bedroom looking down at the body of my father's wife where she'd tumbled either just before or just after she'd been killed. Her eyes were open, and her mouth, too, was open, as if caught in a cry of surprise. She was wearing her nightgown, and the fabric was now stretched stiff with blood across the bloated front of her. The smell was bad, the astringency of spilled blood mixing with the high sweetness of decay, underlaid by a meaty tinge that seemed to invade my body through the very pores of my skin even though I was trying to hold my breath.

So he's killed her, too, was my thought. I didn't see my father anywhere and assumed he'd once more fled in his guilt from the scene of this murder, leaving me for a second time to stumble on the ruins he'd made of a good woman's life, someone who'd deserved far better than she'd received from him.

Then I saw him. One naked foot was visible near the door to the master bath. I stepped into the room, my feet-that-were-not- my-feet carrying me gingerly around the dark rust stain on the carpet, where I could look over the edge and see my father fallen, also in his pajamas. Now I saw the blood and brains and skull bits blasted across the wallpaper on that side, dried trails running down to the floor from the place where the blast had concentrated, as though someone had thrown a balloon filled with the stuff as hard as he could against the wall, and there it had burst.

My father, on the floor, lay with what remained of his face turned upward, both blue eyes intact, somehow retaining their sadness despite the opaque film of death. The blinds were pulled and no lights were on. The stillness of the scene was inviolable. I had a terrible urge to go out the way I'd come and gently close the door behind me, the way you do when you've intruded on an intimate scene.

With the door closed behind me, it almost seemed that the black disorder of the universe could still be contained and prevented from overflowing out of that room, spilling through the door, and pouring in a torrent down the stairs into the world to consume us.

CHAPTER 8

My father's body was laid on a slab, then incinerated to a pound or
so of ash. Maybe it wasn't even his ash. My brother, sentimental, had
an idea of scattering the remains on our mother's grave. They don't
let you scatter ashes just anywhere, I told him, and in any event,
why force them to spend eternity together? If Caroline Maxwell
had lived, she'd have left him by now and married some other man,
probably been divorced again. But Teddy didn't want to hear it.

Meanwhile, Dot's sister had arrived in town and arranged a
memorial service, at which, as the funeral director informed us as
politely as possible under the circumstances, the Maxwell family
wasn't welcome. While the Coopers of Ohio struggled to come
to terms with their grief, we held our own shabby funeral home
visitation for Lawrence.

I sat in the front row while the sad music played, surfing the
Internet on my phone. Teddy, beside me, was likewise silent, his
movements slow, like those of someone who'd been drugged.
Tamara had decided to stay home with Carly, no one having yet

figured out how to explain to her the sudden death of her grandfather and his wife. Car stopped by and spent a few minutes pacing between the chairs and the urn, then offered his condolences to Teddy and shook my hand, whispering in my ear, "Let's talk." But no one else came, not even the police detectives whose inquiries I'd so far stonewalled.

Neither Teddy nor I had mentioned Jack Sims to the police. I hadn't even told my brother about our father's promise to deal with Sims, or what he'd shared with me about his idea for escape. I couldn't know whether he'd been targeted by someone within Bo's organization, or whether the killing had been ordered by a person outside. I didn't yet know which nightmare I hoped was true.

The morning after the funeral, I walked out of my office and a homeless guy, familiar and harmless, stepped into my path. I had a buck in my pocket and gave it to him. As I did, he slipped something to me. It was a "crack phone," as we'd called them at the PD's office, the prepaid kind you could buy at any corner store, no data plan, no frills. I quickly slipped the phone into my pocket, circled the block, and headed straight back to my office, abandoning my plans for a mid-morning coffee.

At eleven-fifteen it rang, and I pressed "Talk."

"You know who this is," the voice said as soon as I'd answered.

Wilder had a Southern-accented voice, higher than I expected, but I knew the regionalism was a put-on. He'd grown up not in the Deep South, but in Southern California, where he'd honed the arts of grand larceny, extortion, and murder from an early age. He'd made his connection with the Aryan Brotherhood in his twenties during his first extended stint behind bars, also acquiring there a spread of tattoos that, according to photos introduced in evidence at one of his trials, covered the gorilla-like masses of his upper body with swastikas, lightning bolts, and nooses.

Upon his release from that first imprisonment, he'd earned a reputation for brutality and cruelty notable even within that hateful syndicate, eventually rising to control the biker drug trade in most of the state, a position that he continued to hold despite the life sentence he'd earned a few years ago for a series of remarkably brutal and brazen murders.

"The man who killed my father," was my response.

"You've got no business accusing me," he said in a reasonable voice, soothing and convincing and all the more dangerous for being so.

I made no reply. But it didn't matter. Wilder went on: "If it makes you feel better, I can verify exactly where I was at the moment your father was killed. They keep good records of my movements. Very detailed. Anyway, I was calling to pay respects, not to invite abuse."

"And not to warn me I might be next, right? If you did, there was no need to call. As usual, the message came through loud and clear."

Again, Wilder went on as if I hadn't spoken. "I'm contacting you directly in an effort to avoid any mistakes. Misunderstandings can be unfortunate. That's because they generally need clearing up."

"Right." Anger made my voice break. "The way someone had a misunderstanding with my father, and it's been 'cleared up.' Believe me, I understand you."

He didn't bother telling me I might be wrong.

"I'm a businessman first and foremost. Always have been, underneath it all. Now, personally, I don't have much more to lose. Sure, they could put me on death row, but I'm used to living with a target on my back. Fuck, my life expectancy'd probably *increase* if I got moved to North Seg. So there's not much they can take from me. You, on the other hand . . ."

His voice trailed off.

"Your man Jack Sims made abundantly clear what I have to lose."

"How's that?"

His surprise sounded genuine. Just in case he truly didn't know, I told him about Sims's clumsy but effective intimidation at the baseball game, and my father's determination to deal with him. Wilder remained silent as I spoke.

"And that was the last conversation I had with him. Either he approached Sims, or he didn't get a chance to," I said, wrapping up.

"It may be Sims is a problem," Wilder at last responded, seeming to choose his words with care. "But if your father thought he could take things up directly with him, that was his mistake. Your pops ought to have known better."

"So Sims killed him."

"If he did, his balls have grown a lot bigger than when he was in here. Now I've got to ask you something real important, and if you lie to me, Maxwell, I'm gonna know it. I understand you're the one who found the bodies, and the one who called the cops. In the heat of the moment, did you tell them anything about Jack?"

"I'm not stupid."

"That doesn't answer my question, does it?"

I answered through gritted teeth. "No, I didn't tell them anything."

"That's good. Jack always was a man of limited imagination. It served him well behind bars, but a man's got to have brains in his head to thrive out in the world. You've told me some things I didn't know. One way or another, justice will be served."

"What's that mean?"

"It means just that."

I had the sense of being caught in a whirlpool. If Sims had killed my father and Dot, I didn't want him dead. Such an outcome would only emphasize the meaninglessness of their slayings. I wanted the killer alive, spending the rest of his days in prison.

I switched gears. "Tell me why you've got me representing Jane Doe."

His tone was one of quiet anger. "You really think you got a pair, don't you?"

"Seems a fair question, and I think I deserve an answer. You see, there's a difference between a man like Jack Sims and me. His kind of job is easy. Slip into some people's house at night, shoot the inhabitants in their sleep, slip back out. Doesn't take much thought—just do as you're told."

"You could learn a thing or two from that point of view."

My pulse throbbed inside my ears. I was astounded that this man could speak to me this way after, for all I knew, having ordered the murder of my father and his wife. We were all expendable—and one day I, too, would be disposed of. The worst thing was that Bo must have understood I knew this, but figured I'd never have the guts to grab the wheel and try to swerve from this slow-motion ride to hell. I didn't pretend to know what justice meant. I'd been a defense lawyer far too long to have any definite ideas in that regard. My relationship with my father had been immensely complicated in life, but now my father was dead, and those complications had ceased.

Revenge was all I wanted now.

"I gather you knew the victim. Randolph Edwards."

"That's not much to his credit," Bo answered. "Or mine."

"Or hers. How'd a kid get tangled up with your crew?"

"Edwards wasn't part of my 'crew,' whatever that means."

I reminded myself that Wilder wasn't aware of Sims's having been on the scene before the crime. Or if he knew Sims had been there, he didn't realize I knew it.

"You wouldn't be paying me to defend her if you didn't have some sort of interest. Let's cut through the bullshit."

"I've never been a fan of bullshit," Bo said, his voice thick with warning.

I was now playing the part I needed to play to learn what I needed to know. At the same time, however, I was aware of crossing a line I'd never crossed before, speaking words that would mean my bar card, and possibly worse, if there was a wiretap on this phone.

"I'm supposed to defend her, but I don't know what my marching orders are. If there's one thing no lawyer has the stomach for, it's guessing. She won't talk to me, won't even tell me her name. *You* won't talk to me. And yet it's been made clear to me in no uncertain terms that I'm to do the right thing, or else. So how the hell am I supposed to know what the right thing is?"

"You read too much into the situation. The first thing you got to remember is maybe the girl doesn't have nothing to do with me. Maybe it's like—what do you call it? Pro bono."

"You said Edwards wasn't part of your crew. But he did time with you, and I'm guessing when I get the autopsy report I'm going to see some AB tattoos. If I were the government, the way I'd see the case is Edwards got out of prison and decided he wanted to walk away, start a new life for himself. But the only way you leave the Aryan Brotherhood is in a box."

"Right as far as it goes. But I never heard of the Brotherhood using a girl to do a man's job. Especially a black girl."

This was the essential paradox of the situation, as I'd realized from the beginning, that an African-American teenager should have murdered a white member of the Aryan Brotherhood and then have her defense paid for by that organization.

Bo went on. "Now you listen to me. And I'm only going to say this once. You told me she hasn't been talking to you. The way you said that, you almost made it sound like a bad thing. But in my mind, the right to remain silent is one of the most sacred rights we have in this beautiful justice system."

I wanted to respond with any number of comments, the first being that no one tells me to muzzle my clients. But I held my tongue. As Wilder had boasted, he had little to lose. The thought of the misery this man could bring down on my family was almost enough to make me reconsider my as-yet-inchoate plan for revenge.

That he didn't have much to lose didn't mean he had no weaknesses, however.

"I hear you," I told him. "I've always believed in the right of silence myself. It's not easy working in the dark, but on the other hand, there's something to be said for liberating a lawyer from bad facts. There's no dispute she shot the man. It's not as though she could tell me anything that would get her off the hook. I'm more concerned about finding out who gunned my father down."

"I told you, I'm working on that," he said impatiently. "Justice will be done."

"Will it?" I remembered the hypothesis I'd shared with my father about the structure of Wilder's business, with one trusted lieutenant on the outside and another whose job it would be to make sure the first lieutenant stayed within his scope of power. "With my father gone, I'm wondering who's left on the outside that you can trust. Maybe you're wondering the same thing. Maybe that's why you called."

"I don't 'wonder,'" Bo said. "When you're on the wrong side, you'll be the last to know."

My blood was pounding. Before I could muster a reply, the phone beeped in my ear.

Wilder's voice was gone.

CHAPTER 9

In the aftermath of the murders, I had little appetite for legal work. Even on a busy street at the height of the midday rush, the world seemed to have receded behind an invisible screen, muffling sound, slowing everything to the dulled pace of my thoughts, weary and overburdened from constant fear and lack of sleep. More than anything else, I wanted to be with my family, with Teddy, Tamara, and Carly, preferably far from Wilder's reach. But there was nowhere for us to go. I had to earn a living, and so did Teddy. We'd been ridden by men like Wilder all our lives. Maybe we should have been used to it, but I couldn't resign myself.

My feelings for my father were too complicated to produce an emotion with a simple name. Not that I was so naïve as to think grief was ever simple for anyone. However, it's hard to believe that many sons, looking back, would be able to find the multitude of reasons for self-blame that I did in those weeks after Lawrence's death.

This was in no small part because his demise was something I'd actively desired most of my life—during those twenty-one years when, like the rest of the world, I'd blamed him for my mother's murder. I'd spent so long wishing to be fatherless that it was difficult not to regard what had happened as delayed gratification. There were moments, even, when I caught myself feeling a sense of relief. I now saw that our reconciliation had been an eyeblink compared with the length of our estrangement.

~ ~ ~

I owed a visit to my client, Jane Doe. In preparation for this visit I printed out color copies of the picture I'd taken of Jack Sims with Carly. I'd intended to crop my niece out of the photo, yet some instinct told me to leave her in.

My client was still on the jail ward at the hospital. I rode the elevator up to 7D, showed my bar card and driver's license, submitted to the usual search, and was admitted to the room where she remained on suicide watch, the self-inflicted wound on her neck still heavily bandaged.

"I broke my promise," I said. "I told you that next time I came here I'd call you by your name."

Her eyes narrowed, showing a mixture of belligerence and boredom. This told me she'd resigned herself to being alive, at least. Her voice was as flat as her affect. "I'm going to fire you, I decided. Go with the public defender."

This struck me as a promising sign. "That would make my life much simpler. But let me show you something first." At first she made no move to take the photograph of Sims and Carly from my hand, as if nothing I could show her could possibly be of interest. Then her eyes locked on Sims's face, and her hand jerked toward the picture. She arrested the motion, however, a door seeming to slam closed on the fear that in that unguarded moment had filled her eyes.

"Who's that supposed to be?" she asked, turning her face away.

"A man named Jack Sims. He was an associate of Bo Wilder's in prison."

A silence followed, filled with the tension of unspoken things. I sensed her wanting to make some retort, but none came.

She swallowed—painfully, it seemed, because the action brought tears to her eyes, and her hand went to the bandage at her throat. "What happened to her?" she finally asked in a voice very different from her voice of a moment ago.

I managed to keep the fear out of my voice. "I'm not sure. I only wanted to see if you recognized the man."

I held out my hand for the picture, wanting it back, but she wasn't ready for me to take it yet. She folded the page down the middle, making a crease between Carly and her abductor, leaving only Carly visible, on her shoulder Sims's disembodied hand.

I wondered what she saw there. She wouldn't identify Carly as my niece, my niece's skin being dark enough that no outsider would guess we were related. No, Jane was more likely to glimpse herself in that photo, or, rather, the child she must've been before evil entered her life.

What'd he do to you? I wanted to ask, but knew I'd get no answer. If I was going to learn anything, I'd have to let the questions come from her.

"She's in danger, isn't she?" she said. "Did someone stop him?"

Not understanding what she meant, I shook my head. "I'm afraid you're the only one who can do that." I spoke gently, then paused. "I know Sims was there the night of Edwards's shooting. How he's connected to you, I can't guess. The police don't know about this, though. At least not yet. And I don't intend to point out to them the witness my investigator found. Still, if one person saw you with him, others probably did."

She stared at me. "You ought to be telling me to keep my mouth shut."

"Keeping your mouth shut's guaranteed to get you life in prison."

"Not keeping my mouth shut will probably get me killed."

I could only shrug. "It's possible you're not as easy to kill as you think. And judging by recent events, it seems death's a risk you're willing to take."

"That was a mistake. I'm *not* going out that way." Her voice was emphatic.

"I'm very glad to hear it." Mine was emphatic, too.

Shifting gears, she asked, "Where'd you get that picture?"

"It's my niece in the photo. And she's why Wilder thinks he can count on me to help you keep your mouth shut."

"You're saying they threatened your family."

It made her angry, I saw. She wasn't cynical or indifferent about my troubles. The picture of Carly, I intuited, had brought my situation into alignment with hers.

"I'm no more interested in furthering the plans of these men than you are," I assured her. "It wasn't your idea to shoot that man, was it? Just tell me that."

Quickly, her anger reverted back to wariness, and I saw I'd made a mistake trying to steer the conversation back to what she'd done. I waited for her to speak—if she was going to speak—but her jaw remained set. Her eyes sought the corner of the room.

I stayed a few more minutes, waiting to see if she'd relent and tell me what I needed to know to save her life, but she said no more.

~ ~ ~

Returning to the office, I shut it up for the day and drove across the Bay to my brother's house, arriving just after 4 P.M. Tamara and Carly were out. I found Teddy sitting on a lawn chair in the backyard, a half-dozen beer bottles scattered around him.

Hearing my greeting, he turned his head. Then he nodded and gestured toward the house—an invitation, I took it, to fetch myself a beer from the fridge. "Tam and Carly went to her mother's this morning," he said when I came back out. "Tam hasn't let me tell Carly yet about Dad and Dot. I'm not sure how long she intends to keep it from her. Maybe the rest of her life."

"I don't know how you can make a child understand death. Let alone murder. I can't understand it. It might be better if she doesn't know—if she just thinks they simply went away."

"You're probably right," Teddy said. He sounded unconvinced.

For a moment neither of us spoke. At last I put the question to him as gently as I could. "Are they staying at Debra's tonight?"

"Tam just said they were going there. I didn't ask her when they were coming back. But she had stuff packed, so I'm guessing it won't be tonight. I didn't argue with her. I'd have done the same if I were her. Oh, Leo. What have I gotten my family into?"

"I'd say the better question is who and what Dad got himself mixed up with. If you know anything about it, now's the time to tell me. There must have been things he didn't want me to know."

Teddy shrugged, seemingly torn. "There was something," he finally said. He regarded the empty bottle in his hand. "How about you get me another beer."

I fetched two more. When I came back out he was sitting lower in his chair and seemed to have resolved something.

"Did it surprise you that none of Bo's crew showed up at the funeral?" he asked.

"Not really. I never thought of Dad as part of that crew. I mean, Bo protected Dad inside prison, but Dad never spilled blood for them. From what I understand, a person's not part of the Brotherhood unless he's killed someone to get in."

"It's not always an either-or thing," Teddy said. "Need has a way of changing old fixed ideas. You were right about our cover story—it *was* a bunch of bullshit we told you about running Bo's rental properties. I mean, I was doing that, but it's not what Bo needed us for. He wanted someone he could trust to keep an eye on the guys who were supposed to be keeping *their* eyes on his business."

"That's not good," I said. It was, in fact, horrible, exactly what I'd feared. "I can imagine those guys wouldn't like the idea of an outsider looking over their shoulders, assuming they ever found out."

"I don't see how anyone could keep it a secret, or that Bo even wanted to. In fact, I think the point was them knowing he was checking up. Bo would give Dad little errands, people he was supposed to talk to, projects he needed to verify. Dad was his eyes on the outside, so to speak. But you know what I think now? I think Dad's real purpose was to be like the canary in the coal mine. Because, as you say, it was an obvious provocation, sending a guy like him to look over the shoulders of these big badass white supremacist ex-cons. Everyone knew Dad was protected. So as long as he stayed alive, Bo could be sure his protection was still good, and that his organization was still under control. But the minute something happened to Dad . . ."

"He'd know the game was on."

Teddy shook his head slowly. "There are only two possibilities. Either Bo withdrew his protection, or the forces arraying themselves against him didn't give a shit."

"So, basically, you're telling me we may have inserted ourselves into a war."

"Could be killing Dad was just a way of sending a message. To Wilder. There might not have been anything personal about it, in connection with us."

"It was pretty fucking personal to me," I retorted.

"To me, too, obviously," he quickly assured me. "I'm just trying to say this could be the end of it as far as we're concerned. As you said, Dad wasn't really part of Bo's crew, and neither are we. We're on the sidelines now."

"I don't intend to remain on the sidelines. Because if it's not Bo, it's going to be some other asshole breathing down our necks. I'm tired of it, and I'd think you should be, too."

"What's that mean?"

"I'm wondering if, between the two of us, we might be able to put together a case."

"What do you mean?"

Instead of answering his question directly I said, "How long have you been working for Bo—a year and a half?"

"Around that." Teddy still seemed uncertain.

"Even though you've been on the periphery, during that time you must have gained some knowledge of how his organization works. Who the players are, how the money moves."

Teddy made a helpless gesture. "Dad probably could have laid it all out for you, but I mostly minded my own business. I stayed at the rental office, took payments, sent out maintenance calls. That was really the extent of it, as far as my involvement goes."

"The rental office." I let a measured skepticism tinge my voice.

"Yeah, the rental office." Teddy's annoyance was clear. "Is it so unbelievable that a guy like Wilder would maintain a legitimate business?"

"No. Those guys almost always have something that looks straight enough on the surface. It's called a front. Money comes in dirty and it goes out clean. I could see how a rental business might be just the thing for laundering moderate amounts of cash. Tell me this: Do you have access to the leases?"

"Sure."

"Does every tenant pay the amount that's written in the lease?"

"No." Teddy spoke as if this were nothing unusual. "We advertise one rate, but then we give the tenant a discount. It builds goodwill. The long-term tenants, especially, we send them increase notices every year. But most are still paying the rents they paid when they first moved in. Way below market. Sometimes a fraction of what's listed. We came in thinking we were going to fix all that, but Bo told us don't rock the boat right away. And he's right. If we tripled their rent, these people would have nowhere to go."

I felt a near-crushing disappointment at my brother's evident lack of acuity. It was hard to believe anyone could be so obtusely innocent. No prosecutor who retained any memory of Teddy's brilliant courtroom performances could possibly accept this current show of naïveté as genuine.

Nor did I believe it. "Don't play dumb," I told him. "You were keeping the books, accounting for the cash money Bo's men brought in by crediting it across the rental accounts of tenants who were getting a discount. *Right?*"

Teddy looked both devastated and guilty. Tears welled for a moment before he mastered them with the aid of a long pull of beer. "Dad was so cocky, he couldn't see that Bo was using him. He thought he could write his own ticket. But I saw what Bo was doing, and I kept my mouth shut. Not that Dad would've listened. I wanted so much for it to be legit. I wanted to be able to support Carly and Tam. . . ."

He broke off, took a last swallow, and dropped the bottle to the grass.

When he was able to speak again, his tone was fatalistic. "There was a reason I never had kids before, and it wasn't what you think, that I cared about work too much. It was that I knew having people depend on me would lead to errors in judgment."

"I depended on you."

"No. You would've depended on me, if I'd let you. But I didn't. I kept you at a distance. I thought it was the best thing I could do for you, that I could shove you out of harm's reach. And look what happened. It's my fault you're in the mess you're in."

"Shut up," I told him, though a part of me responded urgently to this confession, which scraped an ancient wound. I thought again of what Car had told me when we interviewed the witness who'd placed Jane Doe and Sims together—that Teddy's weakness, the one thing he couldn't stand to lose, and therefore the leverage guys like Santorez and later Wilder had on him, was me.

"Stop feeling sorry for yourself," I went on, putting these feelings aside. "It doesn't matter how we got into this situation. Focus on getting us out."

His voice was plaintive. "How on earth are we going to do that?"

"To start with, tomorrow you need to go back to work. It's important, for now, for both of us to act as if nothing's changed."

He gave me a look of defiance, making clear the impossibility of what I'd asked. Then he seemed to put aside his protest in favor of a more pressing question. "You talked about building a case. What'd you mean?"

It would have to be an airtight case, I realized, with enough evidence to put all of them away forever. The first problem with this was there was no guarantee the police would take our evidence at face value, no matter how ironclad it was. In addition, there was nothing stopping the government from turning around and prosecuting us, contenting itself with the opportunity to settle old scores with Teddy, who, a few minutes ago, had as much as confessed to playing a central role in laundering Wilder's money.

More practically, I doubted my brother's ability to reconstruct Wilder's scheme with sufficient clarity and detail to prove a complex financial crime beyond a reasonable doubt. No, I realized, my idea of bringing the government the evidence it needed to convict Wilder and his associates was a pipe dream. At best, we'd probably end up in prison, which was tantamount to a death sentence, given that Wilder's crew was the main power structure behind bars. At worst, we'd accomplish nothing more than to put targets on our backs for men whose professional identity consisted of an eagerness to commit savage murders.

"I don't know what I meant," I told him, admitting defeat. "Dad told me he had a plan, an 'exit strategy,' as he called it, but he didn't share it with me."

"He wasn't acting like someone who was trying to get out."

"I'm beginning to see that. Jesus, he was so goddamn arrogant, thinking he could pull this off on his own. You have any idea what this so-called exit strategy was?"

"It's the first I've ever heard of it." A note of challenge now entered Teddy's voice. "Sounds as though he told you things you've been keeping from me."

I had to acknowledge the justice of this accusation. So I told him what little I knew, leaving out for now the evident connection between Sims and my Jane Doe case. First, I revealed what I knew about Sims—that he'd been in prison with Dad and Bo—and then, even more significantly, I told him that in the final conversation I'd had with our father before his murder, Lawrence had promised to "deal with" Sims for what he'd done to Carly at the baseball game.

"That same conversation was when he told me about his 'exit strategy,'" I said, concluding my explanation. "It wouldn't surprise me if he didn't have anything definite in mind. You know Dad, always promising more than he could deliver. Maybe he was just trying to keep me from doing something crazy, like running to the cops about Sims."

"You haven't mentioned his name to the detectives working Dad's case," Teddy said, confirming what he already knew.

"No, and I'm angry with myself that I haven't," I told him. "I can't stop thinking of what happened at the baseball game, those awful minutes when we couldn't find Carly."

"So you think Dad confronted Sims, warned him to keep his distance from Carly or else, and then Sims killed him and Dot for it."

"Possibly," I said. "Or maybe it's like what you say, that he was killed because a play's being made against Wilder. I could see how Dad, being an outsider whom Wilder was using to spy on bona fide members of the AB, might have been a natural target."

But, in truth, I didn't think this was what had happened. Our father had believed he was smarter than everyone else, and, as a consequence, had likely underestimated the intelligence of these men whose cunning he ought to have feared. For this, he'd paid the ultimate price. The important thing now was not to repeat his errors.

"Or maybe someone found out about Dad's 'exit strategy,' and cut him off to prevent him from compromising the organization," I said. "Or simply to punish him for having the audacity to think he had a choice."

"They thought they owned him," Teddy agreed.

I looked at him. "Bo had Russell Bell murdered because he wanted Lawrence on the outside, working for him. If Bell had lived to testify in the retrial, we both know Lawrence would have been convicted."

I went on to explain my theory that Sims could have been Bell's executioner, having been paroled just in time to pull the trigger. "You know, I doubt Lawrence would have given Sims the kind of thank-you he expected. And ingratitude is just a hair's breadth from disrespect, after all."

Teddy vigorously rubbed his brow, then his face, as if our speculations had left a tangible residue of fear on his skin. I felt it, too. Evening was falling, we were no closer to an answer than before, and none of the possible theories we'd come up with held any comfort for us. The common element seemed to be that we were screwed. Still, knowing this as a certainty felt, in a certain beery light, like progress.

I decided to stay, and we ordered a pizza. After we'd eaten, Teddy called Tamara and said good night to Carly over the phone. Sitting outside by myself in the cool evening, I tried unsuccessfully not to listen to his end of the conversation, conducted in the family's small kitchen on the other side of the window that opened onto the backyard. I overheard no talk of Teddy heading there at any point, nor of his wife and daughter returning here.

It was a while before he came out with another pair of beers, his face grim and heartbroken. In the silent interim, I'd been trying to understand my reasons for withholding my conversation with Wilder from my account of facts relevant to Lawrence's death. I'd vowed not to repeat my father's mistakes. Wasn't withholding vital information from my brother breaking that promise?

And yet I couldn't truly blame Lawrence for keeping us in the dark, because I knew his arrogance hadn't been self-interested. Rather, he'd sought to protect us, probably believing that by suppressing dangerous knowledge, he could shield us from the consequences of his acts. Though hampered now by my ignorance of all that our father had chosen not to tell us, I'd no intention of revealing to Teddy the channel that had recently opened between me and Wilder, nor my hope of somehow using Jane Doe's case to improve our situation.

Her case was connected to a vital interest of ours—I was sure of it.

Teddy handed me my beer. We touched the necks of our bottles. "To an exit strategy," I proposed.

"Don't get pissed—but I think I know how he was going to do it," my brother said. "Only the very idea of it scares me."

"I'm listening," I told him.

CHAPTER 10

I woke at dawn on Teddy's couch, hungover and exhausted after a night of desperate dreams. In a repeating nightmare, I'd found myself running down a dark street, fleeing one set of pursuers only to come face-to-face with another group equally bent on doing me harm. Forced to whirl and flee, escaping the rough hands that grabbed for my legs and arms, I'd then chosen a different direction—and run head-on into the ones I'd thought were behind me before. And so on, again and again, like a repeating refrain on a scratched CD.

My body was stiff and chilled, my shirt damp with the drying remnants of the cold sweat that had briefly awakened me around 3 A.M. The door to the master bedroom was open, and Teddy was snoring away, huddled over on one side of the queen bed that filled most of the floor space, leaving just a few feet of walking room on either side. The stale odor of beer and sweat was overpowering. I walked into the kitchen, started coffee in the pot, then stepped into the backyard and surveyed the mess of bottles scattered around the chairs we'd occupied late into the night. The plans we'd hatched seemed foolish in the fog-soaked morning.

Just crumple it all up and throw it away, I told myself, feeling as if someone had done just that to my throbbing brain. I went back inside, poured a glass of water and drank it quickly, then stood over the sink squinting at my reflection in the chrome until I was sure the water would stay where it was.

I heard the bedsprings creak. Teddy was up, moving slowly at first but then with quickening speed into the washroom, where the toilet lid banged and I heard him retch, then spit into the water before he flushed, groaning. I grabbed the recycling bin, carried it into the backyard, and began scooping bottles into it. Next door someone closed a window with a bang, a clear rebuke. I winced, wondering how much of our wild talk last night had been audible to Teddy's neighbors, or to anyone else who might have happened to be lurking nearby. This wasn't mere paranoia on my part. From what Teddy had told me, doing nothing at this point wasn't an option. Thanks to what our father had set in motion, we had the choice of acting now or waiting until bad trouble found us.

In truth, it already had. The bombshell my brother had dropped on me was that yesterday afternoon, he'd had a visit from the FBI.

He'd gone on foot, as usual, to pick Carly up at preschool. On their walk home, again as usual, they'd stopped at a pocket park about halfway between their house and the school. They'd had it to themselves until another father arrived with a little girl around Carly's age. The dads had nodded to each other. Then, as the girls began to play together, the man—whom Teddy described as white, in his early forties, balding, with the compact build of a wrestler—stepped closer to Teddy and surreptitiously handed him a card identifying himself as Mark Braxton, an assistant special agent in charge at the San Francisco field office of the Federal Bureau of Investigation.

Teddy hadn't known what to say. He'd held the card, staring down at it with as much astonishment as if the man had shown him a naked picture of himself, until Braxton suggested in a low voice that he didn't think they were being watched, but just to be on the safe side he might want to put away the card. Teddy would have turned and left him then if he'd been alone, but the G-man had planned his approach perfectly. The little girls were laughing, taking turns bumping down the slide on the play structure, instant friends, and Teddy knew he'd be unable to leave anytime soon without causing a scene with Carly.

His companion, in the end, had left plenty unsaid, but he'd made clear to Teddy that he and his family were in danger, with the Bureau the only friend they had. "I want to express my condolences," he'd told my brother. "Your father was a good man. The day of his murder was the worst one of my career. You've made an admirable life for yourself and your family, but it can't last. If you're worried about the situation and want my help getting out of it, just contact me at this number. I'll do everything in my power to see you don't end up like him."

Braxton hadn't come right out and revealed that Lawrence had been working as a government informant, feeding the FBI particulars about Wilder's operations, but it was the conclusion Teddy had drawn. "If you were trying to get out of a situation like that, would you be meeting with Wilder's guys, showing your face, putting yourself in the middle of their business? Hell, no. When I asked Dad what he was doing, he said, 'Would you rather I be indispensable, or dispensable?' He used to brag that, thanks to Bo, he had what he called an 'all-entry pass.' That meant he could go anywhere, see anything. I told him he was crazy to put himself forward like that."

"So now you think the FBI, not Bo, was pulling the strings," I said.

But I was aware, too, of another possibility—that Braxton merely wanted Teddy to believe our father had been an informant, as a means of persuading him to offer *his* services. For all Lawrence's deviousness, I found it hard to think of him as a snitch.

Yet what other exit strategy could he possibly have had?

Teddy, it seemed, had readily swallowed the confidential-informant theory. But I had another insight, and immediately voiced it. "Obviously there were preexisting conflicts within the organization, given that Bo felt he had to use an outsider like Dad as his eyes and ears. It's possible Dad was not just documenting the organization, but also sabotaging it, planting suspicions and deepening fractures. I could see him going for that."

My father, after all, had been one of the shrewdest people I'd ever known, and possessed all the capabilities the feds would be looking for in a confidential informant. As an exonerated convict, he'd have made a compelling witness. Plus, the idea of planting slow-ticking psychological bombs as a one-man insurgency struck me as the kind of activity he'd have relished, and the one most likely to have gotten him and Dot killed.

In the night, with plenty of beer in us, we'd spun it all out and arrived at the only solution that, under a cloak of darkness, seemed to offer a path—picking up where our father had left off and, somehow, playing the game to the end. This meant, of course, trusting the feds to ensure our safety in exchange for information.

Shortly after my father's release, Teddy and Bo had been in contact, he reminded me, Wilder having reached out to my brother in the same way he'd recently done to me again. This, though, was a fact I hadn't shared with him.

"No offense, but you can't pull this off," I'd told Teddy firmly. "If anyone's going to become a CI, it has to be me."

Now, hungover, I saw our situation in a different light. Teddy's household was surely in danger, just as Braxton had warned. If

Lawrence had been killed because he was suspected of working with the FBI, such mistrust would extend to the son who'd entered the organization at the same time. That nothing so far had happened to Teddy, Tam, or Carly might indicate only that our enemies were watching for him to make a move. Or possibly they were simply waiting for the heat to cool before they rubbed out other Maxwells. Also, it wasn't entirely out of the question that they believed they had nothing to fear from Teddy and thus could bide their time.

My brother joined me outside, handing me a cup of coffee, his eyes bloodshot. "You thought anymore how you want to approach this?" he asked, referring to the first step in our now dubious-sounding plan, which was for me to make contact with Braxton and learn what it would take for him to honor whatever deal he'd promised our father.

I didn't reply. Not right away. It was clear to me I'd lost my appetite for discussing dangerous subjects aloud. When I did answer, I told him I needed to think some more. And I promised to call him later.

Waiting in rush-hour traffic to cross the bridge, I told myself that if Lawrence was working for the FBI, he must have recognized the possible outcomes, understood the risks. He'd taken them anyway, believed this was the only course to protect his family. He'd failed. But his failure had pointed the way forward for us.

I had Braxton's card in my wallet, but now wasn't the time to make use of it. He'd made an overture to Teddy, and the worst move would be to run immediately into his arms, indicating we were desperate for protection. I'd worked as a defense lawyer long enough to believe that all government agents were essentially alike. In any negotiation, they started from the assumption that they were the ones who controlled the outcome. To bargain successfully, you had to make them believe that you had something *they* wanted, usually information they weren't going to learn unless they cut your client a sweetheart deal.

It wasn't lost on me that Braxton had approached Teddy rather than me. I didn't like to admit that this bothered me, but it did. Again, I reminded myself not to overlook the possibility that he was seizing on the murder as an opportunity to trick us into believing Lawrence had been working for the government. Perhaps, in fact, he'd rebuffed the FBI's approach, with Braxton counting on our not knowing this. Before I could ever consider trusting him with our lives, I needed confirmation that our father had been a CI.

The trouble was, only Lawrence and Braxton, along with the G-man's superiors, could have known this fact for certain. Our father hadn't revealed his secrets to anyone.

Lawrence's urn—a sealed wood composite box a little smaller than a shoebox, engraved with his name, date of birth, and date of death—was housed temporarily in my office, on a bookshelf. Having vetoed Teddy's plan to scatter the ashes on our mother's grave, I didn't know what else to do with the remains. For the time being, then, it offered a reproach to me, an emblem of all the emotions that had kept me tossing and turning the previous night.

Sitting at my desk, I slowly came to the conclusion that I had no independent means of determining what my father's relationship to the FBI might have been. Still, I couldn't let the FBI know that my father had kept me in the dark. As long as there was a chance Braxton wanted something from me, I needed him to believe I was the key to unlocking the secrets that my father had been killed to keep under wraps.

The only angle I had on anyone was Sims, who was connected in some way both with the Jane Doe case and, probably, with Lawrence's murder.

Later, when Car and I met at Schroeder's, an indoor beer garden in the Financial District, he told me what he'd managed to learn.

"He's staying in San Leandro. Supposedly with his sister, but if she's on the property there's no evidence of it. He's still on parole, supposedly. But from the company he keeps, you wouldn't know it—the house is biker central. Plenty of known felons. Or so I'd assume. His PO must be a real soft touch."

"In other words, if I'm going to talk to the guy, I shouldn't try to do it on his turf."

"Why would you try to talk to him?" Car asked with deep irritation. "The last thing I need is lawyers messing around in my investigation."

To my knowledge, the only lawyer who'd ever done so in the past was me. Car waited for a beat. "It's especially distressing when the lawyer in question has a personal agenda that he seems to be putting ahead of his client's interest."

"You're talking about the picture I showed the witness last week."

"Yeah, you hit the nail on the head right there. I think it's time for you to tell me what it's all about."

I realized, of course, that he deserved to know. So I told him what I'd withheld before, summarizing Sims's kidnapping of Carly at the baseball game and my father's promise to deal with him, followed closely by the pair of brutal deaths.

"And you've kept this information from the police," Car said grimly. "Or do you plan to sit on it for a while and *then* tell them?"

I didn't shirk his gaze. "I plan to do what I need to do to keep my family safe."

His tone was deeply sarcastic. "So you're going to go talk to this guy. That's your plan."

"You have a better idea?"

I thought about telling Car what Wilder had said: *Justice will be done.* He'd also told me to leave Sims to him. But where justice was concerned, I trusted Bo about as far as I trusted the FBI.

Which was something else I continued to keep my investigator in the dark about.

"I might have one, if you give me a minute," Car said. "Remember, this guy may well realize you suspect him of killing your dad."

He looked up then, as if checking whether I was okay with him talking about my father's murder the same way we'd have discussed any other case.

I nodded impatiently. He went on. "Sims doesn't have a clue that you can place him at the scene of Edwards's murder. That's one potential advantage I can see. He thinks no one can connect him to his old prison buddy's killing."

"And he must think we can't possibly connect him with the girl."

"Which is true, at least for the time being. He's got her so scared about who-knows-what that she'd rather die than implicate him. If you could *just* persuade her to tell you her name . . ."

"I know," I said. "I'm trying. But what about Edwards?"

"I'm working that angle. It's pretty murky so far. I told you before, it appears the guy was still a loyal soldier for the Aryan Brotherhood. It's a safe bet the police know about his prison record, and if they do, they ought to put the pieces together pretty quick."

"What pieces?" I was startled.

"I first was tracing his whereabouts before his prison sentence— basic background work. He'd been sent away in 2000. An address history has him living in a house in San Leandro prior to that. Guess who owned it?"

"I give up." I pretended to check my phone.

Car grinned. "One of Wilder's shell companies owns the house. It's probably part of those properties Teddy and your dad were supposed to be in charge of. The thing is, Bo never lived there himself. But that's not surprising, right?"

"Nope." I saw where he was going. "You've got Sims showing up there, too."

"Bull's-eye." Car nodded. "Edwards and Sims were sent to prison in 2000 for two different jobs. Prior to that, they were roommates in that house in San Leandro. Safe bet they were in the armed robbery business together."

"They joined the AB in prison or before?"

"Likely they had a prior connection. Both their daddies had also done time. But before '98, neither of them had yet been in prison."

"You know what they say—the only way you leave the AB is in a box."

Car shook his head. "If that was the motive, Sims would've done the job himself. It'd have been his death warrant to use an outsider for Brotherhood business. Especially an African-American female."

This was true, of course. "I figure Jane Doe was around seven years old when they went to prison. I showed her Sims's picture. Her instant concern when she saw it was for Carly. She asked right away if Carly was in danger."

"Who wouldn't be worried about her?" Car asked. "These people's threats aren't empty, as the hit on your father and Dot proves. That's why you can't just rush in there and confront Sims."

A wave of fear momentarily clouded my thoughts, but I didn't swerve from my purpose. I made the next jump on my own. "So Jane Doe might have known Sims because she lived in his neighborhood?"

"It's possible. The timing works, in theory. The cross-racial aspect is puzzling, given that this guy is a hard-core white supremacist. But I'm thinking what we have here could well be the key."

"If they knew each other . . . Well, it's hard to imagine."

"The trouble with you lawyers is you always want to do things backward. You get an idea in your mind, then you set out to find the facts to fit it. But I don't work that way, and neither does the real world. We need to trace the players, find the facts, then look for the pattern that connects them. We've already got the prison connection. That's a big one."

"So walk me through it."

"I started with a list of the neighbors who'd have been there around the same time as Edwards and Sims. I included the apartment building next door, the house on the other side, the three directly across the street, and the one in back. I ran background checks on the names of everyone who'd lived at those addresses when our two guys were in the neighborhood."

"And what did you come up with?"

"Nothing much. Just an unsolved murder from 1999, a few months before Sims and Edwards went to prison." Car's tone was nonchalant, as if, to him, such discoveries were routine. But he couldn't hide the excitement in his eyes. "The victim's name was Leann Ward. She lived in a four-unit apartment building next door to your boys. All in all, they were neighbors for at least ten years.

"She worked in restaurants, and in 1999, the year she died, she was employed at a new one on Park Boulevard up in the Oakland Hills. The Plum Tree. It happened to be a cash-only business. The place was held up one Friday night in November of that year by a pair of masked men.

"An interesting feature of the Plum Tree job is they took the restaurant back to front. They came in the rear, rounded up the back-of-the-house staff, locked them in a cooler, and gained access to the safe, all without the customers realizing what was going on. After they'd taken all of the house's cash, they went through to the dining area and forced everyone there to empty their pockets.

"The job was going perfectly until one of the diners refused to hand over his Rolex. Maybe the dude tried some kind of move, or could be they just didn't like his attitude. It ended with one of the robbers shooting him dead. But they escaped out the front and were long gone by the time the cops showed up.

"They cleared about ten grand in cash that night between the till, the safe, and the diners' pockets, not counting the jewelry and watches. Not a bad haul if it had been a clean job with no repercussions. But not nearly the kind of money that can make up for having a murder charge hanging over your head."

I saw where this was going. "And it's especially insufficient if you've got an accomplice on the inside who wasn't expecting anyone to get hurt."

Car nodded. "The security camera in the back had been disconnected. The robbers wore masks and disguised their voices. The getaway car turned out to be stolen and was found hours later abandoned in a busy parking lot. The only lead the police had was the idea that maybe someone on the inside knew the identity of the robbers."

"What happened to Leann Ward?" I asked.

"It's clear the police viewed her as a suspect. But what's not clear is whether she'd begun to talk to them before she was killed. I could reach out to the detective who worked the case and try to learn more. Once I do that, however, word would probably end up filtering back to the DA's office here in San Francisco, and there's no guarantee that the Oakland cops would even talk to me. Up to this point, I haven't left any tracks."

"Good," I told him. "I don't know where this is going yet. Until I do, no footprints is the idea."

"That's what I figured. Anyway, this part of the story ends with Leann Ward turning up dead in her apartment about a week after the restaurant job with a needle in her arm." Car's voice paused. Then he went on, saying, "Her seven-year-old daughter was the one who discovered her. At first it looked like an accidental overdose, but then they found bruising on the body. Anyway, the investigation seems to have dead-ended."

For a moment I couldn't speak, reeling from what Car had told me about Ward's daughter finding her dead, a detail that seemed dredged from my own past, leaving me feeling breathless.

"Sims and Edwards were picked up a month later for different jobs. I don't imagine they were completely off the radar for the restaurant killing, or for Ward's murder. All I know is the police apparently didn't find the proof they needed to make a case."

"You say Ward's daughter found her. That means she must have been there when the men came."

"Who knows?" Car said. "Probably. It's just a detail that didn't turn up in anything I saw. As I said, I could try and talk to the detectives who investigated the case, but . . ."

"Let's not go there yet," I said. I was beginning to sense the outlines of a plan emerging: If Jane Doe could give the police enough information to convict Sims for these two cold cases, perhaps the DA would look favorably on a lenient sentence for the more recent murder.

"The question is, why'd Ward help them, assuming she did?" I asked. "Money? It seems like a crazy risk. She had a good job, one that probably made her enough money to keep her and her child afloat. Why throw it all away?"

Car agreed this was the question that needed answering. "My next step would be to start knocking on doors," he said. "There's one neighbor, Jennifer Sullivan, from back then who's still living in the building now. In the apartment beneath Leann's. But I thought I should check first with you before I talked to her."

"I'm glad you did," I said. I was thinking now that if Car ever needed to testify in Jane Doe's case, there might be aspects of the case I'd prefer him not to know. I needed an angle that could lead to a plea bargain for Jane Doe, which he could help me with.

However, I also needed information I could leverage as black-mail against Sims or as a negotiating position with the FBI for my family and myself. In those two areas, I couldn't rely on Car's help. Rather, I was on my own.

"Look," he said. "It could be the reason the police never made a case against your guys was that they weren't involved. The only connection we have is that they lived next door to Ward."

"With guys like this, isn't that practically enough to convict them of murder?"

"Good point. Which brings us back to the question of you confronting Sims. . . ."

"I want his sister's address," I said, deliberately provoking him.

Car rose, his beer half finished. "You're not gonna get it from me."

CHAPTER 11

The address for Sims's sister wasn't hard to find, as Car must have known. He also knew I wasn't about to rush over there and cause a scene. If I was right about Sims being the murderer, that rash act almost certainly would get me killed, especially considering that Bo Wilder's "protection" hadn't saved my father.

Instead, I decided to focus on Jennifer Sullivan, the woman who'd lived beneath Leann Ward. After I confirmed that she hadn't moved since Ward's death, my initial thought was to call first, but then I decided just to head over there instead.

It was a building off Dolores Avenue in San Leandro. Arriving before 9 A.M., I felt nervous. It was hard to gauge the best time; maybe evening would have been better. I was aware that from the exterior walkway, I could be seen from the rental house next door, which, according to record, was still owned by Bo Wilder.

Jennifer Sullivan was about fifty years old. Over a turtleneck, she wore a man's dress shirt marked by streaks of paint. More was visible on her jeans. A respirator mask hung around her neck. Her blond-gray hair was cut short and her eyes were wary. Understandably.

I introduced myself, mentioning I was a lawyer, explaining briefly why I was here. At the mention of Ward's name, she gave a sigh, then stepped back to let me in.

Her apartment was furnished with secondhand pieces I could see had been selected for both style and comfort. Vertical stacks of landscapes were propped against the wall. I hadn't imagined this possible witness as a painter. But I'm not sure what I'd expected.

"The police asked me every question in the world eight years ago," Sullivan said. "In the end, they just gave up."

"That's one of the reasons I'm here," I told her. "To see if there's anything they might have missed."

We both recognized that this attempt at justifying my presence was insufficient rationale for knocking on her door to ask questions about an eight-year-old killing. Still, she said I might as well sit down. Two of the four kitchen chairs were free of clutter. She microwaved water for tea, brought me a mug with a tea bag in it, then dropped into the other chair.

"What case are you working on that might be related to Leann's death?"

I told her I wasn't free to discuss it. Dissatisfied with this answer, she lit a cigarette.

It was my turn now to ask a question. "What makes you say the police gave up in the end?"

She blew a cloud of smoke, then stabbed out the cigarette in an angry gesture that suggested the police's failure to delve into Leann's murder was simply one in the series of grievances that composed her life.

"I knew her better than practically anyone. Better than anyone else in this building, that's for sure. Every time she or her daughter moved up there, I'd hear it. And late at night after she got home, she used to sit out on her balcony, and I'd sit on my porch, and we'd talk even though we couldn't see each other."

"What was her daughter's name?"

"Alice." Hearing this, I felt brief elation, followed by sadness. Alice Ward. It now seemed no victory to uncover what my client had sought to hide from the world.

"I'd like to find Alice and talk to her about her mother," I said. In the deeper sense, this was, of course, true. "What happened to her after she discovered Leann dead?"

"I heard the yelling and ran down. I saw Leann, lying there with the needle in her arm. Alice was shaking her, saying, 'Wake up, Mommy! Wake up!' but her eyes were open, staring. That wasn't Leann. She was no druggie. I knew right away things weren't what they seemed, that she wouldn't have given it all up for a needle. I got Alice out of there and up to my apartment, called 911.

"I had Alice here with me for a few days. Then Social Services came. I'd love to believe she turned out all right, but I guess I know better."

I kept my face neutral. "Maybe the police were wrong. Maybe it was an accidental overdose, just as it seemed."

She shook her head. "Someone held her down, covered her mouth while they injected her. She couldn't have given herself those bruises."

"I'm a criminal defense attorney," I told her. "We never seem to run out of cases demonstrating that forensic science is an emperor with no clothes. Ideas presented for decades as scientific certainties are revealed to be nothing more than guesses tailored to fit a specific result. Bite marks, postmortem bruising—all tea leaves." I paused. "But let me ask you—where was Alice's room in relation to her mother's?"

"Next to it," Sullivan said. "On the other side of the wall."

"So at least two men break in to the apartment, surprise her mother, hold her down, forcibly inject her with a lethal dose of heroin, and Alice doesn't hear a thing?"

"Children sleep soundly."

"I'll give you that. But you were downstairs, right? And according to you, every time someone moves up there, you know it. Yet you didn't hear anything?"

She stared back at me, then gave a tiny shake of her head.

"If you had, you'd have called the police, right? And you didn't see anyone come or leave that night, or you'd have told the police what you'd seen. Just as Alice would have told them if she'd woken up and noticed strangers in her apartment. But you didn't see anything, and evidently neither did she."

She was becoming angry. "I think maybe it's time for you to leave."

"I'm not accusing you. I'm just stating a fact. If I'm wrong, I'm sure you'll tell me."

"You're not wrong," she said in a flat voice. "I didn't hear anything. The first Alice knew anything was wrong was when she woke up and found her mother dead."

"So maybe there was no disturbance, no struggle."

"She was no junkie, I'm telling you. She wouldn't have done that."

"The week before she died, there was a robbery at the restaurant where she worked. A customer was killed when he refused to give up his watch. You must have known that. There were even intimations she was perhaps somehow involved."

"We never discussed it, but I'd read the news."

She seemed about to say something, then stopped. I expected her to further insist that her neighbor could have done no such thing. But she surprised me by stating, "Obviously, *they* murdered her to keep her from talking."

" 'They' meaning who?"

I could see she was getting uncomfortable with the conversation. But now that she'd spoken this much, she needed to voice the rest of the thought.

She sighed. "There were always guys coming and going. I mean, not *always,* but when they were here, I'd know it. Not that I was listening for it, I just couldn't help hearing. . . ."

"What sort of guys?"

She looked down. "I couldn't generalize."

"How about the ones who lived in the house next door?"

Silence. I waited. Lighting another cigarette, she blew out a puff of smoke, then said simply, "I just told you, there were always men."

"Did you tell the police about them?" I asked Sullivan.

"No. I kept waiting for them to ask me about those guys, but they never did."

"You weren't going to talk about them unless the police brought up their names?"

"Because as far as I know, they didn't have anything to do with her death."

"I didn't mean to imply that," I said. "I'm just asking a few basic questions."

"Well, I'm trying to answer them. I had to go on living here. And in a murder investigation, bringing up names is the same as making accusations."

"They were over here, though? With Leann?"

"I wasn't keeping tabs. I didn't ever talk to her about those men. But, yeah, they were over here from time to time. One night, I was bringing the trash out to the Dumpster and one of them literally ran me over coming out of her apartment late. He kept right on going without a word."

"That wasn't the night she was killed, was it?"

"Of course not," Sullivan said. "I wouldn't have kept anything like that from the police."

When I showed her Sims's photo on my phone, she was unhelpful. "I don't remember if it was him or the other one I ran into coming out of Leann's place that time. Seems to me maybe they both visited up there at different times."

"What about the daughter?" I asked. "Did either of those men seem to be interested in her?"

"No," she said. "If that was the situation, I'd have known. And I'd have reported it," she added, her voice rising in anticipation of my next question about whether she would have told the police if she suspected the men of sexual interest in the daughter.

This denial, like the others, made me wonder if she was conscious, even now, of having deliberately covered her mouth, closed her eyes, and stopped her ears to threat and danger.

I attempted to ask a few more questions, but her willingness to answer them had come to a sudden end.

"I'm not going to get dragged into anything, am I?" she wanted to know as I was heading out the door. "The next time someone knocks, it's not going to be one of them?"

I told her that one of her former neighbors was dead. Giving her my card, I instructed her to call me immediately if she ever saw the one in the photo.

As I walked down the steps, my eyes inevitably went to the one-time dwelling of Edwards and Sims. The porch was still deserted. However, on the hood of my car, a man with a handlebar mustache and tattoos sat smoking a cigarette. Seeing me, he mashed it out slowly on the paint job and slid down.

I walked toward him, my heart jackhammering. As I walked past the house, the door opened. My knees turned to jelly as I recognized Sims. I was trying to imagine how to retreat when the first guy came closer and sucker-punched me.

The world went end over end, like a child's ball weighted on one side. Someone held me under the arms, and I was conscious of my heels dragging. I actually didn't even realize I'd been punched until the horizon righted and I found myself lying on the floor of what turned out to be a van.

I retched, then heard the door close. Someone was crouching over me. "Get up," Sims said as the metal floor rumbled beneath me, the engine coming to life.

When I couldn't, he kicked me in the ribs. I sat up quickly and leaned my forehead against my knees, the world spinning as the van pulled away from the curb.

"You hit him too hard," Sims said to the man in the driver's seat. There were only two seats, both up front.

"He's breathing, ain't he?" was the response.

I raised my head, my ears still ringing, then groaned, closed my eyes, and let my face fall forward against my knees. "I thought we had an understanding," Sims said to me gently. "I thought you got the message last time we talked."

I had nothing to say. This was the man who'd killed my father and his wife.

"You know where we're going?" Sims asked.

Again I didn't respond.

"Could be we're going to Berkeley," Sims continued, light-hearted. "Going to see your brother and his family. Let him know this arrangement of ours doesn't seem to be working out."

Fear went through me. "It's not an arrangement of 'ours.' Whatever it is, it's got nothing to do with you."

"You work for Wilder, don't you?"

When I found my voice, it came an octave too low. "The impression I got when Bo called me after the killings is that he thinks the person who killed my father and Dot might be making a play against him."

Sims laughed. "And if so, what business would that be of yours?"

"You made it my business when you murdered my father and Dot."

"My condolences. Really. But that wasn't a job of mine. You might want to check with Bo. It's possible he's not being exactly honest with you. He tends to tell people what they want to hear."

My blood pounded in my eardrums. I looked up at Sims. I wanted to kill him and wouldn't have hesitated to do so if I'd had a gun.

I gathered my self-control, telling myself I wasn't dead yet, so there could yet be a way out of the situation. Sims was prison-hard, the source of his power obvious in the promise of violence his body held. My power, if any, was less clear.

The van was on the freeway now, cruising just below the speed limit. I was having a hard time not talking. "If Bo finds out you killed my father and Dot, he's coming after you. Same goes for if you harm me and my family. You'd be signing your death warrant."

"Listen to me. Bo knows I didn't kill your pops. Your whole goddamn family has a gratitude problem, as far as I can tell." He snorted. "That's one area Bo and I see eye to eye on."

"You must be talking about Russell Bell." My head ached and I licked my lips. "You know, there's a database where you can research address histories. Put your name in there and that house comes up."

Sims pretended curiosity. "Now what would you be putting in my name for?"

"I don't like surprises," I said. "If I can trace the connection between you and Edwards that easily, you bet the police can, too."

We were nearly through Oakland now, maybe ten minutes from my brother's place.

Sims didn't reply.

My anger made me reckless, I knew. "It did strike me as a coincidence. What I couldn't figure out is why you used a girl to pull the trigger. Then the answer came to me. I figure you just don't have the balls to shoot someone who's conscious."

This drew another snort. "You mean, like now? One problem is I'd mess up my van."

My breath caught in my throat. It was impossible to guess his intentions.

Then he surprised me. "Another is that that little girl'd be left without a lawyer."

All the humor was gone from his eyes, and I saw that we'd now reached a point in the conversation that, for him, was deadly serious. He wanted *me* on this case, for reasons I didn't understand. And something in his eyes told me it wasn't just to cover his tracks.

"The public defender might be able to represent her more effectively than I can," I told him. "In a case like this, a straight-up acquittal is out of the question. To negotiate a favorable plea deal, she's got to be willing to trade information—"

Before I'd finished talking he'd grabbed me by the throat, thrown me to the rumbling floor of the van, and shoved his gun between my teeth. I struggled to breathe beneath the suffocating, menacing weight of him. The metallic taste of gun oil spread through my mouth. There was also another taste, the sulfurous tang of burned gunpowder. The weapon had recently been fired, part of my brain realized.

His words came out in an enraged whisper. "No lawyer I respect goes into a case talking about a plea deal. I don't want to hear about deals. What I want is to hear how you're going to convince a jury to walk her."

I made a sideways movement of my head, as if to shake it, trying to indicate the impossibility of the task he'd set for me. With a gun in my mouth, oral communication was out of the question.

"You're going to try that case, you hear me?" he said. "And the jury's going to come back with a verdict. Now tell me what they're going to say. You have one chance, and if you give the wrong answer, I swear I'll blow off your fucking head, and to hell with the floor of my van!"

He waited an instant, eyes locked with mine as if to show me how serious he was. Then he took the gun away, just long enough for me to mouth the words, every nerve in my body now focused on complying with his instructions. "'Not guilty,'" I said, my voice barely a croak.

He shoved me from him, and I hit my head on the side of the van, then sat up, gasping. With trembling fingers, I tested the tooth he'd jammed the gun barrel against. It was tender and seemed to wiggle in its socket.

"Obviously, you know more about this case than I do," I managed to get out.

"That sounds right to me." Now he chuckled. "Don't you worry about the jury. Leave them to me."

"Oh, Jesus."

"Meaning, you disagree with your brother's tried-and-true methods? You've got to *reach* the jury, is what he always used to say. Least that's what I've heard. With the means at your disposal. If persuasion doesn't work . . . then, well, there are always other methods, more direct ones."

"My brother never tampered with a jury in his life. He didn't need to."

"Believe whatever you want. It's possible none of the rumors about him were true, but, as far as I can see, he never did a damned thing to discourage them."

I'd heard all the rumors and wasn't interested in debating them. Above all, not here, not now, and not with him. Then, before he could stick the gun in my face again, I blurted out the first thing that came into my head. Just three words: "The Plum Tree."

The van suddenly decelerated, exiting off the freeway. Finally, Sims spoke. "Last I heard, they were looking for a couple of black guys for that job."

"Yeah, I heard that, too." I shut my eyes. I was in too much pain and shock; he had the upper hand.

"Pull over here."

We were on University Avenue, maybe a mile from Teddy's place. "I'm not playing games," Sims now told me. "This isn't a puzzle for you to figure out. You've got one job, and one job only: Make sure she turns down every offer the DA makes, then get the case to the jury and spend a week trying it. I'll do the rest."

He reached back and tugged on the handle of the rear door, throwing it open.

"Now get the fuck out."

CHAPTER 12

I walked half a block in a daze, turning every few steps to make sure the van really was gone, that they weren't following me. Then, gripped by a terrible panic, I took out my phone and called my brother. I reached him as he was just leaving to walk Carly to her preschool, she and Tam evidently having returned home. As Teddy listened, I hurriedly described the van and told him to get everyone inside and lock the doors.

"What happened? Should we call the police?" I could feel his mounting anxiety. And his sense of being trapped in the nightmare that had come to define too much of his life. But the trouble was, I had no answers for him. Not to mention, I was on the verge of collapse.

"Just stay home," I told him. "Wait for me." I stood doubled over on the sidewalk, chest heaving, head pounding, the taste of gun oil in my mouth.

After a moment I straightened, took out my wallet, and extracted what Sims would have found if he'd bothered to search me: the card Agent Braxton had given my brother, who'd passed it on to me.

I keyed the numbers without giving myself time to stop and consider what I hoped to achieve. All I knew was that after this morning, a turning point had been reached.

"Braxton here."

I hesitated. "This is Leo Maxwell."

"Okay." There was the shortest of pauses, as if he'd expected my call and was prepared. "Do exactly as I tell you. Get a secure line—a throwaway phone—and call me back on the number I'm about to give you. Ready?"

I took the number down. There was a convenience store on the corner of the next block. I ducked in, bought a phone, ripped the packaging off, and, after waiting for the device to activate, used it to call Braxton as I stepped outside.

~ ~ ~

The instructions he'd given me were designed to bring us to a place of secure privacy. This proved to be a dark-windowed SUV, into which I stepped when it slowed down to let me in.

"I was surprised to hear from you," Braxton told me. "I'd been expecting your brother."

"The government's dealings with my family will have to go through me," I said. "That's the first ground rule."

"That's fine for now," he said. "But if you're going to make conditions, you might want to remember I'm here at your request."

"And before that, you approached my brother," I reminded him.

"So what is it you'd like to talk about?" Braxton asked. He glanced at me as he drove. "You get hit by a truck or something?"

My head was still painfully tender. I'd tried to get some ice at the convenience store but its machine had been broken. "I'd have *preferred* a truck," I said. "But never mind that. For starters, you told

Teddy our father's death was the worst day of your professional life. Clearly, an opening for a recruitment pitch. I'm here to listen."

"Listen to what?" Braxton said. "I'm afraid I don't know what you mean. It's true enough I approached your brother, but that wasn't a professional visit. My motive was personal, because I wanted to express my condolences. Your father was a man I'd come to admire."

I shook my head, unwilling to accept such obvious bullshit.

He went on. "I can repeat to you what I said to Teddy, but I get the sense that my sympathies would be lost on you. After all, he's the one who visited your father in prison all those years. My sense is that you didn't want anything to do with Lawrence until he was getting out of prison and you could no longer avoid him."

His take stung deeply, as it was no doubt intended to do. The source of Braxton's information about my relationship with my father could only have been Lawrence himself. Now, here was his indictment falling on me from beyond the grave.

"People change," I said. I didn't intend just to roll over when it came to his assessment of my failings as a son. "But our family relationships are none of your business. I didn't risk my life to meet with you just to discuss what a great guy my dad was."

"I'm not sure what else we have to talk about."

"How about whether my dad was working for the government? And, if so, whether being an informant got him killed. And if that's what happened, what does the FBI intend to do about it?"

Braxton turned his face for a glimpse of the view as we rounded a switchback near the top of Grizzly Peak. Then, without glancing at me, he said, "Why should I trust you? We know you're in Wilder's camp now, representing his foot soldiers. I don't mind telling you that if and when we fold up his operation, your name will be on the indictment."

Now he did look over at me, his eyes as cold and pitiless as Jack Sims's gaze had seemed a few hours before.

"Is Teddy's name going to be in that indictment, too? You told him to contact you if he needed help getting out of the situation he was in. You also said you'd do everything you could to see that he didn't end up like my father."

"As I said, that was personal, not professional." He paused. "I know you don't want to believe this, but your father was my good friend. On a personal level, I owed him. And his greatest concern before he died was for Teddy and his family. He figured *you* could take care of yourself."

"Look, I'm not here for myself," I informed him. "It's Teddy and his family that are the problem. And my father didn't *die,* as you so euphemistically put it—he was brutally murdered. I should know. I was the one who found them."

"I'm aware of that." His tone was patently insincere, even mocking.

"Think what you like. My guess is you feel a responsibility toward Teddy because my father did. And rightly so, because he *was* responsible for tangling us up with Wilder. My beef is that, to me, it looks as though Lawrence was killed because he was working for you."

Braxton shook his head. "The difficulty I'm having with this conversation is this. What's to convince me you aren't here acting for Wilder, looking to confirm what he suspects about your father but doesn't know for sure? If I were him, and suspected your father'd been passing information to the feds, I'd want to try to learn what exactly he's told us, so I could understand how bad the damage is. I might even send *you* to try to get that information. If Wilder was threatening your family, wouldn't you do whatever he asked, no matter how you felt about the murder of your father and his wife?"

"You're wrong. He wouldn't trust me to make contact with the FBI and not betray him in the process," I said. "The simple truth is, if Wilder finds out I'm talking to you, I'm dead. That is, assuming he's still the one calling the shots."

His answer was curt. "Who else would be in charge if he isn't?"

"The man who killed my father, of course. I assume you already know his name."

"Let's quit playing games. You tell me who you think pulled the trigger and I'll tell you if you're wrong."

"Fine. Jack Sims." I told Braxton in general terms about Sims's threat to our family and my father's promise to deal with him, followed shortly by his own death. He listened to me, saying nothing.

Then, for good measure, I added, "And I can name at least three more unsolved murders that he's committed."

Braxton grimaced in a way calculated to show how small-time he thought me. "Federal cases? And by that I mean, were any of these murders committed in furtherance of a criminal racketeering organization?"

I could see where this was going. "Not that I'm aware. My father and Dot are the only victims I know of who were killed for the sake of the Aryan Brotherhood."

I could, of course, have named Russell Bell, who'd been murdered because Bo wanted my father as part of his organization. But that would have given the government far too much power in an already lopsided negotiation. I needed to save it until we had the framework of a protective deal in place.

"Then take it to a state cop. I'm not interested."

"You haven't told me I'm wrong about Sims. So I gather you already know that he was the one who killed my father and Dot."

"I don't *know* anything. All I can say is that what you've told me is consistent with, and reinforces, the Bureau's conclusions in the matter."

"Has the FBI assumed control over the investigation?"

"Obviously not. To do so would send the wrong signals."

"What's obvious is that my father's role as a government informant would be pertinent in any police investigation of his and Dot's murders. Has the FBI even shared that with the police?"

Braxton avoided answering my question. "We don't currently have anything close to the kind of evidence we'd need to persuade a federal grand jury to indict."

"So why aren't you helping the state police build a case against Sims? An agent's supposed to protect his sources at all costs, right? When an informant's taken out, the full weight of the government's supposed to come down on the person who pulled the trigger, just the same as if one of your own had been killed. Instead, as far as I can tell, you and the rest of the FBI are sitting on your hands. And worse, you're refusing to share information with the police."

"I'm afraid your view of our policies regarding cooperating witnesses is rather shortsighted." Braxton, his face now a picture of patience, reached up to tilt the mirror so we could see each other in it. "Let's assume for the sake of argument that we *did* have direct proof—even ironclad evidence. Are you actually telling me that you'd blow an investigation that has stretched for nearly two decades? For the sake of two murder victims whom I can no longer do anything to help?"

His words—*nearly two decades*—reverberated in my mind, dramatically enlarging the scope of what was at stake between us.

"Just answer me this," I said. "Was my father an FBI informant?"

Braxton seemed to draw back behind the wheel, his face reflexively closing down against my inquiry.

"Or was that just a ploy you were using as an approach with Teddy, making him believe that Dad was working for you when, in reality, Lawrence had told you to go fuck yourself the one time you talked?"

"Your father was a government informant," Braxton finally said, his eyes holding mine briefly in the mirror. He now wore a different kind of look, the expression of a man with a doubtful hand who's just thrust all his chips across the felt.

I found, to my surprise, that I believed him. This revelation, though I'd already suspected it was true from what Teddy had told me, hit me hard—far harder than I'd have believed before he said it. It couldn't help radically changing my view of my father, who he was, and what he'd stood for. In particular, it cast a dramatically different light on the choices my father had made, particularly those that had endangered his family and hastened the end of his life.

"How long?" I asked, my voice catching in my throat.

"Fifteen years." In the mirror, Braxton's eyes were suddenly clouded with emotion; his gaze was focused on the road ahead of us. "Nearly my entire career."

The silence between us lasted for nearly a mile. Finally I said, "Then you must have known him much better than I did."

"I knew him well, and I valued our relationship greatly."

I was first embarrassed by the emotion in his voice, then shamed by the true sentiment behind it. "Then why aren't you moving against Sims?"

"Because there's much more at stake than a pair of murders, no matter how close any of us were to the victims. As I said, this investigation has lasted the better part of two decades. The information your father has provided us over the years will be enough to bring down the Aryan Brotherhood for good. Not just in California, but across the country, both behind bars and outside prison walls."

He spoke with the passion of a disciple spreading the word. I listened to him with the attentiveness of a pilgrim.

Braxton went on. "It's no exaggeration to say that your dad devoted his life to this investigation. It was what kept him going behind bars, and he never wavered in his determination to continue that work once he was free. He wasn't just an informant—he was our eyes and ears at the heart of the most insidious criminal organization in America today. A source like this comes along maybe once a generation. And the quality of his info was second to none."

"Sounds as though he was your ticket to ride."

Braxton refused to be rattled. "Sure. But the information was so good, we couldn't act on most of it, because we'd have blown the source. I watched other agents make the big hits while I kept on putting money in the bank, storing up intel for the big bust. And I put in my time—ten years undercover as a corrections officer, the last ten years of your father's sentence, full-time at the prison and another twenty hours a week at the field office—processing the material your father gave us. You can't imagine more brutal, demeaning work. We were in the thick of it, the two of us. All that time spent together behind enemy lines."

"Except you got to go home every night."

Again he wouldn't take the bait. "And every night when my head touched the pillow I said a prayer that Lawrence would still be alive in the morning when I showed up for my shift. And every morning, waiting to clear security, I digested my stomach lining from the inside. So many close calls, so many near misses."

I hesitated to ask my next question. "Did you have anything to do with getting him out?" I hesitated before going on. "The evidence that my brother uncovered?"

"No. We couldn't lift a finger. Not that your father would ever have asked for that kind of help. He had too much pride to make a request that he didn't know would be granted. What your brother did for him, he did on his own. As far as we know, the evidence he found was genuine and untainted."

I wanted to believe him, but wasn't sure whether I should. Certainly, after fifteen years, the FBI had owed my father his freedom, and far more. With a surge of anger I said, "And you expect me to believe it was his choice to keep working for you, which meant working for Wilder, after he was released from prison?"

"Bringing down the AB was his lifework," Braxton said simply. "Can you really expect him to have just given that up, especially once he was in a position to feed us the kind of top-level information that one day would allow us to close the case once and for all?"

I nodded, just beginning to understand the full tragedy of my father's death—that he'd been killed for devoting his life to a case that would never be complete, and never, ever be closed, for the simple reason that the men who ran the AB were already behind bars and beyond the ability of the government to punish them further.

"Did Dot know?"

"She was an FBI agent," Braxton said. "One of our own, to use your words. After a few years, it got too risky for Lawrence to pass me information directly. So we brought in an agent from the Ohio field office to play the role."

I was astonished. Then, quickly, overcome with sadness. Followed by confusion and uncertainty. "So their marriage was a sham?"

"It was what it was. Only Dorothy could answer that question, and unfortunately, to all of our sorrow, she's gone."

"So what happens now?" I asked, my mind reeling. My headache was getting worse. "If revealing my father as your source is no longer an issue, then presumably it must mean it's time to kick in the doors. Get revenge for what they did to my father and Dot."

"If that was going to happen, you'd be the last to know." The barriers were up between us again. "I've worked this case too long to sink it that way. If there's even a ten percent chance Bo's turned you, it's too much risk for me. And, even if you're honest, we both know these animals can make anyone reveal anything under torture. It's been done before."

I had no choice but to accept this. "So what went wrong?" I asked instead. "Why'd they suspect him? Did they trace Dot's background?"

"No. Not as far as we can see. We've combed through all the data, reviewed all the wiretaps, culled through all the Internet chatter. We haven't found a single indication that either your father's or her cover was blown. We're confident they weren't exposed."

"No indications other than the bullet holes in their bodies, you mean."

"Your father knew the risks. It goes without saying that Dorothy knew them as well. In a war, each side loses soldiers."

I couldn't believe what I was hearing, and I certainly couldn't accept his apparent acquiescence in their squalid deaths as he calmly drove with both hands on the wheel. "You're in some kind of crazy denial if you think their work for you had nothing to do with their deaths. They were exposed. They had to have been, to be executed like that."

"It's going to be hard for you to hear this. But what you told me earlier puts the pieces together in my mind. As I said, we're convinced your father's cover wasn't blown. But Sims is a dangerous man—a killer. From what you just told me, your father confronted him after Sims threatened your niece. God knows what was said, but knowing Lawrence, I imagine it was to the point. Sims didn't appreciate being spoken to that way, especially from someone who wasn't a bona fide AB member. He stewed over it for a while, then he took the only action he knows. He showed up at your father's place in the night and executed the two of them in their sleep. With those same bullets, he fired a shot over Wilder's bow. It's possible that even without our help, the organization's about to implode."

"I can give you Sims. Not for my father and Dot, but for previous murders. But it's pretty clear you don't want him."

"I already said, that's state law stuff. I'm holding out for the RICO trial."

"Right," I said, unable to control what I now was feeling. "You're holding out for the perfect case, the perfect evidence. I've seen enough guys like you in my legal career to know that's never going to come. There's always going to be something else you need, some piece without which the puzzle just isn't complete. And meanwhile, the years trickle by, and the bodies pile up."

"That's not true," he insisted. "I've staked my entire career, my entire life, on this case. I just don't intend to lose it by acting on emotion. Your father should have known better than to confront Sims as he did. For that, I blame him. He screwed us royally. Now we've got to regroup, figure out how best to carry on the battle."

"How about Randolph Edwards's murder? What if I could place Sims on the scene?" I hadn't planned to offer this, especially not without my client's approval. But the time had come, it seemed to me, to test Braxton's capacity for making excuses to justify his refusal to act.

Braxton's face betrayed no interest, but his body seemed to tense, giving off an impression of increased stillness as he drove along the winding mountain road. "You represent the shooter. Wilder's footing the bill."

"Never mind about that. Not even how you know where the money comes from. What I want to know is if I can connect Sims with his old roommate's murder, will you bring down the hammer on him? And, as I said, we can likely tie in at least two old unsolved murders as well. The Plum Tree job."

"Never heard of it."

"Then you haven't been doing your homework, Agent Braxton."

"You get your client to testify she was pulling the trigger on AB business, and I'll present the indictment."

I knew, however, that this wasn't the testimony Alice Ward was likely to give. I didn't yet know why she'd shot Edwards, but my working theory was that it was a revenge killing, because she believed Edwards murdered her mother; Sims must have told her so. But such a murder presented no federal hook.

"You want Sims as much as I do," I said. "He killed an FBI agent, for Christ's sake. Why does it matter whether it's federal or state law he's accused of breaking? Didn't you guys bring down Al Capone on tax evasion?"

"Which happens to be a federal crime," Braxton reminded me. "The kind within the jurisdiction of the federal investigative powers. *I* want this asshole; it's not good enough for me to hand him over to the state police. Besides, the state prisons are the AB's home turf. Federal prison is a different matter."

I no longer feared that Braxton was inventing Lawrence's cooperation in order to entice us to take the step our father hadn't taken. The story he told was too outlandish not to be essentially true. For me, it only deepened the peril of the situation. I realized that, in his continued pursuit of the case that evidently had become his white whale, Braxton would be unlikely to prioritize protecting us.

"You must have wanted something from Teddy, to have approached him," I said. "Tell me what we can do."

Braxton didn't reply immediately. He'd looped around and was headed back down toward Berkeley. "I need someone on the inside. Someone to take your dad's place. Your brother's the natural choice."

"What about me?"

"Wilder doesn't trust you. And with good reason. What kind of access do you have? You're little more than a rubber stamp for guilty pleas of people who in the grand scheme of things really don't matter."

I didn't like this. But I said only, "And he trusts Teddy?"

"Your brother's impairments make him seem harmless. And his reputation from the old days doesn't hurt."

"So your offer to him wasn't the no-strings deal it seemed at first. He was going to have to sing for his supper."

Braxton didn't say anything, but the uncomfortable silence made his position clear. I wasn't going to let any other member of my family be put back in that untenable and potentially fatal situation, and I told Braxton so.

"Well, you've got my card," was his reply.

We were coming back down from the hills into Berkeley, heading toward my brother's neighborhood. "Where do you want me to drop you?"

I told him an intersection six blocks from Teddy's house. But he seemed unwilling now to let the conversation end. "Your brother has to make his own choices," he said. "You've kept your hands mostly clean, but he hasn't. This is the only chance he's going to get to make amends."

"Never mind," I told him. "Just let me out right here."

CHAPTER 13

"Fifteen years." Teddy shook his head in disbelief.

We were in his backyard, braving a chilly wind with occasional spitting rain. Carly was down for her nap, Tamara in the house with her. I'd told her to stay, that she needed to hear this, too, but after the scare I'd put her through this morning, she wasn't about to leave her daughter sleeping alone in the house.

"You never had any inkling," I said.

He shook his head slowly. "Not until Braxton approached me that day at the park."

I'd told Teddy about Braxton wanting to use him as an informant in our father's place. Though worried about his reaction, I didn't think, in fairness, I could keep it from him. I knew that Braxton was always free to disregard my unilateral "condition" and contact Teddy directly, so it was important he be prepared.

"We can't count on the FBI or anyone else to protect us."

"Right. The AB killed Dad and the FBI didn't stop them. But you said Braxton's convinced he wasn't compromised."

"Let's assume, for the sake of argument, that Dad's cover wasn't blown, and that you'd be able to gain access to the kind of information the FBI's looking for. What's Braxton going to do then—pull you out after a few months, prosecute the AB's outside organization, and then let you live happily ever after?"

Teddy didn't answer. He didn't need to.

"He left Dad in place for fifteen years. Fifteen *years,* Teddy. Building evidence for a case that was never quite ready, never going to be good enough. Listening to him, I got the sense he was actually unhappy Dad had been released. At least, he told me the government didn't have anything to do with it."

"I know that's true," Teddy said. "It was all me. And, at the end, you."

"I also sensed it wasn't an option for Lawrence to stop working for Braxton once he got out. Braxton denied it, said Dad was the one who wanted to keep working to bring the AB down, but what was he going to do—just walk away?"

"Well, then we're up shit creek. From what you're telling me, there's no way out except to do what Braxton says. Feed him information until Bo finds out, at which point my whole family ends up dead."

"Stay with me here. Assume Bo didn't know Dad was working for the FBI, and the murders were just what Braxton claims—the result of Dad confronting Sims because he threatened Carly. Assume, also, that neither you nor I agree to work for the FBI."

"Then we get swept up in the indictments, and you and I both go to prison, where we'll be dead men as soon as the evidence is unsealed and Bo realizes Dad was feeding the feds information all this time."

"You're assuming there'll be indictments," I told him. "But imagine this scenario: What if, before Braxton actually finally manages to close the case he's been chasing for almost two decades, a civil war erupts and his targets take each other out?"

"You said something along those lines the other night when we were talking through this. You were wondering if Dad hadn't only been feeding the FBI information about the Brotherhood, but also working actively to sabotage it."

"During our ride just now, I found myself wondering what the government can possibly hope to accomplish by going to trial against a bunch of bad guys who're already serving life sentences. Sure, there are plenty more on the outside, like Sims, the ones without whom the AB couldn't possibly maintain its power anywhere but behind bars. But the ringleaders themselves are already in prison."

Teddy was ready to disagree with me. "I'd say Sims is worth prosecuting."

"Of course. But the government's looking at him from an organizational perspective, not a moral one. Dad's opinion of Sims before the murders was that he was a lightweight, never accepted within the inner circle. If I were Wilder, I'd be worried Sims was looking to change that."

"It seems to me Braxton's probably so deliberate about assembling the case because the only punishment that can mean anything to these guys is death, the way you suggested. And these days especially, death is hard to get in federal court, at least where the defendant hasn't committed an act of terrorism."

"You're overlooking that they have the death penalty in the AB as well. 'Going in the hat,' it's called. Means your name gets put in a kitty with a bunch of blank slips, and whoever draws it has to do the job."

"Why don't you tell me what you're thinking?"

"Braxton struck me as fairly ruthless, willing to tolerate the loss of a once-in-a-lifetime source or even a fellow agent, provided his goals are served. The question that keeps nagging at me is this: What kind of law enforcement agency continues to reauthorize, year after year, a fifteen-year investigation that hasn't led to a single prosecution?"

"One that's willing to play the long game," Teddy suggested, shrugging.

"But what about one for whom the goal isn't prosecutions— which would serve only a symbolic purpose—but rather disruption, sabotage, and counterinsurgency? And that brings me back to what we were talking about before—Dad's 'exit strategy.' Something tells me it didn't involve taking the witness stand in federal court."

"Your theory is he intended to turn the bad guys against each other."

"It'd be a lot easier to start a war and get them to kill each other than to persuade a jury to sentence them to death, then convince the Court of Appeals and the Supreme Court to affirm it. After that, if you're lucky, you're looking at a trip to the injection chamber fifteen years after the case is tried. More likely, the sentence ends up being overturned thanks to the work of some clever defense lawyer. Or maybe, in the meantime, the Supreme Court finally decides the death penalty's unconstitutional, and then the bad guys are right back where they started. In prison with smug looks on their faces. Kings on their thrones."

"If that's what Dad was trying to do, then something went very wrong."

"I know," I said. "But, on the other hand, it seems he was on the right track confronting Sims. Bo doesn't trust him, and with good reason. If I'm right, and Dad's and Dot's covers weren't blown, then their murders mean the civil war has already started. Dad pushed the right button—it's just that Sims took it out on him."

The screen door flapped, and Tamara came out. She stood at the edge of the patio looking up at the dismal sky. Teddy gave me a significant look and went to comfort her. But before he could take her in his arms she turned and went back inside.

~ ~ ~

The next morning I went to see my client at the county jail, where she was now being housed after her release from the locked ward at San Francisco General Hospital.

We were left alone in a small consultation room with windows all around us, guards walking by every few minutes. They'd given me a thorough patting-down before letting me in. I hadn't argued when the deputy'd demanded my pen.

The wound was closed now, on its way to healing, covered only by a gauze pad held in place with tape. Her previous air of belligerence and boredom was almost gone. Her eyes were guarded but alert, as if she were genuinely interested in my visit.

"I had an interesting day yesterday," I said. "I spent the morning with a woman named Jennifer Sullivan. Later, I ended up on the floor of a van with a gun in my mouth."

"How did you . . ." She stopped talking and simply looked at me.

"Sullivan told me your name. I won't use it if you don't want me to. She doesn't know what you've done, but she remembers you."

Alice Ward slumped, looking down at her hands, then glanced up. "So what happens now? My lawyer rats me out?"

"I don't have any plans to do that. I've learned a few things about your past that I'd hoped we could discuss."

"I don't want to talk about any of that."

"I don't see how we can avoid it. The police are going to find out who you are. I'm not going to tell them, but someone will recognize you eventually. It's lucky your fingerprints aren't on file. That gives us time."

Her forehead rested on her hands, her arms encircling her face. Her voice seemed to come from somewhere far off. "I ran away."

"When?"

"A few days after they came for me. That was the first time."

I wanted to ask what she'd heard that night, whether she'd truly been asleep while Leann's murderers did their work. But I knew better than to ask such a question. "I know you found her body."

Just like me, I wanted to remind her. But I knew using it right at this moment would be a misstep. Besides, I wasn't sure I was ready to discuss that experience with anyone who knew what it was like.

She lifted her head to face me. "She OD'd, okay? She was nothing but a junkie at the end."

"That's not what the police thought. They decided it was murder, that someone held her down and another person gave her the injection, a deliberate overdose. Sullivan didn't see your mother as a drug user."

"Jenny didn't see a lot of things. Not for lack of trying. That nosy bitch was always peeping out her blinds. I was there. I was just a kid, but I saw."

"Saw what?"

She shook her head. "We're not going there. Nope."

"Fine. Then let's talk about something else. Why don't you tell me what happened with your living situation after Social Services picked you up, after you ran away that first time."

She remained resistant. "Why do you need to know all this stuff?"

"You're on trial for murder. Yesterday your buddy Sims put a gun to my head and told me he's expecting me to put up a defense. As if I didn't know that already. I'm a defense lawyer. That's what I do."

"But what defense could there be? You know I killed him."

Her gaze was level now, frankly confrontational but also curious, and, for the first time, not without a glimmer of hope.

I took my time answering. "There's always a defense. Not always a total defense, but often a partial one. For instance, if you were insane and couldn't tell right from wrong when you pulled the trigger, or you were so far gone mentally that you didn't know pointing a gun at a man and pulling the trigger would kill him, then you could be not guilty by reason of insanity. That's a complete defense. An insane person can't be convicted of any crime."

"What if I knew what I was doing and I meant to kill him?"

The set of her jaw made clear to me she'd do it again if given the chance.

"Then, hypothetically speaking, you acted with malice, which means you're guilty of culpable homicide. There are different degrees of guilt, though, and where you fall on the spectrum has a drastic effect on the penalty you face."

I paused to see if she was following. She seemed to understand.

I went on. "You're charged with capital murder. 'The unlawful killing of a human being with malice aforethought.' That's our starting point, and it carries a mandatory life sentence. If the killing isn't deliberate or premeditated, it's second-degree murder, and the sentence is fifteen years to life.

"Where things start to get interesting is voluntary manslaughter. That means you killed him in the heat of passion because you were provoked. The classic example is the husband who walks in on his wife in bed with another man. It could be any extreme provocation, though. If you're convicted of voluntary manslaughter, the sentence is between three and eleven years."

Her face seemed to glow for an instant, then the light went out. "What happened, happened."

"But no one knows what went down before you shot Edwards dead, or why you were running. My investigator's found plenty of witnesses to show that you were dashing like a madwoman through traffic. What they don't know is what Sims said to you before you ran. The only source for that evidence is you."

"You mean I testify at the trial. Admit I shot him and tell the jury why."

"That's the best way to present a heat-of-passion defense in a case like this. It's a safe bet Sims isn't going to testify. You don't want to go to prison for the rest of your life, do you? . . . Alice?"

Rather than answer my question, she switched tracks. "You said Sims put a gun in your mouth. Shouldn't you be making sure I *don't* talk?"

"That's what he wants. But you can't beat a guy like that by doing what he wants. You've got to neutralize him."

"Good luck with that," she said.

I regarded her a moment. Then, prodding her from a different direction, I said, "It wasn't an accidental overdose that killed your mom."

"You said that. You didn't know her. You weren't there."

"I know the circumstances. I know what you know."

"Listen to me: She killed herself. No sense trying to blame it on others. She made the fatal choice."

Her toughness, though, struck me as an act, covering up what had to be a deeper sense of betrayal.

"You mean when she agreed to help them knock over the place where she worked. The Plum Tree."

"Did you come here to show off what you've dug up, or are you interested in hearing what I've got to tell you?"

I made an apologetic gesture.

"She was so nervous that day. She made me French toast. That's how I knew something bad was gonna happen. I could hardly eat. Finally, she came and she sat beside me and put her arms around me and told me she was doing it for me. Without telling me what 'it' was.

"A kid knows lots that she isn't supposed to know. I went off to school as usual that day, but when I came home, she wasn't there. I wasn't surprised—at least that's how it seems to me now. Part of me expected her never to come back, because of the way she'd been in the morning. As long as I can remember, I've always had the feeling that one day she'd just be gone.

"Around one in the morning that night I went next door to Jack and Randolph's. They had the blinds down. They were drinking beer. 'Go to Jack if anything ever happens to me, like if I don't come home when I'm supposed to,' she'd always said. 'Jack has no choice but to look after you. He owes me.'

Alice's mimicry of her murdered mother sent a shiver down my spine.

She went on in her own voice: "Of course, it was like so many other lies she told. I don't know how I knew they had something to do with her not coming home that night, but I did. I knew they'd been wherever she was.

"'My mom didn't come home,' I said when Randolph answered the door. They were hyped up, but looking burned out at the same time. I knew later that it must have been because they'd just shot a dude and were starting to think about what had gone wrong, probably blaming each other.

"Jack came out of his chair so fast. 'What did she tell you?' He started to shake me, his eyes crazy. 'What the fuck did she say?'

"I was crying. 'Nothing,' I said. I kept repeating it.

"I managed to, like, convince them that I was there because she'd told me to come to them if anything ever went down. She'd acted as though it was no big deal to trust myself to these white guys even though we barely knew them.

"Finally Jack stopped looking as if he was going to kill me. Now, he laughed. Not a nice laugh, either. He was laughing at my mom for ever having believed he gave a shit about her or me or anyone other than himself.

"'Go home,' he said. 'Your mom must have had to stay late at the restaurant, but she'll be along. If she isn't, though, you need to remember one thing.'

"And here he bent low and poked me. 'If she doesn't come back, and the police come instead, you don't say anything about Randolph and Jack. You just keep whatever she told you between us. All of it.' Next he gave me a look, a real scary one.

"'Now what are you going to tell the police?' he wanted to know.

"'Nothing,' I answered. I wasn't crying anymore.

"'Good girl,' he told me. 'Now go home.'

"And so I did, and before morning she came back. At first, she was manic—cleaning the apartment, doing laundry, throwing shit out. It was like time stopping. No breakfast, no school, no nothing. She didn't go to work the next evening. When I tried to talk to her, she didn't seem to hear. She'd hug me and hold me, but it was like being hugged by a robot. She was scared to death."

Here Alice's voice stopped. As if she'd run up against a wall.

"A week passed between the Plum Tree job and your mom's death," I offered.

"That week," she said, shaking her head. Again her voice stopped, then rose in sudden protest. "Talking about this makes my brain hurt."

I could see the pain on her face.

"You've got to talk about it."

"You want me to tell you what happened the night she died. You probably want me to say that I lay awake and heard what was happening and didn't move a muscle to stop it. Well, it isn't true. I didn't hear a thing."

"I don't want you to say anything but the truth."

"The truth is, I woke up and found her dead."

I nodded, reading in her eyes the terror of that moment. I was someone who understood exactly how it must have felt. I wanted to comfort her, but knew any gesture I might have made would probably have been misinterpreted, squandering the small reservoir of trust I'd built. And, even if trust weren't an issue, I wasn't her therapist. I was her lawyer. More strongly than ever, I wished it weren't me with this case.

"How'd you reconnect with Sims?"

She looked up. "There are questions you might not want answered."

I didn't say anything, as her words echoed my thoughts about the case.

She sighed. "It wasn't very long before I put the pieces together, just the way you did. Jack had warned me about the cops. Plus, I'd seen how my mom acted during that week after she came home."

She shook her head. "So I decided to kill him."

I wasn't sure I'd heard her right. "What?"

"My mom was everything to me. With her gone, I didn't have anyone left in the world. I finally ended up with a cousin who didn't give a shit about anything other than the check she got from the government every month for keeping me. I didn't know where Mom first crossed paths with these men, or how they got her to break the law for them, but I knew she wouldn't have done it if she'd felt she had a choice."

I couldn't find the words to say what I was thinking, so again I said nothing.

She studied me critically. "You're telling me you never thought about revenge?"

"Thinking about it and following through with it are two very different things."

Her eyes held mine, at last seeming to acknowledge our kinship. But was she referring to my mother's murder or that of my father and Dot? Whatever her meaning, the idea of vengeance, for her, was a powerful one.

"Your dad was in prison until you figured out he didn't do it. That meant you never had the chance. I did. I was walking home from school one day and Sims drove up next to me in this big Buick.

"'Hey, baby girl,'" he called through the window. 'Need a ride?'

"'Thought you were locked up,' I managed to say.

"'You thought wrong. I'm a free man now. I was just driving along, feeling lonely, and whoa, there's a familiar face. A pretty one, too. You're gonna have your mama's looks. Hell, you got them already.'

"'I'm not getting in any car with you.'

"'Seen Randolph lately?'

"'He out, too?'

"'They let him out a whole year before me. You believe that?'

"'You both ought to be locked up the rest of your lives.'

"'Why would you say that?'

"'Because of my mom.'"

Here she'd stopped, she said, turning to face him, her fear gone, replaced by the anger over having to spend the past ten years without the only person who'd ever loved her.

"'I could tell you a thing or two about what happened. It was a bad situation, but not like what you probably believe. Still, you remembered my warning. You kept your mouth shut.'

"'Cops say someone held her down and stuck that needle in.'

"'I can help you with that,' Sims said. 'I didn't know who did it, then, but I've learned me a thing or two since. You know what they say: It's never too late for justice.'"

She hadn't believed him, she said, but decided to play along. He'd come get her that weekend, he promised, and they'd go for a drive, have a good long talk. He'd tell her everything then. But the first thing she had to do, he'd said, was to get him a gun. Could she do that?

Saturday he picked her up after work from her part-time job at the Mrs. Fields cookie shop. The first place he drove was to the big cemetery in Oakland where her mother was buried.

He parked near the grave, but they didn't get out. "'You got the gun?'"

She showed it to him. Her heart was racing, her palm slick with sweat.

"'I know what you're thinking. You're telling yourself this is your chance. *Do it.* Well, I'm telling you the same thing. If you think I killed her, now's your chance. I know you're strong enough, and you're right about one thing—your mama's murderer doesn't deserve to live.'"

Here he'd waited for a few beats, just long enough to prove that he, not she, was in control.

"'Put it away,' he said. 'I didn't kill her. But I'll take you to the man who did.'"

In San Francisco, Sims had found a parking spot on Van Ness. Before getting out he'd told her to give him the gun, which he pocketed. She'd had to hurry to keep up with him as they approached Myrtle Street. "'They ought to be about finished now,'" he'd said, not telling her what he was referring to. "'You remember what he looks like, don't you?'

"'Who?'" Part of her still hadn't wanted to get it, why she was here with him.

"'Edwards. The guy who killed your mother. That's right, sweetheart. Randolph lied to me, said he had nothing to do with it. But I learned the truth. He killed her. He didn't trust her like I did. I knew she wouldn't talk, wouldn't rat us out, but then he lost his head. And the feds knew this. So they used it to get him to start working for them, which meant protecting him from the consequences. He ain't never gonna face justice. You gotta go now, if you want to catch him.'"

She'd stood frozen in place.

"'Come on. He held her down and he covered her mouth and he stuck that needle in her arm, all while you were sleeping in the next room. And then he left her there for you to find. Go ahead, just run on down there and do what's got to be done. Squeeze the trigger—once is enough. Now, go—run!'"

In that moment, something about the alley focused her rage. One minute she was standing beside Sims, and the next it was as if she were being swept along on a wave of anger, her feet pounding the pavement. The world had gone silent. The cars seemed to stand still as she ran between them, and there he was—Randolph Edwards, stepping out the front door of the cheap hotel, looking like a man in a hurry to be somewhere else.

She couldn't even remember how the gun had come to be in her hand. But there it was. She didn't know what she was going to do with it, had formed no intention. And then, like an echo, Sims's words reached her brain: *Once is enough.* Suddenly, she was across the street, and Edwards was standing in front of her, turning to look at her.

She raised the gun and shot him in the face.

CHAPTER 14

Back at the office, I reviewed the case file and sent an email to Sloane asking for several pieces of evidence that I'd requested to be produced, but which hadn't yet crossed my desk. The documents I hadn't received included dash cam videos from the responding patrol cars that day. It was possible these might reveal witnesses the police hadn't corralled.

Half an hour after the renewal of my request, my in-box pinged with a testy message from Sloane informing me that the videos and several other documents had been burned to a disc and put in an envelope with my name on it weeks ago, and that the envelope was still there, waiting to be picked up from the front desk of the DA's office. Certain that no one had told me that it was there, I swallowed my annoyance, grabbed my coat, and walked briskly through the fog and wind to the Hall of Justice, arriving just minutes before the office closed.

Back at my desk half an hour later, I dropped the CD into my computer and waited for the contents to load. Along with several pdf files, it contained three clips that were the dash cam recordings I'd asked for.

Each showed a variation of the same scene, but with different timing and angle, determined by the position of the police cars the cameras were in. I was quickly able to identify the footage from the first car on the scene. The clip showed the view out the windshield as the patrol car negotiated busy streets at reckless speed, headlights and taillights flashing by until the vehicle braked to an abrupt stop. Twenty feet ahead, Alice Ward sat on the curb in front of the Motel 6 with her hands behind her back.

Nearby, Edwards's corpse lay in a pool of blood, the gun beside it. At the edges of the frame, bystanders appeared, some running, others frozen. Car doors slammed, the picture shaking as two uniformed officers ran out, weapons drawn, threw my client unresisting to the ground, and spoke to a man who'd been near her moments before. As the police ran up, it looked to me as though this person took something from his pocket and showed it to them. A badge, I figured. But the image was too indistinct for me to be sure.

I paused and replayed in slow motion the clip of them throwing her to the ground. I wasn't positive, but it appeared she was already cuffed before they touched her. My heart was beating faster now.

I had the case file open. It contained the police reports with the names of witnesses who'd been interviewed, and their statements. I'd been hoping to match statements to faces, but soon realized this would be impossible. There was no mention of anyone having cuffed the suspect before the police arrived.

I watched the videos again and again. In the first clip, perhaps six people were shown at a distance, in addition to the guy I'd noted. In the second, offering a more oblique angle along the sidewalk, a crowd had begun to form at the corner half a block away. The third clip showed a similar throng gathering in the other direction,

Alice no longer visible among a cluster of officers. I slowed each one down, zooming in on the individual witnesses' faces.

The shadowy figure from the first clip wore dark jeans and what looked like the waterproof shell from a ski jacket, this garb offering a stark contrast to the suit he'd been wearing during our conversation. He appeared again in the second clip, shouldering through the crowd at the end of the block, a phone held to the side of his head. For just a second, he glanced back, and I was able to zoom in on his face. The picture was grainy, but I knew I was seeing FBI Agent Braxton.

Until I heard Alice's story and saw the dash cam video, I'd lacked a satisfactory explanation for what Edwards was doing in the Tenderloin the night she'd shot him. An FBI agent at the scene suggested that her story of what Sims had told her was true—that Edwards was a snitch. This was also, of course, a plausible motive for murder, though it raised the question of why my client was needed to pull the trigger. But that was the state's problem, not mine. The police's concealment of Braxton's presence, particularly if I was correct that he'd been the first law enforcement officer on the scene and the one who'd handcuffed my client, was exactly the fault line I needed to begin chiseling into the DA's case.

"I want the three of you out of town during the trial," I told Teddy and Tamara when I went to their house for dinner at the end of that week.

It was Friday evening, and we were sitting at the kitchen table, Teddy and I having finished the dishes while Tamara put Carly to bed.

"I can't just run away," Teddy said. "How's that going to look?"

"It'll look worse if you stay and become a target for reprisals based on the defense I plan to present." I hesitated before going on. "The thing is, depending on how the testimony goes, none of us may be able to come back."

"But what does your trial have to do with us?" Tamara asked.

She deserved to know the whole story. "It's starting to look as if the man my client murdered may have been an FBI informant—just like Dad. Today I sent notice to the FBI that I intend to call Braxton as a witness. The feds will fight my subpoena, but it appears he may have been the closest eyewitness to the shooting. I don't see how the case can go forward without him. I don't know what he'll say, but my instinct tells me to push the button and keep pushing it."

"But what if he pushes back?" Teddy asked. "You're worried he's going to retaliate, and expose Dad's role as an informant?"

"It's always possible. But I think he's got too much invested in Dad's years undercover for that. The alternative is pretending I don't know what I know. I've been warned that it's my job to keep my client from telling what she knows. They've threatened Carly. My fear is that if I give in now, then we're always going to be at the mercy of these guys."

Tamara wasn't buying it. "Why can't you just withdraw?"

"Because that would be an admission that I've outlived my usefulness. Don't get me wrong, I've given serious thought to the idea, not least because the state bar would probably view my decision to remain on the case as a serious ethical breach. There's a decent chance that when this case is over, I won't be a lawyer anymore. That might even be the best-case scenario. But I also think I'm the only lawyer who can fully exploit the weaknesses in the DA's case."

"What weaknesses?" Teddy's skepticism came with the full force of the anger behind it. "You're sitting here telling us we may have to move away, start over, presumably sell our home, and you're doing this because you think you're the best lawyer for this girl who's guilty as hell?"

Feeling suddenly too upset to remain seated, I went to the back door and peered out the window. Then I turned, determined to make them see the truth. "What's the alternative? There's no time for her to start over with another lawyer. As for our family, we can't expect to win a fight with a prison gang, which is what we'd have if I backed out. The AB is far more ruthless than we could ever be. That's its strength—but also its weakness. If I can get Braxton on the stand, it's possible I can use him to make the Brotherhood implode."

"If we aren't safe here, how are we going to be safe anywhere?" Tamara asked. "I mean, in this day and age, if they want to find us, they can. Right?"

I had no good answer. "All I can tell you is that the Brotherhood's power stretches only so far. Bo Wilder's the only guy with the power to order a hit in a different part of the country. But even if he's gone, and one of the local foot soldiers was to meet us on the street, it's possible he'd be obliged to kill us."

"So you're saying we're never going to be safe in California." Tamara's voice now was hardening with blame.

"I'm sorry," I told her. "But I think recent events have made that clear."

She only nodded, too overcome to respond. She took Teddy's hand, and he put his other hand on top of hers on the table. Then he shot me a look that transferred all her anger and resentment onto me, filtered through his consciousness of his own powerlessness to protect her.

"We've lived here all our lives," he said. "Now you're telling me that we have to leave? I suppose you've got someplace picked out for us to go, some new life."

"No," I said. "I don't. I'm sorry. I'm just starting to come to terms with this myself."

"You don't know what's best for us," Teddy went on in the carping tone I'd become familiar with after he was shot, when I was managing his life because he wasn't yet capable of managing it himself. "You're not a father, you're not a husband. I don't think you should be telling me how to keep my family safe."

"Leo's right," Tamara said. I had to strain to hear her soft voice. "He is. We can't stay here. They burned Leo's office. Then that man grabbed Carly, and now they've murdered your father and Dot. Whether you cooperate with them now or not, it's only a matter of time before they'll come for us."

For a moment Teddy seemed to hold his breath, both hands gripped in his wife's. Then, finally, with a shuddering exhalation, he let the held breath out.

Tamara wrapped her arms around her husband and held him tightly.

"What about Braxton, the FBI?" Teddy asked without hope, returning his wife's embrace. "The Witness Protection Program?"

"I've thought about that, but the only conclusion I can come to is that we'd be trading one ruthless master for another. The FBI seems to regard its informants as resources to be used up, to be squeezed until their last drop of usefulness is extracted—not so different from the way Bo Wilder views us. Remember, Braxton kept Dad as an asset in place for over fifteen years."

"And the Witness Protection Program?"

"Braxton holds the key to that kind of thing. For the reasons I just told you, I wouldn't trust myself—or anyone I cared about— to him. He's been chasing his goal too long not to be willing to sacrifice us in service of the cause. And my guess is that no information we could give him would ever be good enough for him to pull us out. He might dangle the idea of relocation in front of us like a carrot when he needed to, with the only result being that we'd be signing on to spend years in the same situation we're in now—with the added danger of knowing that if anyone in Wilder's crew finds out, it's our death sentence."

"I'm not living that way," Tamara said vehemently. "I won't."

Teddy, his head still leaning against her, closed his eyes briefly and nodded. "They couldn't protect Dad," he said. His tone now was resigned. "There's no reason to believe they'd be able to guarantee our safety."

"But what about us?" Tamara said. "What's to stop them from prosecuting Teddy, from prosecuting you?"

"Nothing," I told her. "I'd say because we're innocent, only that's never stopped the feds before. All we can do is make their job a lot more difficult by not giving them the evidence they'd need to hold over us."

For a few minutes, the silence in the kitchen was profound.

"Where would we go?" Teddy finally asked.

I had to laugh. Teddy'd been wrong to think I'd had it all planned out, because the truth was, I hadn't given the future a thought. My mind ran up against a brick wall when I thought of living anywhere other than the Bay Area. Rationally, I knew that people lived in other places, but it was hard to think of those people as real, or those places as anything other than pictures on TV. I was a thirty-four-year-old man who'd never so much as taken a vacation outside my home state, a fact that probably said volumes about the ways in which my life was broken, about how I'd never managed to move past the grim events of my childhood.

"I don't know," I told them. "Somewhere we can stretch a dollar. You two come up with ideas. In the meantime, when's the last time you had a vacation? My trial starts in three weeks. You should take Carly to Disneyland."

I knew how flippant this sounded, but I needed them out of harm's way.

Teddy gave me an abject look conveying his sense of betrayal.

"That's not a bad idea," Tamara said.

CHAPTER 15

I couldn't expect that my client would remain anonymous, and on the following Monday a call from Jillian Sloane put an end to my ethically questionable dreams of trial by ambush. "She shuffled through a number of foster parents after her mother's death, and was eventually placed with a distant relative of her mother's," Sloane said. "She took off from there six months ago. This wonderful person went on cashing the checks from the state and never bothered to report her missing. A social worker checked up on the household last week and found Alice gone."

"She's just a kid. Why not charge her with voluntary manslaughter and let the case go to juvenile court?"

"I'd need to have a good reason to do that," Sloane replied. "And you haven't given me one. Instead, I received a call from the U.S. Attorney's Office about a subpoena you sent to the FBI. Care to fill me in?"

"The witness's name is Special Agent Mark Braxton."

"Justice isn't going to let him testify," she said. "Not a chance. And a state court judge won't have the authority to make an FBI agent appear."

"Yet you could make these problems all go away just by reducing the charges and transferring the case to juvenile court."

She was too smart to tell me it was my witness, and therefore my problem. If she'd done her homework, and I had to assume she had, then she knew the mess the police had made for her. None of the reports mentioned anything about Braxton's presence at the scene, even if the dash cam video seemed to show him displaying his credentials to the officer who'd written one of the incident reports in my file. And, having watched the clip repeatedly, I was certain Alice had been handcuffed when the SFPD first rolled up.

"I'm sorry, Leo," she said, breaking in on my thoughts. "That's not going to happen. Your client gunned down a man in cold blood. We're going to trial."

In response to my subpoena, I received, ten days before trial, a letter bearing an impressive United States Department of Justice seal. It gave me formal notice that Braxton wouldn't be permitted to testify, stating that as an employee of the Justice Department, he was protected by sovereign immunity. Therefore, federal regulations authorized the agency, in its sole determination, to decide whether or not he would be granted permission to testify in a state court criminal proceeding.

This permission, the letter informed me, was denied because I'd failed to provide a detailed summary of the testimony I expected him to give. If I provided a sufficiently detailed summary, the letter stated, my request would be forwarded to the appropriate authorities for further consideration. Unsurprisingly, the boilerplate letter took no position on the question of whether Braxton had been anywhere near the scene of the shooting that night.

Knowing the law, I'd expected this. Attaching the letter, I immediately filed a motion with the court to compel Braxton's testimony, and, along with it, a motion for a dismissal of the charges, citing *Brady v. Maryland*, the Due Process Clause of the Fifth Amendment, and the Sixth Amendment's Compulsory Process Clause. These all, in theory, guaranteed my client the right to subpoena any witness, even one who happened to be an FBI agent.

One week before trial, Judge Ransom, to whom the case had been assigned following my client's arraignment, held a hearing on these and other pretrial motions. One of these was the state's motion to amend the information to include my client's real name. Armed with a binder of cases I'd researched, including one from federal court in California and another from state court in Georgia—neither fully supporting my position—I met my client in court expecting a quick rebuff to my Hail Mary pass. I knew from my research that a state judge had no power to force Braxton, a federal government agent, to appear and testify, no matter how vital his knowledge might be to my defense. The only remedy he could give me would be to dismiss the charges. But I was certain no elected judge would do that.

Ransom was in his late sixties, with a drinker's face and a philanderer's reputation, one bolstered by his four ex-wives, at least two of whom had either appeared or been employed in his courtroom. Ransom's mask of detached intellectualism was a facade covering his hunger for approval and admiration. The lawyers laughed at his jokes, and sometimes this worked in their favor. The defendants, with much more at stake, often did not laugh. The trick was to script the action so that the role this judge was offered would be an interesting one.

I'd crafted my motion to this end, opening with a quotation from a nineteenth-century legal treatise about the right of the courts "to every man's evidence." After Ransom summoned me to the lectern, I began in a similar vein.

He waved at me as if shooing a fly. "Enough. I get that. But what's this FBI agent going to say?"

"I shouldn't have to disclose my defense in order for my client to exercise her Sixth Amendment right to call witnesses. My word as an officer of the court—"

Cutting me off, Ransom finished my sentence for me: "—isn't good enough. Come on, Mr. Maxwell. You're asking me to dismiss a murder charge because some guy won't come to court. You knew that was going to be the result when you subpoenaed him. It was preordained. You also knew the only possible remedy I could give you was dismissal. Maybe the only point of this is to manufacture an issue for appeal, but you're going to have to tell me what he knows that's so important if you expect me to even consider dismissing this case."

"If the ADA doesn't know it already, she's not going to hear it from me. If she does know and hasn't disclosed it, then we've got a serious *Brady* violation. So I'll defer to Ms. Sloane. Let her answer—if she can."

The judge's face tightened with anger. After a moment's reflection, however, he shifted his gaze to Sloane, nodding for her to speak. I saw the slight possibility of his shifting the target of his anger from me to her.

Flushing, she rose.

"There's nothing this FBI agent could conceivably say that changes the basic facts. Several witnesses saw the defendant run up and shoot the victim at close range. It's an open-and-shut case."

The judge turned his focus back to me. "You're not suggesting the FBI put her up to it, are you, Mr. Maxwell? Because that would hardly be a defense. Not to a murder charge."

"Why was she running? What was her state of mind at the moment when she pulled the trigger? The answers to those questions are tremendously relevant, and Agent Braxton's testimony is essential to answering them."

"You're saying he was present at the scene of the crime?"

Six spectators filled the back pews of the courtroom. I'd recognized one as a beat reporter. The one in the suit with a briefcase was no doubt a lawyer from the U.S. Attorney's Office, serving as Braxton's eyes and ears. The others were unfamiliar to me, but I had to assume that what was said here would be relayed to Wilder within hours.

"That would be surprising, Your Honor, considering that none of the police reports mentions Braxton's name. But, yes, to answer your question, I have reason to believe that he was present, notwithstanding the failure of the police incident reports to record that fact."

"Your client, it seems to me, would be the best person to testify about her own state of mind."

"Reversing the burden of proof is hardly a remedy for the deprivation of my client's Sixth Amendment right to call witnesses."

Ransom's brow furrowed. He shuffled the papers before him and found the document he wanted.

"I'm going to deny the dismissal motion. However, we can revisit the issue after trial. Let's take up the state's motion to preclude the defense from presenting evidence or argument regarding the victim's 'alleged' association with the Aryan Brotherhood. Mr. Maxwell hasn't drawn any connection between wanting to call an FBI agent and the prison gang issue, but if I were a betting man I'd put money there's something there."

Sloane stepped back to the lectern. "The only conceivable reason for the defense to introduce evidence of gang affiliation is to suggest the victim somehow deserved to be killed, and to turn the jury against him. The victim's character is completely irrelevant. There's no plausible claim of self-defense here, so the victim's past involvement in violent acts is also beside the point."

"I don't see how we can keep it out of the case," I responded when Ransom nodded for me to speak. "The state has listed the autopsy photos as exhibits, as usual. I didn't bring copies with me, but I think the DA will agree with me that Edwards's body is covered with racist tattoos. The man had Adolf Hitler's face depicted on his back."

Ransom didn't allow himself to smile. "I notice you didn't file the usual defense motions to keep those photos out."

"My client and I feel that the jurors need to learn all the facts, not just the ones the prosecution wants them to hear."

"In the future, Mr. Maxwell, please refrain from making sound bites in my courtroom."

"Yes, Your Honor. I don't intend to use Edwards's gang affiliation as character evidence; that would be improper. The relevance is to motive. My client had no motive for murdering Edwards. There are plenty of other people who did, however."

"Wait a minute. Are you disputing that your client pulled the trigger?"

I demurred. "The state has the burden of proof on that question."

Ransom sighed with exasperation. "Fine. You'll be given limited leeway. But you're not going to put the victim on trial in my courtroom."

"I understand, Judge."

With these matters decided—or, rather, punted for future consideration—Ransom dispensed with the remaining pretrial motions, granting and denying the routine requests filed by both sides. He concluded with a series of housekeeping matters, discussing the familiar ground rules for the trial, procedures for selecting the jury and introducing exhibits, all of which had the enervating effect of a coach's pregame admonitions.

After the hearing, I had a few minutes with my client. Jail had worn her down. She was looking more tired each time I saw her. Her skin was ashy, her hair a static frizz, and she seemed to be losing weight, although the impression may have been due to the hopeless, withdrawn look in her eyes. In her mind, the upcoming trial was merely a stopover between these months in the county jail and a lifetime of imprisonment.

"What's this about an FBI agent?" she asked when we were alone.

"Remember last time, when I asked you who first put the handcuffs on you? You said it was all a blur. You just remember sitting on the curb, and the police grabbing you. Well, the video appears to show this FBI agent was the first one on the scene. Mark Braxton. I've met him. He's been investigating the Aryan Brotherhood for the last fifteen years. If I'm right, it can't have been a coincidence that he was there with Edwards when you shot him."

"So what would he say anyway? He saw me do it? How's that help?"

"The point is that sometimes the witnesses who aren't summoned end up being more important than the ones who are. That's called 'reasonable doubt.'"

"Am I going to have to testify if you can't get him to come?"

"Possibly. The trouble is, they'll ask you where you got the gun, and you've already told me you got it from someone in advance and brought it to the scene. That's pretty damning evidence of premeditation."

"Okay," she said. "I mean, it's just ..."

Her voice trailed off.

"You don't have to go through with the trial. The ADA's offering you fifteen years. That's a lot of time, but it's not forever. If you don't want to fight it, I can go back to Sloane and tell her you're accepting the offer she made last week."

"No," she said. "I want to go to trial." But she sounded unconvinced.

I couldn't help wondering whether her answer would be different if she'd had a different lawyer. Still, I'd given her every chance to take a deal if she wanted one.

The time had come to broach another delicate subject. "There's one more thing we need to discuss," I said. "Sims, when he threatened me, hinted that he plans to attempt to influence the jury, probably with threats. This has to be disclosed to the judge and prosecutor so that measures can be taken to protect the jurors during the trial."

She looked at me with shock. "He'll kill you," she said. "Or your family. That little girl—"

"Which is probably the reason I ought to withdraw from the case, but I'm not going to do that. Not unless you tell me to."

She thought a moment, then looked at me and shook her head.

"Okay," I said.

"So when are you going to tell them?" She was indicating more trust in me than I'd so far felt, along with an untapped reservoir of courage.

"As soon as my brother and his family are out of town. Probably Friday. I need to make a few other arrangements first."

"What about my testimony?" she asked. "Can't I just tell them Sims gave me the gun?"

"No." Having told her story one way to me already, she couldn't un-tell it, and I couldn't un-hear what she'd said. I might have been a gang leader's go-to lawyer, but I wasn't going to make the same mistakes Teddy'd made. I prided myself on playing by the rules, and I intended to go on doing so until the end—even if those rules would mean the end of *me*.

I went on: "What you can do for me is rehearse. I want you to picture yourself on the witness stand. I want you to hear yourself telling your story, in your own voice. From beginning to end, starting with your mother's death and ending with how you got my number. We'll run through it in the evenings once the trial starts. Do that and you'll be as ready as you can be."

She seemed unconvinced. That made two of us. I took her hand and pressed it in a gesture of reassurance, the only emotional connection I could offer her. Then I stood and went through the ritual of knocking on the door to be let out.

CHAPTER 16

The arrangement we'd finally settled on was that Car would accompany Teddy, Tamara, and Carly to Disneyland, ensuring that they traveled in safety and, to the extent possible, that they maintained anonymity at all points of exposure. Like most negotiated compromises, this one made everybody unhappy.

"I'm a PI, not a bodyguard," Car told me with frustration when I first suggested the idea to him. "I don't even have a concealed-carry permit. And even if I did, I don't own a gun."

"I can't let them go without knowing someone I trust is watching them," I said over coffee. "Can you? Because the alternative is they go alone, or with some kind of hired security guard who'd cost a fortune. As for going alone, I don't even know if they're up for a simple trip like this under normal circumstances, much less when they might be walking targets. They're going to need help."

"Well, that goes for all of us. Shit, Leo, you know how your cases usually go down. You get some brainstorm at the last minute, you need an investigator to run out and work a miracle for you.

That's my job. Who's going to do my job if I'm down in Anaheim playing Mickey Mouse?"

"I'll do it myself. I'm not asking you because I want you out of the way. You're right, I need you here for the trial. But Teddy needs you more. Remember what you said to me at Wendy's that night? We're going to want someone on our side as ruthless as the people who're going to be coming after us. Your words. You may not own a gun, but whatever the situation, I know you'll do whatever you have to do. Shit, you don't have to stay with them. Just be there."

Car gave in, as I'd counted on. "But you're the one who's going to have to explain to your brother why he needs a chaperone to take his family on vacation. You've got to find a way to make it right. The old Teddy, he never would have been able to stand the idea that he couldn't take care of his own family. I hate to think how it's going to make him feel."

"Let me worry about that," I told Car. In truth, my brother's pride wasn't high on my list of concerns.

When I broke the news to Teddy, however, his response wasn't what I'd expected. If anything, he seemed relieved to share some of the responsibility, not just for the safety of his wife and daughter but also for the ordinary trials of travel. This, I reminded myself, was a man who, because of the risk of seizures, the DMV didn't trust behind the wheel of a car.

Teddy's acceptance of the new reality affected me deeply. Seeing him nod, clear his throat, and look down, I felt my throat seize, my eyes sting, and I had to stand and busy myself pretending to wash my hands at his kitchen sink.

I'd had plenty of reminders of my brother's diminishment, so I ought to have been used to the new Teddy by now. When I looked at him, however, I still saw, at first glance, the bearlike figure of my youth, the brother I'd looked up to with such a tangled regard that he'd seemed almost mythic to me, remote, inaccessible, and fiercely talented. When I'd begun my career, I'd merely been seeking my brother's approval. The last thing I'd expected was to feel pity for Teddy Maxwell.

Despite all the ways that he'd been diminished, however, I'd come to believe that his loss was outweighed by his gains: a loving wife whom he loved in return, a beautiful daughter, a caring regard for others that, to the old Teddy, would have seemed a sentimental indulgence.

Now, everything that mattered in his life and mine was at risk through my actions. My only solution was to send them away for a vacation that, even if my plan worked, would do little to guarantee their long-term safety.

I shut the water off but still didn't feel ready to face them.

It was Teddy who finally spoke. "We'll be all right," he said. "This situation isn't your fault, and you're doing your best to get us out of it. I'm more worried about you, staying here. Who's going to be looking after you if Car's with us?"

"Don't worry about me," I said.

I heard a rustle of fabric, then felt a hand on my shoulder, turning me. Tamara drew me toward her, pulling me into a silent embrace. I met my brother's eyes over her shoulder as I hugged her.

She released me, and Teddy put an arm around each of us.

"Carly wants her uncle to go in and say good night," Tam said.

~ ~ ~

I had one more stop to make. Sitting in my Saab outside Teddy's place, I thumbed Braxton's number into a burner phone. He answered on the second ring.

"This conversation isn't happening," I said, not bothering to introduce myself.

"That's right. You and I don't have a single word to say to each other. I plan to let a federal grand jury do my talking for me where you're concerned."

"You haven't indicted anyone in fifteen years. You're not going to start with a lawyer who's trying to salvage the life of a sixteen-year-old girl."

"I'm sure you believe your intentions are upright and noble. But that doesn't change the fact that you've chosen to lend your talents to the furtherance of a criminal racketeering enterprise."

"I didn't call to argue. I have a proposition."

"I'm the one who makes the propositions here."

"Don't worry, I'm not ambitious where snitching's concerned. I'll let you take the credit, or you can always blame me if we crash and burn; odds are, if that happens, I won't be around to say any different. I'll be in People's Park in half an hour. Oh, and, Braxton, try not to look like a narc."

Half an hour later, as promised, I'd taken up a position between two homeless camps, sitting with my back against a young redwood tree, the hood of my sweatshirt up, like a college kid who'd smoked too much bud and needed to chill until it wore off. Braxton, awkward in running clothes, jogged up on the sidewalk, circled the park under the streetlights, then rested with his hands on his knees, gasping somewhat, before walking into the relative darkness beneath the trees and stretching against a neighboring trunk.

I spoke quietly: "I can give you Jack Sims on the murder of Russell Bell, in furtherance of the AB's goal of having my father working for them on the outside. But I think you already know all about that. You know because my father knew."

Braxton went on stretching.

"Sims also killed my father and Dot. You know that, as well. The fact that you haven't moved on him yet tells me that you're after a bigger target. I've been thinking about this for a long time, and the only conclusion I can reach is that, where the Aryan Brotherhood and similar organizations are concerned, the FBI's goal isn't prosecution. Because what good does it do to convict a man of a crime when he's already serving a life sentence? Hell, Bo Wilder would probably have just as easy a time running his criminal empire from inside a federal prison."

"There's always the death penalty," Braxton said.

"How's Justice's record on that? Actual terrorists aside. Don't get me wrong, I agree with you that these guys are the worst of the worst, but we both know the death penalty's no sure thing. You could convict Bo Wilder tomorrow, but there's very little chance of that sentence ever being carried out. Plus, a trial would just give him a stage to recruit more members and expose any assets that you may still have within his organization."

Braxton seemed to freeze for a moment. Then he bent to his stretch again, pushing against the tree with one leg braced behind him as if he could push it down. "I don't think you have any idea what it's like to bring a major investigation to fruition," he said. "Let's talk about something you do know about."

"I know that against an enemy like the AB, justice is an elusive concept, and the normal rules don't seem to apply. Especially when you've lost one of your own. When punishment isn't possible, when the enemy can't be any more incapacitated than he already is, then revenge is the only thing left to fight for. But I think you made that decision a long time ago, even before Dad and Dot were killed. I think this ceased being an ordinary investigation—with arrests and indictments and prosecutions—around the time you began to work on it."

"So what is it, if not an investigation?" Braxton said.

"You've been running a domestic counterinsurgency, working to sabotage and destabilize the AB, using informants like my dad. And like Edwards. I know you were present at the scene the day Edwards was killed. It doesn't take too many inferences to guess why you were there."

"Did your father tell you that?"

"No," I said. "But he's not a snitch. He never was. He was a fighter."

Finally, Braxton's shell seemed to crack a little. "That he was," he said, lowering himself to the ground, now sitting facing me from five feet away.

On the other side of the park, a drum circle was starting up, its insistent, unskilled beat seeming to electrify the chill evening air.

"I know my dad better than you think," I said. "I just can't see him pledging fifteen years of his life to snitching on the AB. What I can imagine is his dedicating all that time and more to the mission of sabotaging these fuckers from within."

"What's this deal you're talking about?" Braxton asked. "You've got two minutes before I need to break off this extremely insecure meeting and get back to my run."

The fact that he was here at all had told me what I needed. I knew I'd gained his interest. Now I just wanted to close the deal. "It's not information you care about," I said to him, "though you pretend it is. You're really waiting for just the right opportunity to drop the biggest possible bomb on the Aryan Brotherhood. You figured my brother was your best chance to do that. The thing is, you figured wrong."

Braxton's lip curled. "You're the guy I should be dealing with, huh?"

"My father and Edwards were your best assets in the AB's organization. Normally, losing them would represent a tremendous blow. But being in a disadvantageous position also brings certain possibilities to light. You're now in a situation not unlike your targets. The same as these guys running criminal empires behind bars, you've already lost everything there is to lose. So, if you've learned anything, it should be that the person with nothing left to lose is probably your most dangerous adversary."

"If you're trying to get me to confirm or deny that the Bureau still has informants in the organization, it won't work." Braxton started to rise. "Tell Bo Wilder I said hello. You may even get to see him in person one of these days."

"I'm sure Bo and his pals are pretty eager to know whether my father and Edwards were their only rats. I can't help them. You're the only one who knows."

Braxton laughed. "You're damn right. And I don't share, not with crooked lawyers."

It was easy to control my response. That's because I'd sensed the undercurrent of excitement in his voice, which told me he saw where I was going but was holding back, trying to make me think he didn't want to play.

"You wouldn't spill anything," I told him. "That's exactly the point." My tone was even. "It's why I sent you the subpoena. One of the reasons, anyway. The chief reason, of course, being that you're the key eyewitness to Edwards's murder and can testify that Alice Ward was hysterical, in a panic."

"You're forgetting one thing. You can't make me take the stand."

"No, but you can choose to. Surely your boss will let you if you tell him why. It'll be just the stage you need to accomplish your goal. Think of the lead: 'Today, on the witness stand, an FBI agent denied that the FBI currently has confidential sources in place at the highest level of the Aryan Brotherhood.'" I paused, then went on. "Who's to say that my father didn't tell me all he knew before he died? My experience tells me that the questions I ask in cross-examination often prove more meaningful to my listeners than the answers a witness gives."

"It sounds to me as if you're looking for some kind of understanding that I'll give testimony favorable to your client. Such an agreement's not possible. What I say may be favorable, or it may be unfavorable. But if I do agree to testify, I'm not going to lie. You'll get the truth . . . and your client may not like it."

I started to speak, but he held up a hand. "You're hoping I'll tell you what I saw. But it's not going to happen. And whatever I have to say, you'll hear it for the first time when I take the witness stand—assuming I do. I just want to make sure you comprehend the terms. I'm not your friend, and I'm not your client's friend. You need to realize, I don't have the slightest interest in helping your client avoid prison."

None of this was what I wanted, but I felt my only choice was to go along. "Fine. Ms. Ward's willing to take her chances. So when will I have your answer?"

He rose from the ground, brushing himself off. "I have to get clearance from the director. This may have to go all the way to the Attorney General's Office, which puts it above my pay grade. You'll know I've agreed to testify if my name is called and I walk into the courtroom and up to the witness stand. If you don't see me, then, well, you'll also have your answer."

CHAPTER 17

The start of Alice Ward's trial was delayed by a day, owing to extra security procedures instituted in response to Sims's threat to tamper with the jury. I'd revealed this tactic, and the need to take it seriously, during a conference in judicial chambers last Friday afternoon.

After hearing me out, an angry Judge Ransom had initially proposed to remove me from the case on the grounds that, in his view, I'd become a potential witness against my client. This would disqualify me from also being her lawyer. Sloane, for her part, insisted she had no intention of informing the jury of Sims's threats. Finally, Ransom cooled down enough to admit that the situation wasn't my fault, especially after I'd explained that my family had been threatened, too.

"And you don't feel that's a conflict of interest?" he concluded.

"If it's not me in the chair, it'd just be some other lawyer, maybe someone who'd be more intimidated by these kinds of tactics. The threats have nothing to do with my client. She deserves the best possible defense."

"And you simply happen to be convinced that you're the one who can give it to her," Judge Ransom said.

I chose to interpret this comment as not requiring a response. As for the judge's other questions, I respectfully declined to answer them.

"Any chance of your client reconsidering and taking that deal?" Sloane inquired after the conference.

"I'm afraid not," I told her. "She's determined to take her chances."

"You really think you can beat a murder charge? Or are you banking on an ineffective assistance claim based on Sims's threats against you?"

"I don't try cases to lose them," is what I told her.

"Look, if he's threatened you, he must have threatened her. Come on, Leo. Do the right thing. Step aside. Let the PD's office take over. The judge told you just now he thinks you should withdraw. I wouldn't oppose a continuance."

It would be a lie to say I wasn't tempted. Every attorney wishes at some point for the whole complicated weight of a looming trial to suddenly be lifted from his shoulders, and last-minute pleas were common enough that such a reprieve felt tempting, within reach. But I knew that postponing the trial would only postpone the inevitable for Alice Ward, and for me. I might not live to see the retrial, but I was pigheadedly certain I was the only lawyer who could win her case. And winning, it seemed to me, was the only way out—for both of us.

I spent the weekend working out of an office I'd borrowed from a colleague, splitting my time between there and the jail, having deemed my own place unsafe now that a warrant had been signed for Sims's arrest.

The jury would be sequestered. "It's an overreaction, I'm sure," Ransom had informed the lawyers on Monday. This was when he'd called us back into chambers to discuss the special protocol he was using, a series of safeguards normally reserved only for gang cases.

"But I've got to stand for reelection next year, so I don't intend to have an incident on my watch, or even the possibility of one. They'll be bused back and forth to the hotel, and their meals will be brought in."

As a result of this extra hardship that jury service would entail for those chosen, culling the panel took longer than usual. After a day and a half of the same questions repeated again and again, we'd ended up with a collection of fourteen retirees, widows and widowers, hourly workers, and students. All they had in common was that none of them had been able to dream up a good enough reason to get out of it. These men and women would be tasked with deciding Alice Ward's fate.

Finally, on Tuesday afternoon, Sloane rose to give her opening statement. She worked without notes, seeming relaxed, entirely confident in her case and in possession of the courtroom, assured of her ability to command the jurors' attention. I glanced covertly at my client, dressed in a borrowed pantsuit that made her appear even more diminutive than normal, my expression reinforcing the advice I'd shared with her before court this morning: *Don't react*.

Sloane was competent and professional, beginning with a summary of the known and provable facts, all succinct and damning. She efficiently narrated the circumstances of the shooting itself, establishing that the defendant had run deliberately up to Edwards and shot him in the head without a word. This made it more than clear that there was no possibility of the shooting's having been an accident, nor a crime in the heat of passion; rather, it was a willful, premeditated killing. Sloane then transitioned into the state's burden of proof, running through the elements of the crime, including the state's responsibility to prove beyond a reasonable doubt that Edwards's murder hadn't been the result of provocation or committed in the heat of passion.

Suddenly, she switched tracks. "Now I want to talk to you for a few minutes about what the state doesn't have to prove." Here she paused, gathering the jurors' attention as she prepared to discuss the weakness at the center of the DA's case. She waited until she had their maximum focus.

"You're probably asking yourself, why would a young woman commit such a horrific crime? Throughout this trial, I'm going to be as honest with you as I can. And the honest answer is, I don't know. I doubt any of us ever will understand completely. But it's important for you to realize that the presence or absence of a motive doesn't necessarily have anything to do with the question of her guilt.

"Alice Ward knew the victim years ago, when she was a child. Then he went to prison for six years. She didn't see him again until the day she shot him. As you listen to the evidence, I want you to think about how much time six years is. Time for thought, time for reflection. Time for planning. Time for premeditation.

"Of course, even six seconds can be enough time to premeditate a murder. Or to have second thoughts. The evidence is going to show that in those few seconds before the murder, Alice Ward made a final, deliberate choice, and it was an irrevocable one. At the end of this trial I'll stand here again and ask that you return a verdict of guilty on the charge of first-degree murder."

Sloane sat down. I was already on my feet, moving quickly to usurp the jurors' attention from Sloane's last words.

I didn't waste words. "Randolph Edwards lived in the house next door to the apartment building where Leann Ward and her daughter lived. They had one of the second-floor units. It was a cramped one-bedroom. Leann was a single mother who waited tables. Some nights her tips were good. Others, not. But even on the good nights, it probably seemed to her that there was never enough.

"Leann's death is on the books as an unsolved murder. She was found with a needle in her arm. The cause of death was a heroin overdose. I say 'she was found,' but her daughter Alice was the one who discovered her unresponsive body. She was there in the next room, sleeping or trying to sleep, the night her mother was killed. The needle was still in her mother's arm the next morning when this young girl went to wake her. Leann's eyes were open and her skin was cold."

Here I moved over to place a hand on Alice's shoulder, allowing the jurors the chance to look at her—and, I hoped, to see her for what she was: a scared teenager who ought to have just gotten her driver's license. I'd prepared her for this moment, and she tentatively raised her head.

"At first, it looked like an accident, a single mother who'd yielded to the pressures of trying to support a daughter on an unreliable income in an uncertain world. But the medical examiner's reports show marks on the victim's neck and bruising on her wrists, indicating she was held down. The death was ruled a homicide. No one was ever arrested—though that doesn't mean the police and the authorities don't know who did it. But let me first go back and give you a picture of Leann's situation in the period preceding her death."

Sticking closely to the parts of my client's story we'd rehearsed, I briefly summarized what I knew about the Plum Tree holdup, Leann Ward's role in it, and the circumstances of her murder after the job was botched. Then I told the jurors about Sims's and Edwards's imprisonments on unrelated charges.

"You see, the FBI was interested in these men. But the federal government was after a bigger target than a pair of murderers associated with a local restaurant heist gone bad. The Aryan Brotherhood had started as a prison gang. But by the time Sims and Edwards went to prison, it had become one of the largest organized crime syndicates in California. What this meant was that the FBI needed reliable, long-term informants inside the organization.

"There's no dispute that my client killed Randolph Edwards. She pulled the trigger. However, I expect the evidence to show that she was provoked, and that she acted in the heat of passion. As you listen to the evidence, I want you to ask yourselves why the state, represented here by Ms. Sloane, who says she wants to be honest, is trying to hide or obscure so many key details, beginning with what happened at the Plum Tree years ago and ending with an FBI agent being an actual witness to the shooting.

"At the end of this case, I'm confident you'll see that Alice Ward was provoked by calculating men expert at manipulating others to do their dirty work for them. Men who don't mind spilling blood if it serves their goals. Men like Jack Sims and his counterparts in the FBI."

CHAPTER 18

I'd bought a half-dozen prepaid cell phones before Teddy and his family's departure with Car for Anaheim. They'd driven my Saab down, and were staying in a rental condo that we'd reserved and paid for under an assumed name through an online site. That evening, after opening statements, I checked in with my brother.

He picked up on the first ring. "Still having fun?" We'd talked twice already: once on Friday, when Teddy'd called to confirm their safe arrival, and again on Monday night.

"One of us is," he answered. "We spent yesterday and today at the amusement park. Leo, I can't handle these crowds. After an hour my head feels as if it's going to explode. Tomorrow's a rest day. We're going to stick close to home, float in the pool. And watch our backs."

"That's probably a good idea." I then briefly filled him in about the tack I'd taken in my opening statement, and how I'd worked in a mention of Jack Sims's name in open court for the first time, sug-gesting a connection to the FBI. However, as I'd already informed my brother, there'd been a warrant out for Sims's arrest since Friday afternoon.

"I'll tell Car. Don't worry, he's already on his toes."

"Where is he now?"

"Went to get groceries. He ought to be back soon."

I could tell from Teddy's voice that things weren't going so well on that front. "I know the situation isn't ideal," I said, trying to sound understanding, apologetic, and unyielding all at once. "But, from a selfish point of view, I don't think I'd be able to do this if he weren't there."

"Car's not a man with a lot of patience for human weakness," Teddy said. "He's like you. He remembers how I used to be, and he keeps expecting me to take charge. But unlike you, he hasn't come around to the way things are these days."

"It may seem that way, but people have a funny way of express-ing loyalty. You know, after Dad and Dot were murdered, Car told me the story of how he first came to work with you. That court case you were working, the shooting he was involved in. He talked about coming clean to you and you offering him a job."

"No shit." The line was silent for a moment. "I'd forgotten all about that."

"He hasn't," I assured him. "Car is who he is. He's unforgiving, and he's caustic, but he's very, very good at what he does—and I wouldn't trust anyone else to keep you and your family safe. He and Tam getting along okay?"

"Like oil and water. So, I guess about as good as you'd expect."

In the background I heard a door thump open, and Carly's voice asking Daddy who he was talking to. Teddy let out an exasperated sigh. "It's Leo, darling," he told her. Then, more distinctly: "Here's Carly to say hello."

"Uncle Leo?" Carly asked, and as soon as she heard my voice she began breathlessly telling me about all the Disney princesses she'd seen over the last few days, several of whose names I hadn't even heard before, and all the rides she'd been on. For more than a minute I couldn't get a word in, even during her brief pauses, which were filled with rapturous intakes of breath ending in renewed bursts of speech. Despite my fatigue and worry, I stood there with a smile, recognizing I'd be happy to go on listening to such nonsense for hours.

Finally Teddy intervened, taking back the phone and sending her back to bed, no doubt to dream of what new wonders tomorrow might bring. "As I said, at least one of us is having a good time. We're safe here, Leo. I don't think there's anything to worry about. Just make sure you nail these bastards to the wall good and tight so that we can come home and be done with this forever. It's time for all of us to stop being afraid."

I couldn't have agreed more.

~ ~ ~

In the morning, the first police officer on the scene described how he'd received the dispatch call and raced there, his testimony hewing closely to the narrative in his report.

Once Sloane had finished with him, it was my turn to question Officer Rick Martinez.

"In your report and in your testimony, you included all of the details that you considered important, correct?"

Predictably, he jousted with me, and we went back and forth with lofty abstractions for a few rounds, alternately grappling and returning to our corners. The point of it wasn't to secure any admission from him but to wake the jurors up to the fact that this witness might be hiding important information.

At last, I cut to the chase. I had the dash cam video cued up and ready to go. After obtaining the judge's permission to admit the video into evidence, I played it for the witness and for the jurors. I let the clip cycle through once, then ran it again in slow motion, freezing the image near the beginning where it showed Braxton standing just a few feet from Alice Ward.

"Who's that man?" I asked, zooming in.

The cop took a sip of water. "He didn't tell me his name."

"But he must have offered you some identification, didn't he?"

The officer admitted that he had. "It showed he was an FBI agent."

"You testified that your partner handcuffed my client. But that isn't true, is it?"

"Sure it is. He cuffed her. Everything in my report was the truth. I didn't lie."

He shot a glance at Sloane. At the same time, I raised my hand in a slight wave, a way of calling attention to the cop's discomfort, so fleetingly revealed.

"Isn't it true that Ms. Ward was already cuffed when you and your partner took her to the ground?"

Martinez admitted that they'd discovered as much after they'd tackled her. He further admitted that his partner had gained a set of brand-new cuffs that day, since the FBI agent hadn't stuck around long enough to retrieve the pair he'd abandoned on Alice Ward's wrists.

"You testified earlier that you secured the gun. But isn't the complete truth that, before you arrived, the FBI agent had already done so?"

"Look at the video. You can see it lying on the sidewalk there."

"My point is, you've got no idea who handled that weapon before you arrived?"

"I have a pretty good idea that your client handled it some when she used it to shoot the victim."

Just in case the fact wasn't already completely obvious to the jurors, I now went about the task of forcing Martinez to admit that he hadn't mentioned the FBI agent in his police report, nor in his testimony under direct examination by the DA.

"I want us to be clear here. The reason you didn't mention the federal agent who was present is that he told you he wanted his name kept out of the official record?"

The witness reluctantly agreed that this was the request made. "No further questions."

Once Martinez's partner had taken his oath, Sloane again focused on the details of the victim lying there on the sidewalk with half his head blown off, the gun just a few feet away, and my client sitting on the curb. Again, I had no problem establishing both Braxton's presence at the scene and his swift departure.

Other routine witnesses followed: a paramedic; the medical examiner who'd performed the autopsy; the forensics expert who confirmed Alice's fingerprints on the gun and gunshot residue on her arm. Sloane's strategy for the moment seemed to be to bore the jurors into acquiescence. This gave me little to do but wait for her to call a witness who mattered, and to study the jurors.

Applying what I'd learned of them from their answers to the lawyers' questions during voir dire and from the online research I'd conducted Monday night, I tried to intuit their prejudices and inclinations. My goal was to decide which were the likeliest candidates to step forward as my client's champions once the case was handed over to them.

I also couldn't help giving thought to Sims's promise to "reach" the jury. Whatever precautions had been taken in sequestering the jurors, I remained concerned. Better than anyone else in the courtroom, I knew just how dangerous Sims was. They might have been sequestered, but those closest to them weren't.

Plus, with each day that went by without Sims being taken into custody—and, on the flip side, without any contact from anyone in Wilder's organization—I grew more uneasy. The defense strategy I'd plotted and announced to the world during my opening statement yesterday amounted to a declaration of war on Sims, Wilder, and their crew.

Having begun that war, I'd have preferred to keep my enemy in sight.

I didn't have to wait long. Thursday evening, after the first full day of testimony, a drunk stumbled against me on the sidewalk. Exuding stale cigarette smoke, he moved away with a sober, unhurried gait. I watched him go, then looked down at the disposable cell phone he'd pressed into my hand.

It rang later that evening as I was in my borrowed office, prepping one of my first witnesses—Alex Rosen, the man Car and I'd met with at Wendy's, the one who'd placed Sims with Alice Ward near the scene of the shooting. Car's last task before leaving for Anaheim had been to serve him with a subpoena.

After informing Rosen that the subpoena obligated him to testify whether he liked it or not, I'd apologized for the way Car and I had treated him. I also made him realize it was in his best interests to know, before he took the stand, what I was going to ask. He wasn't happy about testifying, but I'd made clear that it would be better for him if he appeared voluntarily rather than being dragged into court.

"Give me a minute," I said, hoping he wouldn't run out on me before I returned.

I went into another room and closed the door.

"Yeah," I said.

"That's all you got to say is 'yeah'? My guys usually show me more respect, even when it's just a cover for betrayal."

"I'm not 'your guy.' But at least with me you know what you're getting."

"I'm not so sure," Bo said. "But we'll leave that discussion for another time. You're a busy man. You've got court in the morning, and only so many hours between then and now. Me, on the other hand, I've got nothing but time."

I heard a vague threat in this, but realized there was almost nothing that the man could say to me that would have no ominous overtones.

"The real reason I'm calling is that I checked into what we were talking about before. You raised suspicions about someone close to me's possible involvement in the murder of your father and his wife. I didn't want to believe this. But it turns out you were right. And we both know who we're talking about."

He'd caught me off guard, and his confirmation of my suspicions stunned me, stirring anger in my chest. "Thanks for checking," I said. My thoughts were racing. "But I'm not asking for your help. I didn't need you to tell me what I already know."

"You suspecting and me telling are different things. I suppose next you're going to say you can take care of it yourself. Bullshit. You don't have the right. Plus, you try to make a move without my okay, you're in the same position as him. Your name goes in the hat, and one of my guys draws the slip."

He paused, and I waited for what was next.

"Second, you don't have the balls. Third, whatever you might try, there's a good chance you'd wind up dead." Suddenly, he shifted tack, going on in a more reasonable tone. "You don't want to be in my debt, I get that. What do those white-collar assholes call it? 'Leverage.' Try to think of it like that."

I still didn't reply. What was the point?

"I can't control whether a man feels a sense of obligation," Wilder continued. "But I do know that it can be a pretty cold and lonely place for the man who won't accept a hand that's offered him. Especially when it's my hand."

My mouth was dry, but I found my voice. "Whatever help you're offering, I don't want it. There's nothing more to discuss."

Bo sounded unsurprised. "You speaking for yourself? Because, you know, you're not the only one who's lost a father."

"I'm speaking for myself and my brother."

"How is Teddy doing? How's that family of his?"

I didn't respond, wanting to end the call, but aware that I needed to keep listening.

"They ought to take some time for themselves, a little vacation. The lesson I've learned is that you've got to live life to the fullest, every minute. Because in the blink of an eye, it can all be taken away. A knock comes on the door, none of us knows when—and you could end up in a place like this. Or somewhere worse, even."

His tone turned contemplative. "Like, if I had a kid Carly's age, I'd probably take her down to Anaheim, see Disneyland."

I was struggling to breathe, even if none of this should have been unexpected. "Whatever beef you've got with me, it's about me. Leave my family out of it."

"You don't get it, do you?" He gave a short, unpleasant laugh. "Protection's what I'm offering, not threats. You're a fool not to accept it when I'm offering, especially with an animal like Sims on the loose. It's an ugly world out there. Think about it."

Before I could make any response, the call went dead.

I waited until my breathing slowed, then I went back out to finish prepping Rosen.

CHAPTER 19

In the morning, the prosecution presented the testimony of six civilian eyewitnesses, several of whom had been gathered outside the Gangway, a sailor-themed bar across the street. With each, Sloane took a minimal, formulaic approach, prompting the witness to describe where he'd been standing, what direction he'd been facing, and, finally, what he'd seen. She ended each examination by having the witness identify the shooter as Alice Ward, sitting at the defense table beside me.

When it was my turn, I used the notes Car and I had taken from the pretrial interviews we'd conducted to tease out, with varying success, as many details of my client's emotional disturbance as I could.

One witness, I knew, had missed the precise moment of the shooting because he'd turned his head to see who was chasing Alice, a fact the DA had glossed over. Hearing the gunshot, the witness then had looked back in time to see Edwards fall. Another, catching sight of Alice running out of the alley with a handgun clutched in her fist, had thought she was deranged, possibly a random shooter. Most of the six had been too preoccupied with their own terrified reactions to observe or register Agent Braxton's actions in the moments before the police showed up.

A sense of vertigo began to suffuse the courtroom, as the same event was repeatedly narrated with subtle shifts in the frame of reference. None of the witnesses had any clue whatsoever why my client had done what she did.

Sloane's next witness was Dunham, the detective who'd investigated the case. Having proved a crime had been committed and that Alice Ward was the one who'd committed it, Sloane now sought to offer the jurors a plausible motive for an otherwise senseless act.

Using certified public records, Sloane led Dunham through a recital of the known facts of Alice Ward's life. These included her single mother, the San Leandro apartment, her next-door neighbors Sims and Edwards, her mother's overdose, and, finally, the police's suspicion that Leann was murdered. The intended implication was that Alice Ward might have blamed Edwards for her mother's death. Although I could have objected on numerous grounds as Dunham testified beyond her personal knowledge, I allowed all of what she said to be entered into the record.

Next, Sloane used Dunham to introduce evidence of Alice's placement in various foster homes, painting a picture of a shattered life, offering the jurors a plausible motive for revenge. Wisely, however, Dunham made no mention of the Plum Tree job; I assumed she knew about Leann Ward's connection to that unsolved murder. I could have attempted to wade into the subject on cross-examination if I wished, but if I did, I'd only be reinforcing the DA's point that my client harbored a long-held motive.

Instead, I began with more recent history. "Jack Sims has been a person of interest to the local authorities for some time, has he not?"

Dunham studied me. Mannish and imposing, she was dressed in a dark suit over a gray silk shirt. "Define 'of interest.'"

"Well, isn't it true that he's a known member of the Aryan Brotherhood?"

Sloane, sensing an area of danger, objected. So I countered with the obvious fact that she'd mentioned the victim's gang membership in her opening statement. The judge allowed the question.

"That's correct."

"What's the Aryan Brotherhood?"

Probably she'd been asked similar questions so many times under different circumstances by prosecutors that the answer simply rolled off her tongue. "It's a criminal organization whose members engage in narcotics distribution, firearms trafficking, money laundering, and acts of brutal violence."

"Edwards joined the Aryan Brotherhood while in prison, correct?"

"That's the usual route of entry. It started out as a prison gang, and, essentially, it still is."

"But one that's grown to control an extensive network of illegal activities in the outside world, true?"

Dunham admitted this was so.

Next, I confirmed with her the following: that Edwards, the victim, had likewise been a member of the AB, and that he and Sims had been known associates after each had gotten out of prison. Which suggested that they'd both remained active in the AB. She didn't disagree. I introduced the pictures of Edwards's corpse stripped naked to reveal the AB tattoos that covered his back, including the jumbo-sized portrayal of Adolf Hitler.

"Now, Detective, as part of your investigation, you've made some inquiries into the source of the funds that are financing my client's defense, haven't you?"

Sloane was instantly on her feet. "Your Honor," she began in a tone of strident objection. Then she stopped short.

"Hold on a minute. You're talking about the money that's going into your pocket?" Judge Ransom asked in a tone of personal affront.

I didn't mind the jurors' hearing it. Over the last three days, they'd been lulled to sleep again and again by the DA's humdrum presentation of her case. I felt it was time, now, to wake them up.

"That's exactly what I meant, Your Honor," I told him.

"Answer it," the judge instructed the detective. "It's Mr. Maxwell's funeral."

"I've looked into the matter," Dunham said, seeming to relish what was coming.

"And you've learned that the money to pay my fee is being supplied by the Aryan Brotherhood, haven't you?"

The jurors looked appalled, as if the script had changed suddenly from droning facts to shocking reality.

"That's right," Dunham said with a slow smile. "Wired the same night she was arrested."

I had a strong urge to ask her more, to find out how deeply she'd delved into matters that, more than arguably, were protected by attorney-client privilege. But I'd made my point. I'd committed myself to falling on the sword for my client's sake. Now, I had to finish the job.

"Why in God's name would the Aryan Brotherhood be paying to defend an African-American teenager from murder charges for killing one of its members?"

Sloane objected at this obviously unanswerable question. Ransom sustained the objection with a stern admonition to me, but that didn't stop Dunham from responding. "Ask her," she said, her eyes flashing to my client.

It was arguably a remark incompatible with Alice's right to remain silent. I objected and asked the judge to strike the remark, which he did. But I didn't allow her to throw me off.

"I'm asking you," I said. "It doesn't make any sense, does it?"

"Maybe you can enlighten us," she replied, again ignoring Sloane's objection and the judge's forceful and immediate response of "Sustained."

I nodded solemnly, letting her and the jurors know that I intended to. I let this promise hang in the air before moving on.

I stepped closer to the jury box, positioning myself now directly in front of it. "If Jack Sims had been present at the murder scene," I began, "that would be a fact of interest to you in investigating the shooting of Edwards, a fellow member of the Aryan Brotherhood, correct?"

"I have no knowledge of his being present."

"But it would be of interest to you if he was, wouldn't it?"

"I'm always interested in the presence of any witness to a murder."

"Jack Sims lived with Edwards in the house next door to Alice Ward's apartment building when she was a little girl, before her mother died, isn't that true?"

Dunham had no other choice but to confirm this was so.

"So, am I right that you have no idea what Sims, if he was there at the murder scene, might have said to my client in the moments before she shot Edwards?"

Again, Sloane objected. But my point had been made.

I moved on, without waiting for Dunham to fill in the blank.

"In response to some of the DA's questions, you talked about events that occurred years ago in Alice Ward's life. I want to focus right this moment on more recent history. Please tell the jury what happened the day of Ms. Ward's arraignment."

"She tried to kill herself," Dunham said.

"How?"

Grudgingly, Dunham described Alice Ward's brutal self-attack, which I'd now seen on video numerous times. Through all of this, Sloane sat silent, though I'd expected to draw her objection. Getting her hits in where she could, Dunham made sure the jury understood that it was my pen Alice had used.

"She attempted to kill herself immediately after I'd spoken to her about exchanging information for the possibility of a reduced sentence, isn't that true?"

Sloane's objection was strident, and the judge's rebuke of me even more so.

"All right, then let's move backward," I said to Dunham when Ransom had finished instructing the jurors to disregard my improper question. "Alice's mother's killers were never caught, correct?"

"Or killer. But yes, it's my understanding that the crime remains unsolved."

"Isn't it true that at the time of her death, Leann Ward was working at a restaurant called the Plum Tree?"

Before Dunham could answer this question, Sloane stood and lodged the obvious objections: hearsay, lack of personal knowledge. But I was prepared. Soon after learning Jane Doe's identity, I'd submitted a Public Records Act request for the police incident reports from the Plum Tree robbery, a route that had allowed me to obtain the documents without alerting the DA.

In response to her objection, I now offered these reports into evidence. With the judge's permission, I used Dunham as my mouthpiece, forcing her to read into the record the official Oakland Police Department narratives summarizing what was known about the perpetrators. The courtroom thus learned that they'd been masked and armed with multiple weapons, including handguns and shotguns; that they'd come in through the back door, which presumably had been left open; and that they'd killed a man and escaped with a modest amount of cash, along with jewelry and other items seized from the customers. I pointed out that Leann Ward's name was on the list of witnesses, and that the robbery had taken place just a week before her death.

"Was Sims or Edwards ever a suspect in the Plum Tree job?"

"I have no idea." Dunham's facial expression was tight; her eyes were uncertain. She was beginning to piece together the contours of my defense.

"To your knowledge, was either of them ever arrested in connection with it?"

Dunham admitted that no such arrest had been made.

"Isn't it true, in your experience, that the police have been known to go to great lengths to protect a confidential informant?"

"Not cover up a murder," Dunham said. "Never."

"All right, the police wouldn't. But what about the FBI?"

"I don't know. I don't have a thing to do with the FBI."

I had one more question, which would be a deliberate echo of the abuse she'd thrown at me the day of Alice Ward's attempted suicide. "In your experience as a law enforcement officer, what's the worst thing that can happen to an informant in a murder case, even a cold case like Leann Ward's death?"

Dunham held my eyes, her gaze locked with mine so intensely that I sensed the jurors fidgeting uncomfortably in their chairs.

"Sometimes they turn up dead," Dunham finally answered.

I nodded sadly, then offered a frank, appraising glance at the jurors. "No more questions."

CHAPTER 20

After Wilder's warning from jail, I'd spoken with Car, letting him know that it was possible they were being watched. He hadn't noticed anything, he told me, and in any case, they were keeping close to the condo. "They're wondering how much longer we're going to have to stay here. Tam's especially anxious to leave, but everyone's nerves are frayed. Are you completely sure this is necessary?"

I told him that I was, even though I remained uncertain. "The prosecution rested its case today," I said. "We're looking at tomorrow and Monday for the defense witnesses, with the case going to the jury Tuesday. Who knows how long they'll be out."

"Could be five minutes," Car said.

"Or five days."

"And who's to say it'll be safe to return after the verdict's in?"

I didn't have an answer. And I didn't want to say what I feared: that it would never be safe, especially if I couldn't get Braxton to testify as I'd planned.

Because of this concern, my next call after my talk with Car was to the FBI agent. "I'll need you tomorrow," I said when he came on the line.

I steeled myself for bad news, but his answer at least gave me hope.

"I can't do it tomorrow," Braxton said. "I've got tentative approval for the plan, but it needs to be kicked up one more level for the final go-ahead. We're talking Monday at the earliest."

My insides fizzed with the familiar panic of an underprepared lawyer. I needed the weekend to prep my client for her testimony. I'd hoped to call Rosen first, followed by Braxton. Tomorrow was too soon to be putting Alice Ward on the stand. "It has to be tomorrow," I told him. "I need you on the stand before my client. That's just the way it has to be. You'll have to expedite the process."

There was a pause, then Braxton said he couldn't make any promises. He wouldn't know until mid-morning if he had authorization to testify. "And even then, remember, this may not turn out the way you've planned."

That was my problem, I said, not his.

~ ~ ~

With the state having rested Thursday afternoon, I called the defense's first witness Friday morning. Trembling, Alex Rosen took his place on the stand.

He said his name, swore the oath, and stated where he lived. Without further preamble, I directed his attention to my client, Alice Ward, and asked him if he'd ever seen her before. He identified her as the person he'd seen in the city the night of the shooting. "She was walking down the sidewalk with this guy. Big muscles, shaved head. Mustache. Scary-looking dude."

Rosen went on to repeat what he'd told me about the guy having his arm around Alice Ward and talking to her in a low voice as they went, then giving her a little pat on the back before returning alone the way they'd come.

"She stood there for a moment like she was in a daze. Then suddenly she started running up the alley, up Myrtle Street," Rosen said. "I couldn't help watching her. By this time, the guy was gone. I heard her yell something, then she raised the gun and fired. I saw the victim fall, and then I started running."

I had a blown-up mug shot of Sims, and showed it to the witness. "Does this appear to be the man you saw talking to Alice Ward?"

"Yes, that's him. I'm sure of it."

With this, I sat down. Sloane had evidently detected something in his testimony that aroused her prosecutor's instinct, because her first question was accusatory, in a tone that presupposed wrongdoing: "What were *you* doing in San Francisco that evening, Mr. Rosen?"

I objected to the question as irrelevant, but the judge allowed it.

Rosen answered with a sheepish grin. "Trying to score some smack."

I stood and objected again, moving the judge to strike the testimony as irrelevant and prejudicial. Ransom agreed, and instructed the jurors to disregard it. But I knew he was doing this only for the sake of any eventual appeal my client might file. There was no way to un-ring that bell.

Sloane had more tricks up her sleeve. She asked Rosen when he'd first seen the photograph of Sims he'd identified in court today; he was forced to admit that the first time he'd seen it was the previous Thursday evening, when he'd met with me in his office to prepare for his testimony today. From here, she easily picked up the scent, establishing that I'd met with Rosen one other time. Rosen testified that a man he knew as a sometime dealer had convinced him to talk with a private investigator—whom he couldn't name—and then with me.

I cringed with each step she took down this chain, seeing the inferences she was setting up, the implication that Rosen had exchanged testimony for drugs. And, in truth, she probably wasn't far off the mark, at least as concerned his motivations that night for speaking with me. At the time I'd thought I was smart to take advantage of Menendez's street presence to locate a witness I wouldn't otherwise have found. Now I was paying the price.

"Did Mr. Maxwell show you anything during this meeting at Wendy's?" Sloane asked.

"A picture on his phone," Rosen said. "The man and a little girl. Except that time, he told me the guy in the photo *wasn't* the guy he was looking for. He didn't have the mug shot then."

"And then when he met you last Thursday, he told you the person in the mug shot *was* the guy, correct?"

"He showed me the mug shot and I told him that was the guy I saw."

"Last Thursday night, did he put those two photos side by side, the mug shot and the personal photograph from his phone?"

I stood on numb legs and objected at Sloane's use of the phrase "personal photograph," though I knew my objection served only to draw the jurors' attention to her insinuation that I'd been trying to influence this witness, perhaps even attempting to protect one of the racist gang members who were paying my fee.

"He didn't show the one from his phone again, no. Just the mug shot."

"In your initial meeting, you identified the person in that photograph as the man you saw?"

"That's right."

"And after you identified him, Mr. Maxwell told you it wasn't the guy?"

"Correct."

"And then a month later you met Mr. Maxwell again, and he showed you another photograph, and he made it clear to you that this *was* the guy, right?"

"I guess."

"And that's the testimony you gave today in response to Mr. Maxwell's questions, correct?"

"Correct."

"Sitting here today, can you even tell us whether the men in the two photographs were one and the same?"

Rosen was already shaking his head before she finished her question. "No, ma'am, I sure can't tell you that."

"No more questions," she said, a flush of victory on her cheeks.

I took my time making my way to the podium, trying to show the jurors that I was unruffled by what had passed. In truth, however, this had been one of the worst moments in front of a jury that I'd ever had.

I took the mug shot of Sims and approached the witness. "Mr. Rosen, what doubts, if any, do you have regarding whether this mug shot of Jack Sims shows the man you saw talking to Alice Ward that night?"

"No doubts," he said. "I'm sure that's the guy."

I could have run though it all again, establishing that I hadn't promised him anything, that I hadn't influenced him in any way, and that he'd made the identification of his own free will. But this would have served only to prolong the bleeding.

"No further questions," I said.

~ ~ ~

"Is your next witness ready, Mr. Maxwell?"

"Give me a minute, Your Honor." It was only ten-thirty, too early to break for lunch. I scanned the gallery, my eyes skipping over rows of spectators before coming to rest on Braxton. As my eyes met his, he smirked, his superior gaze seeming to comment on the debacle of my last witness and to promise more of the same from him.

I turned to face the court, my pulse racing. "The defense calls Agent Mark Braxton."

With open disbelief, verging on shock, Sloane watched him rise and move to the stand. Judge Ransom peered over his reading glasses at the new witness. I did my best to gather my thoughts as Braxton raised his right hand and was sworn in.

Because he was my witness, the rules of evidence didn't allow me to lead him as I normally would do with a law enforcement officer. This meant I had no choice but to ask open-ended questions, which under the circumstances felt like standing blindfolded on the edge of a cliff. The risks were high. I couldn't know whether Braxton was here to help me or to burn me, and his attitude so far was no guide.

Braxton identified himself as an FBI agent working out of the San Francisco field office, and confirmed his presence outside the Motel 6 in San Francisco on the night of Edwards's death. Having progressed this far, I drew back, retreating from the lectern to the defense table.

"Tell the jurors what you were doing on Larkin Street that night."

"I was present at the scene as part of an ongoing investigation."

"What organization was the target of that investigation?"

"The Aryan Brotherhood."

"Explain to the jury what that is."

"A ruthless criminal racketeering organization. It started out as a white supremacist gang in the California prisons. However, the AB has grown beyond prison walls and expanded nationwide. It now controls a large swath of criminal activity in the outside world, from drugs to prostitution to guns."

"At present, who's in charge of the organization in California?"

"In prison, the AB is headed by a man named Bo Wilder. He's currently housed at San Quentin, serving a life sentence for a series of brutal killings. On the outside, a man named Jack Sims appears to have recently taken control after an internal power struggle. His position isn't secure, however. There remain tensions between the prison factions and the outside elements. I suspect that the power struggle hasn't fully sorted itself out."

"Describe to the jury how the FBI goes about investigating an organization like the Aryan Brotherhood." Again I felt the trepidation of jumping off into the unknown.

Braxton's response was testy, spoken with the seriousness of an acolyte addressing an unbeliever. "Three tactics," he said. "First, traditional responsive policing, investigating known crimes and trying to bring the perpetrators to justice. Second, wiretaps and other surveillance. And third, the use of confidential informants."

"Was Randolph Edwards an informant for the FBI?"

Braxton now hesitated. I wondered if he was having second thoughts. Then, as if I'd dragged the answer from him, he answered somberly, "Yes. Yes, he was."

A wave seemed to pass through the jurors, jostling them awake.

"How did Edwards come to be an informant?"

Braxton told the jurors briefly what had gone down at the Plum Tree, and explained that the FBI, by virtue of its preexisting operation, had been able to tie Edwards and Jack Sims to that robbery and murder. "We'd had those two on the radar for a while. Sims was already a target of our investigation because his father had been a founding member of the AB in California, a lifer who'd died behind bars. We figured it was only a matter of time before he joined up. But, first, he needed a spell in prison.

"We picked Edwards up after Plum Tree and offered him a choice. The first was that he and Sims could both do time for a couple of two-bit jobs we knew about. Once inside, they would take advantage of Sims's connections. From there, first inside prison and then continuing on the outside, Edwards would be working for the Bureau. Otherwise, he could go up on capital murder charges for the Plum Tree killing and take his chances on death row."

"So when Edwards was killed, the FBI lost an informant?"

"That's correct."

"But the Bureau still has at least one informant left, doesn't it, Agent Braxton?"

Now was the time for the U.S. attorney who'd accompanied Braxton to put a stop to this line of questioning—if he was going to stop it. However, he remained seated in the back row, turning the pages of a document he held in his lap.

Braxton didn't answer right away. Then, seeming to choose his words carefully, he said, "No. Edwards was the only currently active informant remaining in the AB's organization."

"Edwards and Sims were sent to prison around the same time?"

"Yes."

"The FBI took care to arrange that they went down on seemingly unrelated crimes?"

"That was intentional, yes. It was important that Edwards and Sims go into the prison system at the same time, again because of Sims's AB connections. However, we wanted the timing of their imprisonment to appear coincidental."

"Am I correct that either of them could have been charged with capital murder in the Plum Tree job based on the information the FBI had?"

"Correct."

"Instead of passing that information to the local authorities, the FBI concealed it?"

"We kept it in our pocket, yes. Ready to be trotted out if and when it needed to be used."

"So the FBI protected two highly dangerous criminals from capital murder charges?"

"That's correct. But it was at the service of a broader investigation."

Sloane stood, at last, and objected to this line of questioning as irrelevant and prejudicial, moving that it be stricken from the record. The judge called us to a sidebar conference, and, under cover of white noise meant to prevent the jurors from hearing our conversation, asked me what I thought I was doing by bringing this "circus" into his courtroom.

"It's not a circus," I told him, while Sloane listened intently. "It's my client's theory of defense. I expect to show that Ms. Ward was provoked and manipulated into committing this homicide by Jack Sims. This testimony is relevant to showing that Sims had a strong motive for wanting Edwards dead."

Now my cards were on the table. Ransom, after some thought, turned to Sloane as if seeking her advice on how to handle a prickly situation. "If that's his theory, I don't see how I have any choice but to allow him to proceed."

The trial had taken a turn Sloane hadn't expected, and she was rightly pissed at being sandbagged. With Braxton's appearance, she'd found her prosecution suddenly at risk of being derailed by a criminal defense lawyer apparently acting in concert with an FBI agent who'd readily admitted to protecting two men from the consequences of committing multiple murders. She concisely and angrily stated her objections, then stalked back to the DA's table.

I returned to the lectern and, with a few more carefully chosen questions, established that Sims's and Edwards's conditions of imprisonment had been the same. They'd been released within a year of each other, each having served between five and six years of an eight-year sentence.

"What was the status of their membership in the AB at the time of their release?"

"Each of them had become a full-fledged member of the Brotherhood."

"And Edwards, presumably, continued to provide the FBI with information about the Brotherhood once he was out of prison?"

"Yes, although it wasn't the quality of information we might have hoped for. Sims, because of his willingness to inflict suffering, had risen quickly in the organization, while Edwards lagged behind. A penitentiary is a ruthless place."

"Edwards didn't have the stomach for it," I suggested.

"He was fulfilling his obligation to the Bureau," Braxton said. "We don't condone participation in criminal activities, especially if it involves harm to others. Obviously, given the AB's activities, and its expectations of its members, Edwards, while inside, couldn't avoid wrongdoing entirely. But the purpose of having him in place was to bring down the AB, not to further its hateful purposes."

"Was he your only informant at this time?"

Again Braxton hesitated, trying to intuit where I was going. "No."

"What concerns did you have for Edwards's safety after he and then Sims were released from prison?" I asked.

"In a word? Sims. There's always the concern that an informant may have been compromised. Sims definitely suspected Edwards after they got out of prison. At first I thought his suspicions went back to the way they'd been set up for prison, that something about how those arrests and prosecutions had been handled was suspicious to him. It also could have been the simple fact that Sims knew Edwards could hang the Plum Tree job around his neck anytime he wanted. But it turned out that wasn't it. It all went back to a woman named Leann Ward."

"The mother of my client, Alice Ward, the defendant in this case."

"Correct. Leann was found dead of a drug overdose a week after the Plum Tree job, and the medical examiner classified it as a homicide. Once we connected Edwards and Sims to the Plum Tree, it was natural to suspect that Ward was the person who'd helped them gain access, and that after the job went bad they'd killed her to prevent her from making a deal. As it turned out, there was something about Leann Ward that I didn't know at the beginning, something that made Jack Sims extremely wary of Edwards after she turned up dead."

"And what was that?" I said when it became clear the FBI agent was waiting for another question from me before he'd go on.

"Edwards believed he was the father of her child."

As he spoke these words, Braxton looked directly at my client. His eyes were eager and observant, but emotionless.

My next question had evaporated from my mind. I was aware that Braxton had possibly just pronounced Sims's death sentence at the hands of the Aryan Brotherhood. Whatever else you might say about Bo Wilder, it was clear to me he wouldn't tolerate one of his men using another man's daughter as her father's executioner.

Turning to my client, I saw she didn't seem to notice that the FBI agent, the jurors, and everyone else in the courtroom were staring at her.

Without warning, Alice Ward jumped up, knocking over her chair.

The first deputy to reach her pinned her arms and slammed her onto the carpet facedown. In the jury box, there was obvious consternation. For his part, Braxton hadn't moved a muscle, except that his eyes had followed Alice's blind flight toward the door of the detention cell where she'd attempted suicide weeks before.

CHAPTER 21

At Judge Ransom's order, Alice was returned to her holding cell. After a few minutes, I was permitted to join her. I found her shackled, her teeth chattering, her arms squeezed between her legs by her restraints.

"I'll take the deal," she said. It was hard for me to hear her, she was speaking so softly.

"We don't know if he's telling the truth or not." I went down on my heels in front of her, my eyes seeking hers. "He's trying to mess with your head, the way Sims did. They're both bastards, two sides of the same coin."

"Doesn't change what I did."

I had no answer to that. Nothing would change it, as long as Braxton was telling the truth. And I had no reason to believe he wasn't.

"We can get a paternity test," I told her. "The results might take a few days, but—"

"It's not the first time I heard that," she admitted. "Another girl passed me the message, right after. 'Jack said for me to tell you that you killed your daddy yesterday,' she said to me. 'The only thing left for you to do now is kill yourself.' That's what Jack wanted, and what I was trying to do. But I fucked up suicide the way I fucked up everything else. Two with one stone, he thought."

"We have to go back out there," I said, and then I made a reckless promise. "It can't get any worse than this."

But who was I to say whether things couldn't get worse? For instance, she might be convicted of first-degree murder. That, on top of believing she'd likely killed her father, would probably send her over the edge.

Still, I had unfinished business with Braxton. Even if the judge was willing to postpone the trial, I doubted the FBI agent would return tomorrow. This was my one and only shot.

"You have to," I told her, lifting her by the arm. "Let's go back out there together and show the jurors what you're made of."

I knocked on the door and we were readmitted to the courtroom. The jurors weren't present. I pleaded briefly with the judge to allow her restraints to be removed. After consulting with the deputies, Judge Ransom acquiesced. Next, I asked him for permission to treat Braxton as an adverse witness. The ADA objected, but the judge, after a moment's thought, granted permission. I helped Alice into her chair. She didn't attempt to rise when the jurors were readmitted.

Standing beside her, my hand protectively on her shoulder, I carefully studied the jurors' faces as they filed in, trying to read their reaction to what had happened and thus determine my next move. In their eyes I saw concern and pity, overlaid with shock. All of them had been deeply affected by what they'd witnessed a few moments before in the courtroom. They sat shaken but alert, without a trace of boredom or disengagement. Not one of them looked at Braxton, still sitting there on the witness stand. Only a few glanced at the ADA.

At the defense table, Alice's chin was clamped against her chest, her body was hunched like a question mark, her eyes were fixed on her hands in her lap. A shudder passed through her. She seemed to gather herself tightly, the better to contain it.

"The FBI doesn't care about the random murder of a diner in a restaurant, does it, Agent Braxton?" I asked once the jurors had all been seated.

He blinked at the shift in tone. "It's not that we don't care. It's that sometimes true justice can only be achieved through roundabout ends. We're a federal agency, and our jurisdiction only extends to the violation of federal law."

"You're saying you couldn't find a federal law to charge Jack Sims with for the Plum Tree robbery? How about the Hobbs Act?"

Braxton was silent. At any point, Sloane might have objected to this line of questioning, but she made no attempt to do so.

"You could even have sought the death penalty for use of a firearm resulting in a murder, couldn't you?"

Again, Braxton chose not to answer. I glanced at the jurors and saw that they'd interpreted his silence correctly as an admission. They were gazing at him now, several sitting with folded arms, all evidently dismayed by what they'd heard.

"In fact, as far as you're concerned, any crime not committed in furtherance of the Aryan Brotherhood isn't worthy of your attention, correct?"

"That's not true. Our operational priority is to bring down one of the most vicious criminal organizations in the state of California over the last fifty years. No one murder is justifiable, but we're talking about an organization that drops dozens of bodies each year. You've got to look at the big picture."

"And the way you achieved your operational priorities in this instance is by helping prospective members of the Aryan Brotherhood remain free to commit more crimes, free to victimize innocent Californians when they might have been safely locked away in prison the rest of their lives, or on death row, isn't that true?"

"I don't answer to you, and I don't need to sit here and listen to this."

"Answer the question," the judge instructed him.

Braxton made as if to rise.

"Deputies," Ransom said sharply.

The deputies who a moment ago had flanked Alice Ward now advanced toward the witness stand, glancing at one another uncertainly.

"That's good," Ransom told them. "Just keep him company up there. Mr. Maxwell, proceed."

I asked for the question to be read back. When the court reporter had done so, Braxton answered. "When you're fighting an enemy that prides itself on ruthlessness, you've got to be *more* ruthless. When his only value is loyalty, you've got to make him disloyal. When the only thing he respects is blood, you've got to show him blood. And when your enemy thinks he has nothing to lose, you have to give him something, if only so that, later, it can be taken away."

"And you gave Jack Sims his freedom, didn't you?"

"Not permanently," Braxton answered.

Having exhausted this line of questioning, I decided to move on. "Earlier, you'd begun telling me that Sims had become wary of Edwards because of a woman named Leann Ward."

"That's right."

"Edwards had a relationship with Ms. Ward and believed himself to be the father of her child."

"Correct. We covered that."

"Jack Sims killed Leann Ward?"

Sloane now objected, basing her opposition on the agent's lack of personal knowledge.

"But the state introduced this topic," I responded. "When Detective Dunham was on the stand, Ms. Sloane asked her numerous questions regarding Edwards's possible involvement in Leann Ward's murder, because the state evidently believes this murder supplied my client with a motive to kill. Now that we're trying to make our case for provocation, however, the DA doesn't want the jury to hear that Sims may also have been involved. That's fundamentally unfair."

"The objection is more straightforward than that, Mr. Maxwell. It's a matter of the agent's personal knowledge." He now turned to Braxton and, to Sloane's evident frustration, rephrased the question. "What knowledge, if any, do you have regarding the identity of Leann Ward's killer or killers?"

Ransom's use of the plural "killers" didn't go unnoticed by the jurors, I observed. Though he surely hadn't meant it to, the question tipped the playing field in favor of the theory I was developing, which was that Sims and Edwards had both been involved and that Sims had then lied to my client, pleading innocence and putting it all on Edwards as a way of provoking her into killing his onetime partner.

"Edwards never spoke about her murder, and I never broached the subject. But my opinion, for what it's worth, based on all the facts and circumstances and my experience, is that Sims and Edwards must have acted together, to prevent her from going to the police about the Plum Tree killing. I don't believe either of them could have pulled off her murder alone. Not without making more noise than was made."

I now stepped in. "And you helped the two of them cover it up?"

"'Cover up' implies an active role. So, no, I didn't help them cover up anything."

"You simply declined to share pertinent evidence with the state and local authorities?"

"That's correct."

"Evidence that could have led to the conviction of Sims as well as Edwards for one or both of these crimes?"

"Fair enough."

"In exchange for all this consideration, what did the FBI get?"

"I can't answer that," Braxton said. "Or, rather, I won't. As I said, this is an active investigation. I won't compromise legitimate law enforcement objectives, and I don't see how the answer could possibly be relevant here."

Sloane stood to supply an objection to my question, which the judge sustained, requiring me to move on.

"In addition to shielding informants from state or local law enforcement, the FBI also provides financial incentives in exchange for information, correct?"

"When appropriate."

"Monthly envelopes of cash?"

"Information is a cash business. The whole point is keeping the relationship secret from prying eyes."

"And am I correct that Edwards had been meeting with you to receive his cash payment and deliver his latest information the day he was shot?"

"Yes."

"So what happened to the cash you'd given him?"

"I removed the envelope from his pocket after he was shot."

"And you didn't inform the police or anyone else that you'd done this?"

Braxton was unrepentant. "Correct. At that point, I was still concerned with maintaining the integrity of my source. "

"Isn't it true, Agent Braxton, that the FBI has another informant placed at the highest levels of the Aryan Brotherhood? A man who's spent years behind bars, who'd be compromised if you revealed what Randolph Edwards had given the FBI in exchange for the consideration we've been discussing here today?"

Again, Braxton refused to answer. Again, the judge ordered him to respond.

"No," Braxton said. "No, it isn't true. There are no remaining active sources within the organization."

I had no choice but to move on. "I want to talk for a moment about the oath you've taken here today. An oath to tell the truth. In fact, you'd violate that oath to protect a confidential informant, wouldn't you?"

Sloane objected that the question was argumentative, and the judge sustained her objection. "Mr. Maxwell, please move on."

Frustrated, I said, "You witnessed the shooting?"

"I did. Want me to tell about it?"

This question was a clear challenge.

"I want you to tell the jury about it," I said.

Braxton smiled without humor, turned pointedly away from me, and addressed the jurors. A look of surprise crossed his face as he registered their hostility, but he quickly recovered his pose of indifference.

"We'd finished our business. Edwards insisted on leaving first, as usual.

"A car braking hard drew my attention. I looked out and saw the girl sprinting through traffic across Geary Street. She was nearly run down. The skidding car missed her by about six inches, which she didn't seem to notice. She looked like just a kid, but the gun in her hand was no toy.

"I ran out, and as I reached the sidewalk she pulled the trigger. There was no hesitation. She didn't say a word, barely even stopped running. The gun came up and went off. It was a head shot, killing him instantly. I shouted at her, told her to drop the weapon, but she didn't move. I had my sidearm out of the holster and was prepared to fire. Then, as I came closer, her legs seemed to give way, and the gun slipped from her hand. I caught her and cuffed her.

"It was obvious Edwards was dead. Killed instantly. I removed the envelope of cash from his pocket and finished securing the scene. I knew SFPD would soon be there, and in the meantime I attempted to question the shooter. She'd just taken out one of my informants, and it seemed possible she might have been coerced into doing that. I wanted to know by whom."

Sloane stood and objected. The judge instructed the jurors to disregard Braxton's last statement about Alice being coerced, informing them that coercion was no defense against a murder charge. When Ransom's admonition was finished, Braxton waited as if daring me to ask what my client had said.

I had no choice but to take the dare.

Sloane objected. In response, the judge instructed the jurors not to use any statement my client might have made to establish the truth of its contents—that rather, its only relevance should be to her state of mind.

I had no argument with that.

"She didn't answer," Braxton said, addressing the jurors directly. "She appeared, for all practical purposes, to be catatonic. She kept swaying, as if she was going to pass out. I couldn't get her gaze to focus on my hand when I held it in front of her face. Her eyes were open, but it was as if there was no one home."

Too late, Sloane was on her feet, objecting to an answer that had to register as a hand grenade lobbed into the camp of the prosecution. The damage, though, was done. Evidence of my client's altered mental state at the time of the shooting was now before the jurors. Not only did this testimony bear the stamp of the FBI's authority, but because Braxton's hostility toward my client was so painfully obvious, any testimony from him that was helpful to Alice Ward carried even greater weight than it otherwise would have.

On the cross-examination, Sloane came alive, attempting to undo the damage. But her efforts were too little, too late. Under her questioning, Braxton simply filled in the details he'd omitted during the quick summary he'd provided in his direct examination. Each detail reinforced that Alice Ward been acting out of blind rage up to the moment she pulled the trigger, after which she seemed to lose all animation, "like a puppet with cut strings," as Braxton said.

Sloane had little to gain by attacking Braxton for deliberately sabotaging her murder case. Instead, she worked indirectly, focusing her questions on the voluntary nature of his testimony, trying to make clear to the jurors that he must have a hidden motive for being here. She also took this opportunity to establish that Braxton, at least, had no knowledge of Jack Sims being anywhere in the area the day Edwards was shot.

"If you'd known he was there, what would you have done?" she asked.

"Randolph would never have gone out that door," Braxton said. "We'd have whisked him out of there in an unmarked car. He certainly wouldn't have been exposed the way he was."

Finally, with this much accomplished, Sloane sat down.

As the FBI agent walked from the courtroom, I glanced at Alice. The evidence of provocation was tenuous, lacking that vital piece revealing exactly what Sims had said to provoke her. Nevertheless, it seemed to me this could be inferred.

In theory, it was the DA's burden to disprove that Alice had acted in the heat of passion, not mine to establish provocation. I was more certain than ever that we couldn't afford to put Alice on the stand, knowing this would mean allowing the DA to discover her evident premeditation in obtaining the gun and bringing it to the city that day. There was little to gain and much to lose. The smart plan was to argue reasonable doubt, asking the jurors to hold the state to its burden of proof. I simply had to hope that I'd picked a jury that was willing to do that.

"The defense rests," I said.

CHAPTER 22

Sloane's closing argument was predictable but effective. She hammered on the known, undisputed facts, urging the jury not to speculate regarding Alice Ward's motivations.

"I expect Mr. Maxwell to argue to you that the defendant was provoked. But who provoked her? Surely a defendant can't escape a murder charge by claiming she provoked herself. Even he admits there had to be someone there.

"They've thrown out a name, and even a mug shot. But Mr. Sims is a ghost conjured up by the defendant's lawyer. Two police officers and multiple eyewitnesses testified regarding what they saw and heard. The defendant's lawyer didn't bother showing Jack Sims's picture to any of them. Surely, if Sims were present, it would have been at least worthwhile to ask these witnesses about him. Mr. Maxwell didn't do that. The reason is that Sims *wasn't* there.

"And even if there'd been some evidence that this man was in the city that evening, the fact that none of these witnesses saw him near the scene of the crime is telling. The judge is going to instruct you that the influence of any provocation must have been 'direct and immediate.' How immediate could it have been if he left her so far from the scene that none of these witnesses saw him? Leaving aside the fact that we have no idea what he's supposed to have said to her.

"But these questions are academic. Sims *wasn't* there. The only person who claims to have seen him is an admitted drug addict who admits to having been in the Tenderloin in order to score heroin. Let's talk about Mr. Rosen's testimony for a minute."

Here, she launched into an attack that was all the more effective because she let Rosen's numerous admissions speak for themselves. Rather than accuse me outright of suborning perjury, she simply stated the facts.

"The first time Mr. Rosen met with Mr. Maxwell, Maxwell showed him a picture of an individual Rosen now claims was Jack Sims. According to Rosen, that picture was on Maxwell's phone. After Rosen identified this person, Maxwell assured him that it couldn't have been the man Mr. Rosen had seen.

"Now fast-forward a few months, to their next meeting right before the trial. Maxwell shows Rosen another picture, a mug shot, and tells him he wants him to identify *this* man. And Rosen does identify him, agreeing with Maxwell that this was the man he saw even though he can't say for sure whether this man and the man in the picture he previously identified are the same. And on this occasion, it's the only picture Maxwell shows him.

"After hearing Mr. Rosen testify, I think you'll agree that if Mr. Maxwell wanted him to, he'd claim he saw the president of the United States that evening. Simply put, his testimony doesn't deserve to be believed."

She also addressed Braxton's testimony, of course urging the jurors to look past my attempts to manufacture a defense. "Alice Ward had an obvious motive for committing this crime. She didn't need to be provoked. She'd been planning for years to get back at the man or men who she believed had murdered her mother. We may feel sorry for someone whose life has been poisoned, but that doesn't mean the defendant can be allowed to perpetuate the cycle of violence by taking justice into her own hands. There's no law that permits a revenge killing.

"The state has proved beyond a reasonable doubt that the defendant, Alice Ward, killed Mr. Edwards, and that the killing was willful, deliberate, and premeditated. You've heard all the facts. Now I ask you to follow the law and find the defendant guilty of first-degree murder."

Sloane had homed in on the weaknesses of our defense. Now it was my job to make the jury realize she'd missed the mark. I had nothing written down, but knew exactly what I needed to say. I walked close to the jury box and stood before the jurors with empty hands, presenting myself to them without artifice.

"The defense doesn't have to prove anything," I said, launching into my difficult task. "We don't have to prove that Ms. Ward was provoked, or that she acted in the heat of passion. Rather, it's the state that has the burden of disproving provocation. The state must prove, beyond a reasonable doubt, that Mr. Edwards's death was intentional and premeditated.

"Ask yourself, has the state done this? Has it proved beyond a reasonable doubt that Sims *wasn't* there?

"There's no evidence Alice had any clue who was behind her mother's murder until this night. The only reasonable inference you can draw is that immediately before the shooting, Jack Sims gave her the answer she'd been hungering for all these years. He told her, at last, the identity of the man who'd murdered her mother. That's the sole supposition we can draw from the facts, the only reasonable explanation for what she did. We know how she reacted. Remember Agent Braxton's testimony. Right after the shooting she was 'catatonic.' He waved a hand in front of her eyes, but there was 'no one home.'

"The state wants you to look at this case through blinders—to assume, without any evidence, that Alice Ward all along has held the key to solving this unsolved crime. It wants you to believe that she patiently bided her time, keeping the identity of her mother's killers secret from the police, until, finally, in cold blood, she deliberately acted out a long-nurtured plan of revenge. But that theory doesn't mesh with the facts. How'd she know Edwards was there in the city that night? Where'd she get the gun she used to kill him? All these questions are ones the state leaves unanswered.

"You've heard testimony about Sims's membership in the Aryan Brotherhood, about his various criminal acts. Agent Braxton believes that Sims, along with Edwards, murdered Leann Ward, to cover up a previous murder they'd committed while robbing the Plum Tree. There's no statute of limitations on murder. As long as Edwards remains alive, he holds Jack Sims's life in his hands.

"Sims is a master manipulator, an unrepentant white supremacist, a cold-blooded murderer. Alice Ward, by contrast, is just a teenager—a child with a deep void at the center of her life: her mother's death. Do you think he'd hesitate for an instant to tap into that hurt and pain, to channel that darkness inside her in order to achieve the outcome he wants? How easy it must have been for him to utter the lie that set this damaged young girl in motion.

"We know for certain that Braxton and the FBI helped Sims and Edwards get away with at least two murders. Evidently, granting such killers impunity is part of the government's scheme to bring down the Aryan Brotherhood—even at the cost of innocent lives. In the government's view, the ends justify the means. And what is it, in the government's mind, that justifies allowing Jack Sims to escape punishment for these heinous crimes? It's pretty obvious, folks. Sims has been allowed free rein because the government values the information he, just like Randolph Edwards, has been passing to the FBI regarding the inner workings of the Aryan Brotherhood.

"Agent Braxton denied under oath that Jack Sims was an FBI informant. But Braxton will say anything to protect an active source. If he were to admit a thing like that, it'd be a death sentence for Sims. We all know what happens to snitches inside criminal organizations. Conveniently, Braxton now claims that Edwards was his only source inside the Aryan Brotherhood.

"In fact, it wouldn't surprise me if Sims was the only snitch, and Edwards was targeted for other reasons. I'll give you one—Sims's effort to consolidate his power within the Aryan Brotherhood, requiring taking out possible rivals. The greater an informant's role in an organization, the more valuable the information he provides. And how about another reason—preventing state and local police from using Edwards to prosecute Sims for those old murders, which would take him out of play for the FBI? The feds will do anything to keep Sims on the street, even facilitate the elimination of someone who's both a rival and a threat, a man who might've been having second thoughts about Leann Ward's murder, a man racked with guilt over the death of the mother of his child.

"Alice Ward may have pulled the trigger, but she's not the one who's guilty of Edwards's murder. Sims is the one who 'premeditated' this killing. He planned it, then used my client as his tool to carry it out. He's the guilty party. But he's not here in this courtroom today. As you consider Agent Braxton's testimony, I want you to ask yourself why Sims isn't on trial for this crime. And, more broadly, why hasn't he been brought to justice for the other murders he's committed? It's because Braxton and the FBI protected Sims. It's safe to say that protection's still in place.

"This case is about more than just Randolph Edwards's death. It's about the murder of Leann Ward, about the murder of that innocent diner enjoying his meal at the Plum Tree ten years ago. It's about all the other nameless innocents harmed as a result of Jack Sims being allowed freedom and protection by the FBI. It's a travesty that he was allowed to use the umbrella of that protection to provoke my client into committing a killing that turns out to have been even more senseless than she knew.

"Probably he hoped that once she learned the truth, that she'd just killed her father, she'd want to kill herself—carrying any evidence of his involvement with her into the grave. Thankfully, he didn't succeed. Instead, we've had this opportunity to learn the truth—and the truth is that my client was the real victim in this case.

"It's been my privilege to speak to you on Alice Ward's behalf today. I ask that you recognize that innocent lives aren't worth an FBI agent's dreams of triumph. I assert that the government hasn't met its burden of proof on any of these charges. For that reason, your verdict should be 'not guilty' on each and every count."

~ ~ ~

In her rebuttal argument, Sloane labeled my defense of Alice Ward a "house of cards" and proceeded to deconstruct it. Sims hadn't been there, she insisted, again harping on Rosen's lack of credibility, along with the absence of any other witness putting him at the scene. The obvious implication here was that my client, surely, could have taken the stand in her own defense and told the jurors about Sims's presence, and also could have told them exactly what he'd said.

"All we have is speculation, but Mr. Maxwell's 'inference' isn't evidence," Sloane insisted. While she couldn't comment outright on my client's invocation of her right to remain silent, the jurors couldn't fail to understand what the missing "evidence," in her view, should have been.

This led to her next point, which was that nothing Sims could have told Alice Ward that day would have come as a surprise. Her mother had worked at the Plum Tree. That robbery had preceded her death by only a week. Might her daughter not have drawn the connection between that job and her untimely death?

"As for Agent Braxton and the supposed machinations of the FBI, you should see it for the smoke screen that it is. Whether or not Sims or Edwards was an informant is entirely irrelevant and beside the point. Mr. Maxwell admitted as much during his closing argument when he reminded you that the defendant was the one who pulled the trigger. The murder of an informant is still a murder. The fact that the murder she committed may have served the ends of the Aryan Brotherhood doesn't lessen her guilt. If anything, it makes her crime worse.

"Again, there's no evidence that Sims was there, or, if he was, that he told her anything of consequence that she didn't already know. Even if he had been present, Alice Ward still had a choice. She had plenty of time to deliberate. She could have gone to the police.

"Instead, she carried out an act of revenge, shooting the victim through the head. Leann Ward had been dead for over a decade. This wasn't a killing in the heat of passion. She wasn't provoked. She didn't catch him in the act. Rather, she saw the opportunity for vengeance, and she made the decision to carry it out. She executed him, taking the law into her own hands.

"Don't be fooled by the speculations of defense counsel, by all the smoke and mirrors. Focus on the evidence. Take your time. Consider all the facts. And when you've done that, return a verdict of first-degree murder."

~   ~   ~

It was after 6 P.M. when the judge finished reading aloud the jury instructions. His intended audience was yawning, but rather than break for the evening, the jurors elected to begin their deliberations immediately, with dinner ordered in. Their sequestration from their jobs and families wouldn't end until they either reached a unanimous decision or deadlocked, resulting in a mistrial. This meant that the pressure on any holdouts would be magnified. I had to hope that one or two jurors who'd seemed to be on our side would become my client's advocates in the jury room, repeating my arguments and coming up with new ones to convince their peers.

Alice had been taken into the holding cell, where a female guard was to remain with her at all times. I stayed in the courtroom, in the company of the bailiff, a few spectators, and my disordered thoughts. I spoke with Teddy and confirmed they were all fine, said good night to Carly, then stretched out on one of the benches. The room seemed to swirl around me, a side effect of trial fatigue.

Freed from the obsessive circles in which they'd been traveling, my thoughts returned to my father. I knew even less about his motivations than I did about those of Alice Ward. Now, again, I wondered at them. I wanted to believe that he'd acted out of bravery, heroism. But I knew better.

He undoubtedly possessed courage, yet altruism had never been his style. Informant or no, he'd benefited from his association with the Aryan Brotherhood. Working for the FBI had allowed him to hedge his bets, persuading himself that it was okay to take the protection and other benefits Bo Wilder offered. But I was sure he'd also understood the essential truth of what I'd argued in court today: that, when one looked at the larger picture, his efforts had most likely served to prop up and strengthen the enemy.

I dozed fitfully, then sat up as my phone suddenly buzzed in my pocket. It was just after 10 P.M. The jury was still deliberating. Seeing that the call was from an unknown number, I walked out of the courtroom for privacy.

In the hallway, Sims's voice ran through me like a blade of ice.

"I *was* loyal, you piece of shit. Because of your false accusations, a good man had to die tonight."

He was breathing hard, real stress behind his words. That, more than anything, frightened me. Sims sounded scared, and I pictured a cornered animal, the most dangerous kind.

"What good man?"

"Bo. They got to him—my orders. Had to happen today, before word reached him. Had no choice, had to strike first. I made sure he didn't even see it coming. It was painless. A shank to the base of the neck. He didn't even have the chance to go out fighting. A brave man doesn't deserve to die that way, you asshole."

"I'm sorry." The words escaped me unbidden, a reaction to the genuine grief I heard in Sims's voice and my own awe at the upheaval I'd caused.

"You will be," he said, his voice becoming more measured now. "I should've known you didn't give a shit about your family. Well, Bo Wilder was the closest thing to a brother I ever had, and now, because of you, he's dead."

"That makes us even," I said, though I hardly felt this was so. As far as I was concerned, the job was only half done. My revenge for my father's death wouldn't be complete until Sims, too, was dead on the ground.

Evidently, the feeling was mutual. "I warned you," he said. "I told you exactly what I'd do if you fucked with me. I'm a man of my word. Thanks to you, I got nothing left *but* my word. And I'll be dead, too, before I give that up."

My throat had tightened painfully at his mention of my family. I talked fast. "It sounds as though we should meet, try to straighten things out. I'm waiting on a jury here, as I'm sure you know. You wanted me to put on a case, so I did that."

"I'm four hundred miles away. You're down on my list, but I won't forget you. Bo died fast. In your case I'm gonna make it nice and slow. I just got to take care of business here in Anaheim. Don't worry, I'll bring you a nice souvenir from Disneyland."

He ended the call. But his words echoed in my ears like the tolling of an awful bell. *Souvenir. Anaheim. Disneyland.*

I came unfrozen with a cry that turned the head of a reporter typing on his laptop outside the courtroom. I phoned Car. The call went to voice mail. Next I tried my brother, but he, likewise, didn't pick up. Tamara's phone also went unanswered. I dialed the Anaheim Police Department and, after several handoffs, was connected with a dispatcher. I explained the situation, telling her that I was an attorney in a criminal trial in San Francisco involving gang issues, and that moments ago I'd received a credible threat to the lives of my family members. I gave her the address of the condo and left her my number, pleading with her to have the responding officers call me once they were on the scene.

Shortly after I hung up, my phone buzzed again. For some reason I expected it to be Sims, but it was Judge Ransom's courtroom deputy. The jury was adjourning for the evening, she informed me. Normally, I'd have recognized the failure to reach a verdict immediately as a good sign—the longer the jury was out, the better for my client. Tonight, however, all I could think about was my family, and how stupid I'd been to send them so far away.

In a panic, I again dialed Car, my brother, and, finally, Tamara, but none of them picked up. This couldn't be happening, I told myself—whatever *this* was. Again, in my mind's eye, I saw the slaughterhouse scene I'd discovered at Dot's condo, revisited the stink of congealed blood and decomposing flesh.

Finally, as the deputy let me out of the courthouse, I called Braxton. The call went to voice mail, but after a moment he called me back.

His voice was breathless, his excitement palpable. It was as if he'd forgotten that during the trial I'd done everything I could to humiliate and anger him on the stand, attempting to draw moral equivalence between the Aryan Brotherhood and the FBI agent to whom I was now turning for help in my time of need. "Bo Wilder's dead. He was assassinated in San Quentin forty minutes ago."

"I know." I was walking fast through the chilly evening, blind with terror, my legs directing me toward my apartment. "I can't get hold of my family," I said. Frantically, I explained about sending my family to Anaheim during the trial, and then about Sims's call this evening, revealing that he knew where they were.

"I wouldn't worry about it," Braxton said with the self-assurance of a man for whom "collateral damage" was just another cost of doing business. "Taking out Bo Wilder in a preemptive strike wasn't the solution to his problems. It's only the beginning. The organization is fractured now. Sims has no choice but to continue on this course. He has to eliminate each and every one of his rivals before they succeed in taking him out. For tonight, at least, he's too busy to be settling personal scores."

"But he knows where my family is, and they're not answering."

My voice sounded hysterical even to my own ears. And now, suddenly, I wondered again about what I'd argued to the jury, though I hadn't believed the words as I spoke them: that Sims was the real informant, protected by Braxton to the point of being shielded from responsibility for numerous detestable crimes. Including, perhaps, my father's murder.

"I've had an agent keeping an eye on your family all week," Braxton revealed. "If Sims shows up there, it'll be his last stop on the way to jail."

I felt a surge of gratitude and relief that overwhelmed my doubts. Even in my distress, the double standard of my position wasn't lost on me. Whatever suspicions I might have about Braxton's motivations, no matter how viciously I'd attacked him in the courtroom, I had no choice but to trust the FBI agent with my family's lives on the line, and I was more than willing to do so.

"Call your agent now!" I told him as I quickened the pace of my walking. "Have him check on them. I've contacted Anaheim PD, but who knows how long it'll take them to send a car around. Please!"

"You're asking me to blow my agent's cover. I'm not going to do that. He's not there as a bodyguard to protect your family. He's there to spring the trap."

I realized the full implications of what he was saying. "Are you telling me that you've been using my family as bait?"

"Protection wasn't part of our deal. You had the chance to go that way, but you wanted to play your own hand. Ever hear the term 'moral hazard'?"

"Just have your man look in on them. He doesn't need to blow his cover."

I hesitated before adding another heartfelt "Please."

I was nearly back to my apartment. Once there, I'd have to decide what to do next. My impulse was to rent a car and drive all night, arriving in Anaheim before morning at best. I knew, however, that such a trip would accomplish nothing. If Teddy and his family were in trouble, I was already too late.

Braxton reluctantly promised to have his agent pretend to deliver a pizza. "It's a developing situation, so if you don't hear back from me, just assume no news is good news," he said. "In the meantime, try to get some sleep."

CHAPTER 23

What Braxton had suggested was impossible. With a jury out, Bo Wilder dead in prison, and Sims making threats against my family, there was no chance of my shutting my eyes even for a minute.

I hadn't been back to my apartment all week, but, now, my half measures seemed foolish. Anyone who'd wanted to get to me could easily have done so by following me from the courthouse. The undeniable fact was that I'd survived the week. Even now, when my betrayal of Sims's instructions had become crystal clear, I'd arrived home unmolested, finding the apartment just as I'd left it, dirty laundry on the floor and dishes in the sink.

Sims was four hundred miles away. I hadn't for a second believed that my family was safe, as Braxton had claimed. This left me pacing back and forth, debating what to do, when my phone vibrated again.

"Mr. Maxwell?" It was an unfamiliar voice, emotionless but out of breath.

"Who is this?"

"Detective Jacobs. Anaheim PD."

Something in his voice told me it was bad. "Have you found my family?"

"We're at the condo now. We've got one dead, one wounded, door's wide open. I'm sorry, Mr. Maxwell, but right now we're dealing with an emergency situation. I need to know who did this and where you think he is."

"One dead," I repeated, stunned beyond comprehension. All I could think of was my father and Dot. Teddy and Tamara.

Carly.

"Two white males," the detective clarified. "No ID yet."

"Describe them," I said, my voice hoarse. I didn't want to know, but I had to.

"The deceased, mid-forties, thin, full tattoo sleeves. Shot through the forehead."

Car. It had to be. I saw the scene as vividly as if I'd been there to discover it, and I knew it was my fault, that I'd forced him into a situation that went against his better judgment, making him a perfect target. My insides gave a terrible heave, and I had to spit on the rug to keep from throwing up. Car, loyal to the end, had paid the ultimate price.

The detective was speaking again.

"The other—younger, in his twenties, very fit. They're taking him into surgery as we speak."

I felt a surge of shameful relief. Not Teddy, then. It had to be the FBI agent Braxton had mentioned, the one who'd been sent in to check on my family.

"What about the others?" My lips felt numb. I was barely able to form the words. "There should be a woman, and a heavyset man in his late forties. And a little girl."

"Seems they must have left in a hurry. There's kids' stuff here, but no kid."

"You've got to find them," I urged. "They have to be nearby. He has them."

"So, help me. That's what I called you for. Who are we looking for?"

"Jack Sims is the man who did this. As for the casualties, the wounded one is probably an FBI agent. He works for a man named Braxton, who's based out of the field office here." I began explaining about Sims's ties to the Aryan Brotherhood.

Then a beep sounded in my ear.

It was Braxton.

"I've got to take this," I said, and switched calls without letting the cop get in another word. Before Braxton could explain what was happening, I told him I was on the phone with the Anaheim PD.

"I'm getting on a chopper in a few minutes," he said. "Something went very wrong tonight. I have a man in the hospital, but my first priority is finding your family and bringing them home alive. The minute we have a lead on their location, you'll hear from me immediately. In the meantime, we're sending an agent to you. Our best hope is that Sims will contact you in order to communicate some kind of demand, something we can at least work with as the start of a negotiation."

"What if he doesn't?" I asked. "What if he has something else in mind?"

I imagined Sims driving my family far from the scene of Car's murder in Anaheim, Teddy and Tamara bound in the back of a nondescript van, Carly terrified, all of them becoming more irretrievably lost to me with each minute that passed.

"He's no fool. He doesn't want to end up dead at the end of the day. Being the top dog is still his foremost goal, and he knows even the AB would shun him if he hurt a woman and her child. All I can promise you, Maxwell, is that we'll do everything we can. Now give me the name of the cop down there who contacted you, please."

I did, then switched back to the cop in Anaheim. I answered a few more questions, including describing the van I'd ridden in the day Sims grabbed me. But it soon became obvious that I had no specific information that could help them find my brother and his family. So he ended the call, promising to update me "as soon as we know anything definite."

Bracing for a sleepless night, I paced up and down in my apartment, my fear mounting like a gasoline fire. At last I picked up my phone and called Jeanie.

~ ~ ~

She stood at the window, not wanting me to see her cry, or so I figured. A few inches taller than I was, with wispy brown-blond hair and a beauty that was in her attitude and intellect rather than in any summation of features, Jeanie was the first woman I'd ever kissed. It had happened just once, under extraordinary circumstances when I was fifteen, the moment coming back to me now, surfacing randomly through the raw storm of our shared grief and terror.

"You're sure he's dead?" she asked in a desolated voice that told me her thoughts and memories were in an entirely different place from mine.

Jeanie and Car had been lovers after her marriage to Teddy collapsed. Though no one had more right to be shocked by my brother's transformation into a family man than Jeanie, her pleasure at Teddy's newfound happiness with Tamara was clearly genuine. The tangled threads of her personal and professional life must have made tonight's news all the more devastating.

"There's been no official notification. I had a call from one of the officers responding to the scene, describing a body with full tattoo sleeves, and nothing since then. But, yeah, I'm pretty sure it's him. Car was there. I'm so sorry, Jeanie."

"And now you're telling me it's the man we saw at the baseball game that did this."

She turned, and I now saw that it wasn't grief she'd been seeking to conceal by facing away, but, rather, a ferocious anger at me.

"Jack Sims," I said, forcing myself to hold her gaze.

"You knew what he was and what he wanted the day he took Carly, and you didn't go to the police. You even kept her kidnapping a secret from me. You knew something like tonight was a possibility, and now look what's happened."

"I thought they'd be safe if they were out of town. Car didn't want to be 'babysitting,' as he called it, but I reminded him of everything Teddy's done for him. I thought he could protect them—and I was wrong. It's my fault."

"You're goddamn right it's your fault," she said, taking a step toward me as if she wanted to beat me with her fists. Instead, she grabbed me in both arms, wrapping them around me and squeezing me until the breath sighed out of me.

We stood that way for a long time, each holding the other in a fierce grip, like wrestlers grappling, or like two survivors of the storm that might yet rip us apart. At last Jeanie stepped back, wiping her eyes. "It's a terrible thing to feel so helpless. I can't believe there's nothing we can do except wait for them to call and let us know the others are dead. If they even find the bodies . . ."

I wasn't ready for this kind of talk. I hadn't yet told Jeanie about Braxton, but now I did, explaining my father's secret life working for the FBI behind bars, the FBI agent's apparent loyalty toward Lawrence and my family. I also told her about Braxton's conviction that Sims wasn't suicidal, nor likely to sabotage his bid to take over the AB by harming a woman and child.

Jeanie listened with skepticism, deep in thought, processing the situation with her sharply analytical mind.

"I always figured Lawrence was hiding something. I just never guessed that any secret your father was keeping would raise my opinion of him."

"He was a brave man; Teddy was right about him. There are so many things I'd like now to be able to ask him, so many things I'd like to say. But I'm never going to have that chance. Anyway. Braxton thinks Lawrence died because he confronted Sims, not because he was exposed as an informant."

My doorbell rang. It was a young woman, Agent Sessions, dispatched by Braxton. I surrendered my cell phone and my kitchen table, where she spread out the equipment she'd need to monitor any call that came in.

Jeanie and I paced in despair as it became apparent my phone wasn't going to ring with news of a miraculous rescue. Of course, we hadn't really expected such a call. Better no news, I reminded myself, than the tragedy I feared most.

At last, hoping we could each get a few hours of sleep, I made up the couch for Jeanie. At my request, she'd showed up with a suit so that she could take my place if needed to receive the jury's verdict tomorrow.

I lay fully clothed on my bed, listening to Jeanie toss and turn and to Agent Sessions's restless movements, until, as usual, my alarm went off at six.

CHAPTER 24

When Jeanie and I arrived in court at nine, Sloane was already sitting at the prosecutor's table. She glanced at me with wan sympathy but didn't say anything, her gaze communicating that she knew what was happening. I spoke to Judge Ransom's clerk, informing her that I had a family emergency and might need Jeanie to stand in for me. The jury was deliberating, the clerk informed us. Now that we'd checked in, we were free to leave, provided that we were able to appear back in court at a maximum of ten minutes' notice.

After checking in briefly with Alice Ward, who was being kept in the holding cell adjoining the courtroom, Jeanie and I walked quickly to my office. Once there, she collapsed in my wing chair with her laptop, looking unbearably stressed as she sent emails and made phone calls to clear her calendar for the rest of the week. I paced from window to window. Normally the source of my anxiety would have been the jury deliberating six blocks away. Today, Alice Ward's fate hardly entered my thoughts.

I checked in with Braxton, who had nothing to report. They were running down every lead they could think of, he said. In the meantime, our best hope was that Sims would make contact with me. However, the assurances Braxton offered were empty, and his voice, offering them, sounded grim.

Jeanie knew the basic contours of Alice Ward's case from the news reports. I'd also explained the role Agent Braxton had played in the judicial theater we'd concocted, with such disastrous and tragic results. She passed the morning reading over the news stories about the trial, including reading aloud to me the *Chronicle* piece quoting an FBI spokesperson who said that Braxton's testimony was "unauthorized in substance."

"Who knew where they were staying, other than the three of them, you, and Car?" Jeanie set her laptop aside.

"Just Braxton. Last night, when I couldn't reach them, I called him, and he revealed he had a man watching the condo in case Sims tried anything. I asked him to have the agent check on them. He was the other one, along with Car, who ended up taking a bullet."

"So Braxton knew. And somehow Sims found out where they were."

Her point was all the more forceful for being unsaid. Again my thoughts circled the theory I'd argued to the jury, that Sims, not Edwards, had been the informant Braxton had been protecting all these years. But certainly Braxton wouldn't have sacrificed my family, nor would he have sent his own agent to be gunned down. Even if he hadn't intended the outcome, however, it was plausible he'd deliberately used them as bait to lure Sims, just as he'd implied last night.

"We could talk to his superiors," Jeanie suggested. "From the quote in this article, it sounds as if Justice isn't happy about his testimony in your trial. He blindsided them. Clearly, he's comfortable bending the rules. If you raise a stink, you could possibly get him taken off the case."

I considered this for a brief moment before shaking my head. "He knows the AB better than anyone else. I know it looks bad, but I can't believe he'd sacrifice my family to protect Sims on something like this. We've just to got to wait for his call."

When a call did come, however, it was not from Braxton, but from Judge Ransom's clerk. "We have a verdict," she said.

For a long moment, my mind couldn't attach this word to its context. I'd been expecting Braxton's voice, and I'd anticipated instructions that would bring us closer, one way or another, to answers about my family's fate. The trial had become an afterthought. I was even irritated by this demand on my attention.

Jeanie and I gathered our things and walked briskly to the courthouse.

"What's going on?" Alice Ward whispered when the deputies brought me out. "I heard Sims has your family—"

She didn't get a chance to finish.

"All rise," a deputy called as Judge Ransom took the bench.

"All right, let's bring the jury in," he said, clearly impatient to be finished with this ordeal of a trial, and, more pertinently, to be relieved of his responsibility for these jurors who'd been sequestered because of the threats of a dangerous man. A man who, it now seemed, was all too willing to carry out such threats.

My client was renewing her whispered plea for information, but I shushed her, prodding her to rise. The deputy was bringing the jurors out. Tired-looking, the twelve filed into the box, several glancing somberly at my client as they mounted the steps.

Despite the consuming urgency of events outside the courtroom, my heart had started to speed up with a familiar rush of adrenaline, the world telescoping as time slowed down in anticipation of a verdict.

The forewoman, a pharmacist—a profession I normally associated with hostility toward the defense—passed the verdict form to the bailiff, who in his turn presented it to the judge.

Ransom glanced at the form and handed it to the bailiff to read. "We, the jury, find Alice Ward not guilty," the bailiff intoned.

I waited for him to go on, assuming this was just the verdict on the first-degree murder charge. I figured that in a moment we'd hear that she'd been found guilty of manslaughter, an outcome I'd have chalked up as a win, the best possible result I'd predicted coming into the case. However, the bailiff now handed the verdict form to the clerk and returned to his desk. In a shocked voice, Sloane asked for the jury to be polled, and each of the jurors echoed the verdict the bailiff had read. *Not guilty. Not guilty.*

Not . . .

The judge was now speaking to the jurors, thanking them for their service. But I couldn't track the words, hearing instead the rush of blood in my ears. Beside me, Alice Ward had taken my wrist and was holding on as if to keep herself from floating away.

Sims must have gotten to one of them, I thought. But, in that event, the jury would only have hung, prevented by the lone hold-out from reaching a guilty verdict. It simply wasn't possible for even the most powerful gang leader to engineer an outright acquittal. There's no way he could have managed to threaten all twelve. Yet each juror had just confirmed the unanimous vote.

The outcome of the trial was unreal, inexplicable.

The jurors began filing out of the courtroom. I turned to Alice and numbly shook her hand, thinking of something Teddy'd once told me, a quote probably stolen from some other lawyer: that to win a murder case a lawyer needed only to prove that the victim deserved it and the defendant had been the one for the job. The jurors must have concluded that in taking out a member of the Aryan Brotherhood, Alice Ward had performed a public service. If so, it was the first and only instance of jury nullification that I'd ever seen.

Sloane was staring with open shock at the jurors as they walked out. None would meet her eyes. They knew they'd flouted the law, but one of their number must have been smart enough to explain to the others that they'd get away with it, that no judge could undo a "not guilty" verdict.

As soon as the courtroom doors had closed, Judge Ransom was on his feet, walking out of the courtroom to his chambers, unbuttoning his robe as he went, as if he couldn't wait to leave this fiasco behind. Sloane stepped graciously across the aisle and shook my hand, but her eyes were cold, filled with suspicion, disappointment, and self-doubt.

"You hoodwinked me," she said. "You and that FBI agent."

My phone buzzed in my pocket. "Excuse me," I said, my heart beginning to race all over again.

Jeanie had come forward from the gallery to stand with Alice Ward, nodding at me. I stepped past her toward the rear of the courtroom. Then, as the doors swung open, I caught a glimpse of the throng waiting in the hallway outside.

Reversing, I stepped through the well of the courtroom, answering the call as I went into the recently vacated jury room, waving a hand at the bailiff. It was Braxton. "I talked to Sims. He contacted me directly. I'm back in San Francisco, and I'm on my way to the courtroom. I'll be in there in fifteen minutes. In the meantime, you've got to keep Alice from leaving. I have an order pending from a federal judge authorizing her detention as a material witness in Edwards's murder."

Shit. This meant Alice Ward's legal troubles weren't over. She could be prosecuted again in federal court under the RICO statute if Braxton decided he wanted her. "When did you talk to Sims?"

"Just a minute ago. He called me on my cell."

That Sims would have known Braxton's cell phone numbers set off alarms. "He already knew about the verdict?"

I stepped to the door of the jury room and looked out, scanning the faces remaining in the gallery. If Sims had a man here, he was indistinguishable from the usual courtroom hangers-on. Or he'd left as soon as the verdict was announced. I could see Alice and Jeanie talking at the counsel table, Jeanie's arm now around the girl's shoulders.

"Sims wants to talk," Braxton said. "He's playing games, trying to work the situation to his advantage. That's a promising sign. Means we're dealing with a calculating man—not a desperate one."

I ducked back inside the jury room. "Surely he doesn't think he can walk away from this."

"Come on, Leo. Where's the seat of power for the AB?"

The answer was obvious once I thought of it. "You're telling me that Sims actually *wants* to return to prison."

"The man who would be king has to live in the castle. From the moment someone stuck that shank in Wilder's back, Sims knew that he was going inside. The question is, how does he give himself up without losing face with his 'brothers'?"

Again I had the answer. "By going on a rampage and taking my family hostage."

"I already said, I'm confident he won't hurt them while he still thinks he has a shot at being top dog," Braxton said. "He'll never be accepted as a bona fide leader if he breaks that cardinal rule. That's not to say they aren't in danger. Because, as things stand now, he's apparently used a woman—a Brotherhood member's daughter, no less—to kill a fellow member. Under the code of the AB, such a man doesn't deserve to live, let alone run the show. We've got to find a way to fix that."

"The case is done. The verdict's rendered. It's over, Braxton."

"But your client hasn't told her story." He paused. "Five minutes."

The call went dead. I lowered the phone. I was shaking all over. I couldn't do this, couldn't offer up my client—a child herself—as a sacrifice to save my family, to save Carly. The very idea of it was beyond the pale.

And yet.

I came back out and found Jeanie disputing with Sloane. Alice was still sitting at the counsel table, a deputy looming beside her. "She *can* be released. She was tried as an adult and she was acquitted," Jeanie was saying.

"But she's still a juvenile," Sloane explained with an edge in her voice. "She walked away from her foster placement, and she killed a man."

"She's been acquitted," Jeanie said. "It would amount to double jeopardy to bring that up again in juvenile court."

"But she's been declared a dependent of the juvenile court. That means she remains in custody. She'll have a hearing there to determine whether she'll be returned to foster care or placed in a more secure institution."

Jeanie glanced at me, seeming to expect me to take over. But I remained silent.

Even if Braxton hadn't been on his way here, what was Alice Ward going to do, I asked myself—try to survive on her own on the streets of San Francisco, an AB target on her back? The failure was mine, I realized. I should've had a plan in place, a shelter bed ready to accept her. But I myself had made the mistake of assuming she'd be found guilty of something.

"I want out of here," Alice said. "They can't keep me. I was acquitted." Her voice sounded uncertain, however, as if she knew better.

"You have an order to show me?" I asked.

"We're getting it," Sloane said. "The dependency court judge is at lunch. We're trying to find her. It shouldn't be long."

She'd been caught off guard, so expectant of a guilty verdict that, like me, she hadn't made a plan for what would happen if the jury went the other way. Her insistence on detaining Alice made my conflicted role somewhat easier, freeing me from the disloyal act of keeping Alice in the courtroom until Braxton showed up.

He arrived before the family court judge's order did. His encounter with the sheriff's deputies was brief and to the point. "She's being taken into federal custody under the federal material witness statute," he said, showing identification. "We've got an order on the way from the federal district court."

The order from the federal judge came through on the fax machine. Judge Ransom, whose jurisdiction over the matter had ended with the verdict, still hadn't reappeared in the courtroom. His clerk handed the fax to the deputies, and Braxton showed it to me and then to my client. He explained to her that she had a right to challenge her detention before a federal judge. Now, however, he was hoping to speak with her in the presence of her lawyer.

She glanced at me, then nodded, and we went into the jury room.

When the five of us were sitting around the table, Braxton began by explaining the situation to Alice, who listened without expression. Then he turned to me with an assertion that, to me, sounded delusional, given all that had happened: "My view is that Sims is only pretending to be motivated by revenge in kidnapping your family. In reality, I think his reasons are more calculating. He needs a pretext for arrest. Then, once he's behind bars, he intends to consolidate his power and assume control over the AB. Murdering your private investigator and terrorizing your family can give him the credibility he'll need to do that—as long as he doesn't go too far."

My hostility surprised even me. "There's no standing down from what he's done. There's no 'too far' for him. A bullet's the only deal the government should be thinking of making."

"Put your desire for revenge aside. Would you rather we have a months-long struggle between factions—with innocent bodies falling between them, daily riots in most of California's prisons—until this power struggle sorts itself out?"

"But you're talking about giving him what he wants."

"As far as cementing his control, he's on his own. Wilder's dead. That leaves a power vacuum. And prison's always been the primary seat of power for the Aryan Brotherhood. A cell, for these guys, is the equivalent of a throne. If the death penalty and solitary confinement are off the table, Sims'll come around. Trust me. I know these men. I've been after them all my career. At the end of the day, I can convince him to make the only play that allows him to seize the crown—and keep it."

I didn't want to hand Sims what he wanted, a perch from which to rule the AB from behind bars. I wanted him dead. Or at least that's what I'd have wanted last week, before he'd grabbed my family. *Don't you ever think about revenge?* Alice had asked me. Right now, however, I'd take just having Teddy, Tamara, and Carly home safe.

However, I didn't believe Sims would give up his freedom as easily as Braxton, with all the arrogance of *his* power, seemed to suppose.

"What's the FBI getting in return?"

Again Braxton's silence seemed to confirm that he was on the verge of making a deal with the devil. Assuming, that is, that Sims hadn't already been in the Bureau's pocket for years.

Still, we had to hear him out. I was aware that this negotiation was, at present, the only concrete possibility on the table for bringing my family home. "What exactly are you requesting of Alice?" I asked Braxton.

"Sims needs to save face. The only person who can help him do that is your client. My proposal is that she fires you, and that her new lawyer issues a statement making clear that in her view, Sims had nothing to do with Edwards's killing."

"And if she does this, he'll let my family go? Come on, Braxton. He'd be able to run the AB much more effectively from the outside. That was Wilder's problem. What could you possibly offer Sims that he doesn't already have?"

"You'd be surprised." His tone was level. "Maybe you shouldn't be, though. Didn't you just accuse me in court of protecting the target I was sworn to destroy? It's always possible you were more right than you know."

I held his gaze, seeing now that he hadn't forgiven me for those attacks, even though we'd been working together to serve his purposes. "You're saying that the only way to save my family is for the government to allow Sims to consolidate his power over the AB. With your agreement to do that, he'll consent to being sent to prison. Once he's there, the FBI may even help cement his control. Do I have that right?"

"We've covered up murders before; you pointed that out quite ably during the trial. So, from Sims's perspective, since he's gotten away with murder at least twice before, it's not unimaginable that there might be a way out for him from this mess now."

Again I wondered if this was the result intended all along, if Braxton had secretly been backing Sims from the beginning. If so, then it appeared his ambition was not to destroy the AB, but rather to contain it by placing his informant, someone whom he believed he could control, at the top of its hierarchy.

The idea, to me, was abhorrent.

He continued: "Remember, Sims craves the same power Wilder held. Looking at it from his perspective, who better than the FBI to give him the support he needs to control a huge criminal organization?"

I knew better than to ask again how the FBI hoped to benefit from such a deal. It wasn't lost on me that Braxton's short-lived tactic of sowing chaos had given way with surprising ease to a lesser-of-evils philosophy. By backing Sims, he might purchase order behind bars and peace in the outside world.

I decided that I didn't care anymore about the game Braxton might be playing, where his loyalties lay, or whether he was honest or corrupt. I just wanted him to save my family and protect Alice, and this was the point I pressed now. "If Alice fires me, who's the lawyer that takes over?"

"Unclear. Presumably Sims has someone in mind. Because your defense raised the possibility of RICO liability, we'll have a plausible basis to keep her in custody as a material witness. The new lawyer's assurances that Sims had nothing to do with Edwards's killing will not only be consistent with a defense against federal charges, but also appease those within the AB who may be tempted to believe Sims was involved. Meanwhile, Alice will remain in protective detention. Eventually, we'll announce that we're declining to prosecute, and we'll assist her in transitioning to an independent life."

Alice was skeptical. I didn't blame her. I didn't trust Braxton, either, and I sure as hell didn't trust Sims. But, like me, she seemed to recognize that we had no choice but to accept the plan Braxton had offered. "I don't want him to get a deal, to go on running the AB behind bars. I want him locked up in solitary, or on death row. Or dead. But what I want even more is for that little girl not to get hurt. So, okay. I'm in."

This wasn't how this meeting was supposed to go. I was supposed to be Alice's lawyer, which should have meant preventing her from being used by the government for purposes that could be of no benefit to her, now that she'd been acquitted and there was no credible threat of further prosecution.

Instead, I was sitting by, more or less silently, while she offered, perhaps, to sacrifice herself. "Let's just consider for a moment that he's manipulating us all," I said. "That he has no intention of letting my family go. That, instead, he'll find a way to blame their deaths on the FBI."

I'd expected this to provoke further overconfidence from Braxton, but his tone, instead, turned somber. "You're right. That's why we'll need to take extraordinary precautions. He's supposed to contact me in the morning with the meeting place for the handover, somewhere here in the Bay Area. My agents will be in position, but out of sight, ready to close in if anything goes wrong."

"Alice isn't doing this unless I'm allowed to be present at the exchange."

Braxton held up his hands. "Fine. As far as I'm concerned, Maxwell, it can't hurt to have Sims's attention focused on you. Remember, I'm only doing what I'm doing because the lives of your family members are at stake. I promise you I'll do my best to get them home."

CHAPTER 25

I hereby discharge Leo Maxwell from representing me. . . .

The termination letter, written by me on a sheet of legal paper, was folded in the breast pocket of my suit. With the stroke of my client's signature at the bottom, I'd been kicked off the case I'd won barely half an hour before.

As Jeanie and I walked out of the jury room, leaving Alice in Braxton's custody, I had no doubt that she'd obey my parting advice not to speak to the FBI agent without a lawyer present, but all bets were off as soon as her new lawyer appeared. Jack Sims now had his first wish granted: He'd succeeded in replacing me with a lawyer who, presumably, could be counted on to do his bidding. Clearly, this development served Braxton's purposes as well.

As we emerged, a balding, barrel-shaped man in a shiny suit and thick-framed glasses was just walking into the courtroom. Art Jewel introduced himself as Alice's new lawyer. I'd seen him around, a night-school JD scraping out a tenuous living handling indigent appointments in cases where the public defender had a conflict of interest and whatever personal injury work fell into his lap. His congratulations on my trial win were tempered with condescension. No doubt he believed his fortunes had taken a promising turn.

I didn't disillusion him. Instead, Jeanie and I grabbed my file boxes and got out of there to await Braxton's call.

"Golden Gate Fields," Braxton told me when he phoned at 10 A.M. the next day, after I'd had another sleepless night. "Not the facility itself, but the turnaround at the end of Buchanan Street, past the entrance to the general parking lot. Smart choice for a high-risk meet."

I understood what he meant. Just to the north, Interstates 580 and 80 split, heading to Marin and Sacramento, respectively. To the south were the sprawl of Oakland, the tunnel to Orinda, and the Bay Bridge. Within ten minutes, a driver could easily vanish into this spaghetti tangle of freeways. And with a steady stream of vehicles arriving along the access road for the afternoon racing at the track, Sims could be certain no law enforcement officer would dare risk a long-range shot.

He filled me in on the rest of the details. It didn't take long.

"So how's this going to happen?" Jeanie, who'd driven over before dawn after spending the night at her place, asked when I got off the phone. "We just show up, he hands over your family, and they arrest him?"

"According to Braxton, Sims wouldn't confirm anything, except to promise that he'll be there, and that he intends to give himself up."

"I don't believe it," she said. "I'm coming with you."

I hadn't expected otherwise. Still, I made a vain attempt to talk her out of it.

We met in the IKEA parking lot and rode from there to the meeting place in the back of Braxton's unmarked Tahoe SUV. The complex was tucked next to the freeway on landfill. Along the water were narrow public beaches and a former landfill, the Albany Bulb.

He'd bragged of having a chopper standing by, ready to maintain constant visual contact with Sims's vehicle after the meet. He also promised that he had agents stationed in the parking lot and on the beach. We had no easy way of spotting Sims among the cars exiting the freeway, gradually filling the huge lot that lay between the track and us. We, on the other hand, were sitting ducks in one of about a dozen parked cars at the turnaround.

"He's coming," Braxton announced. "On the other side of the fence."

We'd been watching the entrance road. Now we swiveled as one in the direction of the Bay. Behind a chain-link gate was a large flat lot the size of several football fields, separated from the beach by low mounds of sand. A path skirted the gate, allowing just enough room for a person to squeeze by, but not enough for a car. Trailing a cloud of dust, a brown Bronco was approaching fast.

We stepped out of our vehicle as the Bronco pulled up on the other side of the gate, swerving broadside to the fence to be poised for a quick departure. Sims yelled through the window over the noise of the engine. "Keep your men back! The car's packed with C4. If I see anyone within a hundred yards, I'll blow it!"

My ears were ringing, desperation surging through me like a narcotic. The need to do something was overwhelming. With a strangled cry, I surged forward, stumbling against the fence between us, straining for a glimpse of the car. Clearly, though, my family wasn't there. Jeanie's hand gripped my arm.

"Come on," Braxton told him. "There's no need for that. Where are they?"

Sims's gun was pointed through the window toward me. "Send Maxwell over to me. We need to have some private words. If you do as I ask, he'll be with his family within the hour. If not, he'll never see them again."

"You were supposed to have them here!" Braxton said.

It was impossible to tell whether his surprise was genuine or this sequence of events was prearranged, a piece of theater put on by two schemers.

Sims's eyes shifted to the FBI agent, but the gun didn't move. "Did I mention the C4? Half's here with me. The other half's with them. I've got it wired to a detonator and one of those cheap cell phones. It's set to blow on a sixty-minute timer, running now. If the phone rings before then, the countdown stops. But of course, I can start it ticking again with a second call.

"When I'm free and clear, and I'm sure you're keeping the promises you're about to make, I'll call the number and then send you their location. If I don't get clear, it'll be pretty fucking obvious where they are. Hell, you might even be able to see the blast from here."

"That's *not* what we agreed," Braxton shouted.

"Too bad," Sims said. "You'll still get what you were promised. But I changed my mind. Maybe I don't feel like doing the time after all."

"If you think I'm handing you another hostage, you're crazy. Maxwell stays with me."

"You don't have the leeway to negotiate this one, Agent Braxton. Maxwell needs to do exactly as I say."

Braxton glanced at me. I nodded, and then, without further hesitation, slid through the gap in the fence. Sims leaned over and pushed open the passenger door, and I climbed in beside him, every muscle in my body pumped with blood.

Before the door had finished closing, the throttle roared and the tires spun, spitting gravel. Sims, leaning out the driver's window as he drove, fired six quick shots at Braxton's SUV. Though his aim was wild, at least three bullets struck home with metallic thunks. Then the Bronco was rocketing away, trailing a cloud of dust as we sped across the empty lot, with me struggling to keep from being thrown out the door.

"Now we go down together," Sims yelled. "Or you and I can make a deal."

I braced myself against the dashboard and looked back. In the dusty rear window I saw the Tahoe accelerate toward the gate, one tire flat. The two halves of the gate flew open with the collision, Braxton coming in pursuit.

The promised chopper, however, was nowhere in sight.

Sims floored the accelerator, opening the distance between us and our pursuers, a trio of SUVs now spread out across the dusty lot behind us as we raced toward the grandstands.

"How can I trust you when you just blew off the deal you made with Braxton?"

"That deal's still in place. Don't kid yourself—we're surrounded. No way we're busting out of here." He seemed surprisingly relaxed, driving at sixty miles per hour over rough terrain. He glanced at me. "You didn't think we were getting away, did you?"

"You've got to disarm the bomb."

"I'm a man of my word. Once I'm in custody, I'll make the call. But if the FBI gets trigger-happy, fucks it up . . ." He shrugged. "But that's not what you and I need to be talking about."

I waited. For a moment, steering required all of Sims's attention. He swerved recklessly through the parking area at the main entrance, causing two cars to collide while people ran for cover in his wake. Laying on the horn, he had no choice but to slow. He swerved around a line of parked cars.

"My first thought when I grabbed your family was that you fucked me over, so they deserved to get wasted. Then when I calmed down, though, I started to see that you did what was asked. Not in the spirit of obedience, maybe, but you actually got her off a murder charge. That deserves respect."

"If you think I can do the same for you, you're wrong. You're going back to prison."

"Sure. Surrendering was Braxton's idea, but it suits me. Don't get me wrong, it needs to be a little more dramatic than Braxton wants. But despite what I said back there about not wanting to do the time, I'm no idiot. We all know this ends with me on the inside, calling the shots."

"Alice is going to do what you want. She already fired me. As we speak, the new lawyer's issuing a statement that the shooting had nothing to do with the AB. She'll swear you were nowhere near the scene. We did our part."

"The *first* part. You want to see your family again, you also have to understand that you'll be working for me. I've got to hear you say these words. 'I belong to Jack Sims and the Aryan Brotherhood.' That'll be your oath. You can never take it back."

I felt cold. Angry tears welled in my eyes. "I don't belong to anyone. I never did."

"You belonged to Bo. Bo's dead. I killed him. That means you're *my* boy now."

Clear now of the entrance and the parking lot, he continued from the roundabout at the front entrance of the racetrack at a mad speed onto Gilman Street, then followed the curve of the Bay, where a low breakwater was the only barrier between the pavement and the waves.

The road was bordered inland by a fence, with parked vehicles lined up on both shoulders. In the distance ahead, I saw two police cars with their lights flashing pull into position across the road.

"Why would you ever expect me to work for you after what you've done to my family?"

"You even hear what I'm saying? Haven't you been paying attention? Braxton needs me. He understands that. A power vacuum's no good for anyone. Until order's restored, blood will continue to be shed. He's always been a realist. I can offer him the same deal he had with Bo. He's agreed to my conditions, so I'm giving myself up, going back in to fill the empty chair. In return for certain ... benefits. I thought you were supposed to be a smart guy. I can't believe you don't see your part in the arrangement."

"So you're going to be his mole at the top of the organization."

"Or he'll be mine. I've got to get to the top first. Can't do that out here. Once I'm inside, I'll need Braxton's assistance. He understands that. And he also understands that for me to solidify my position, I'm going to need a man with a clean sheet who'll do what I tell him on the outside. What I'm saying is you won't have to worry about the FBI.

"It'll be different from how it was before. I'll leave your brother out of it. Don't need him. You'll be making more money than you've ever made in your life, enough to rent yourself an office in one of those Embarcadero towers. Hell, I'll send you plenty of legit clients. You and your family will be well paid for the inconvenience you've been through."

The words and the offer they conveyed seemed to pain him in the delivery, but I guessed he was putting his bitter feelings aside for the higher cause of business.

My mouth was dry. "You call the deaths of my father and his wife an 'inconvenience'?"

"I call any man an inconvenience when he stands in my way."

"And if I say no?"

It seemed, for a moment, that Sims intended to ram the police cars. Then he braked, swerved, and accelerated into an opening that suddenly appeared on the left. The Bronco clipped a pair of vehicles, knocking them akimbo as it smashed through the valet line. Thrown against the door, I grabbed my seat belt and fastened it. Sims, securely strapped in behind the driver's seat, sped through this gap toward an opening in the perimeter fence, not swerving for the attendant, who leaped out of the way.

"If you say no," he continued, "then I surrender today without making a call, and a bomb goes off. I can probably live that down—it'll be on the feds. Then, in a few months, after this trouble fades, one of my guys will pay you a little visit. By then you'll probably know just what you want to write in your suicide note."

Row after row of low-roofed stables stretched behind the fence just ahead. Sims held the Bronco into a skidding turn through what must have been an employee parking lot, and, next, coming out of it, careened through a roundabout beneath the track's official observation tower. Nearly rolling the vehicle again, he then wrenched the Bronco around this outpost into a 180-degree turn, a groom diving out of the way as another man shook a rake at Sims. Then he accelerated the Bronco into the stables proper.

"On the other hand, once you agree, your family becomes my family. I guarantee the harassment will stop. You'll be under my protection. Keep in mind that they'll know nothing. Not even your brother. As far as he and his wife and their little girl are concerned, you'll be out."

Between the stables, in a concrete space about as wide as a two-lane road, were a series of pedestals with tie-outs dangling from crossbars, allowing the horses freedom to walk in a circle while their keepers tended to them. Two horses were tied in this fashion directly in the Bronco's path.

"Got to have a little fender bender now," Sims said. "A little something for my boys to talk about, during those long nights after lights-out. Because no one respects a man who just *gives* himself up."

I glanced over.

He was still talking. "How much you think that horse is worth? This is your last chance. Say the words."

"I belong . . ." I began. But the words didn't come. I knew that the lives of my family depended on my accepting the fate Sims offered, but I couldn't bring myself to do it.

Sims didn't brake, didn't slow. The first horse reared as he accelerated past it, a groom racing out to seize its bridle.

Sims's gun was on the other side of him, wedged under his left ass cheek. My hand flew down and pressed the button to unbuckle his seat belt just in the instant before he struck the second horse across the midsection at forty miles per hour.

The vehicle skidded, plowing sideways into the stable. Dust rose from the half-collapsed structure. Sims, his seat belt off, was launched through the windshield, though not so forcefully as to eject him entirely from the car, perhaps because he was thrown against the horse, which had fallen kicking onto the hood.

The horse slid to the ground amid the wreckage, writhing as three men ran up to it. Sims was trapped in the windshield, his head twisted around at a strange angle, looking back at me through the shattered glass.

Behind us, the Tahoe pulled up, followed closely by the other vehicles. Still stunned by the impact, I touched my arms, my face. No blood, but I felt dazed, and my ribs hurt. I realized I was holding my breath, dreading the explosion Sims had threatened.

I stepped from the Bronco and walked around to Sims. He was conscious, a look of dawning panic in his eyes. "I can't move my legs," he said. "Can't feel them." Then, with sudden heat: "Bring the gun. . . . Do it."

I realized what he wanted. An executioner's bullet.

"Where's the phone?" I asked him.

At my feet, the horse lay on its side, pink foam oozing from its nostrils, its chest heaving.

"My pocket." His breath came in strangled gasps. "Please. Hurry."

But Braxton was already there, stepping in front of me, keeping his gun trained on Sims, foreclosing any possibility of the mercy Sims had begged for. He bent and quickly frisked him, coming up with a flip phone. No detonator.

He tossed the phone to me. "Check the call history," he said.

The phone was unlocked. I was able to view the call log, which listed three outgoing calls, all to the same number this morning. The first two calls were to test the switch, I guessed, the third to activate the timer after the bomb was armed. According to what Sims had told us earlier, another call would disarm it.

"Where are they?" Braxton asked Sims. "Teddy and Tamara and Carly. Tell me now."

Several grooms had come out from the stable, looking on with horror at the fallen horse, Sims still lodged in the windshield, the FBI agent close to him.

"Just wait and you'll find out," Sims said, his voice low enough to draw me closer than I wanted to be to that piece of human wreckage. My thoughts of revenge were gone now. All I saw was a pathetic, destroyed man. "Or dial the number, see what happens. Maybe calling the number doesn't stop the countdown. Could be it triggers the explosion." His voice was hoarse. "One way to find out."

Braxton stepped away as a California Highway Patrol cruiser and an ambulance rolled up. He held out his hand to take the phone from me and spoke the number into the radio. Behind him, the paramedics began examining Sims, talking to him in calm voices as they worked to immobilize his spine and extricate him from the windshield. Meanwhile, one of them was testing Sims's extremities for sensation. "Looks like a cervical injury," the paramedic said.

A white-coated man arrived and, in anguish, began to examine the horse.

Braxton had Sims's flip phone in his hand. "We have a StingRay unit in the chopper. We can use that to trace the phone he called."

I knew what a StingRay was from my criminal defense work. It was a surveillance tool commonly used by law enforcement that functioned by mimicking cell phone towers and forcing all cell phones in the area to connect to it, providing real-time tracking.

"The bird's setting down on the infield in two minutes if you want to ride along."

As we rode out onto the racetrack in the Tahoe, I heard the thump-thump of rotor blades and saw the chopper descending.

The grandstands were filled with spectators, many of whom would have had at least a partial view of the scene that had just unfolded in the stable area.

Bending low beneath the wash, we ran to the copter. I found an empty seat and strapped myself in. An agent was in the copilot's seat with a tablet computer on his knees. As soon as we were aboard, the chopper seemed to leap into the air, leaving my stomach and the rest of my internal organs down below.

Braxton handed me a headset. Putting it on, I immersed myself in operational cross-talk. Braxton had the cell phone in his hand, his sleeve pulled up above his watch. "It's been twenty minutes since the first call," he said. "He wasn't lying about the explosives in the car: Just as he said, the Bronco was packed with C4. There's no telling when he started the clock, or even if he's telling the truth about a sixty-minute countdown, but we have to take his threat seriously. If we don't pick up a signal within fifteen minutes, I'm going to ring the number."

The chopper wheeled in wider and wider circles, pitching precipitously toward the ground, my stomach plunging with each turn as familiar landmarks whirled past in dizzying succession: Sather Tower at UC-Berkeley; Oakland's Mormon temple, looking like a spacecraft readied for takeoff. The agent in the copilot's seat shook his head, not bothering to voice the obvious.

The swooping loops of the helicopter brought on waves of nausea that seemed to block my breath. My eyes were only on the man in the copilot's seat. The pilot soon abandoned his spirals outward from the track and flew northward, the engines roaring as the helicopter raced toward the Richmond-San Rafael bridge. We carved a wide inland turn and raced south again to Hayward, where, for the first time, the copilot reacted with attention and focus to the screen in his lap, signaling the direction the pilot must turn in.

We spiraled lower and lower, the pilot refining his course as the man with the StingRay directed him, while squad cars, lights flashing, raced to meet us, turning broadside to block vehicle traffic as the helicopter settled to a landing in the middle of a dirt-bordered street in the Hayward Flat. The copilot pointed out a once-pink bungalow.

Braxton donned a vest one of the officers offered him, and ordered the cops on the scene to cuff me and lock me in the back of a squad car if that's what it took to keep me from following him. Then he disappeared through the weeds at the side of the house. A few seconds later the front door opened and Tamara appeared, my brother limping beside her. Braxton carried Carly, then set her down to run forward into my arms.

Learning the details of their plight would have to wait. Promising that I'd be with them shortly, I walked the perimeter of the crime scene until I found myself face-to-face with Braxton. Seeing me, he ducked under the tape and grabbed my arm, leading me down the residential street, away from the flashing lights and the onlookers.

He seemed to be waiting for me to thank him. "You were going to sell me out," I said instead.

Braxton met the accusation with indifference. "Sims has got his life sentence. It's a shame, in a way. But the truth is, he wouldn't have lasted long at the top. He doesn't have the brains that Wilder had—or the survival instinct."

"He told me the arrangement you made with him. You offered me up."

Again Braxton didn't deny it. "He was going to kill you," he countered. "And your family, too. All I did was convince him it was in his best interest to give that plan a second thought. Because of me, your family's still alive." He paused before going on. "And, anyway, he was going to need the help."

"How can you call what you do law enforcement?"

Braxton stopped walking, turned to face me. His eyes were emotionless. "In a few months, the dust is going to settle. A lot of bodies are going to fall between now and then. Eventually, a new leader of the AB will emerge. At that point, you can expect a visit from the new leader's lieutenant. I expect you to notify me as soon as that occurs."

I stared back at him. This man had used me and my family. He'd used up my father and then he'd focused on Teddy and Tamara, turning them into bait for a trap that didn't spring in Anaheim. Now he'd set his sights on me.

Braxton held my gaze. "Don't you want to finish the work your father started?"

"There's no finish," I said. "You've just proved that. The old faces merely get replaced by new ones. It's a revolving cast. You accepted long ago that you can't stop them, can't deter them, can't punish them, so you've merely adopted their tactics in an effort to contain them. It's a game, and I'm not playing it."

"I'm not playing either."

I suddenly saw him for what he was: not a man, or, rather, not merely one. Rather, he was an instrument capable of channeling the immense power of the federal government, the thumb of a giant that could press down and crush a man at will.

"Don't forget. As long as you're a free man, the AB owns you." He paused, holding my gaze. "And that means I own you. Because the alternative, believe me, is federal indictments for you and Teddy. You've spent your career helping men on the wrong side of the law. For once in your life, do the right thing."

"Do you even know what that is?"

Braxton ignored my question. "They're going to come after you, regardless of what you and I decide." His voice was utterly calm and completely certain. "They'll give you the same choice I've given you, in essence, except their consequences will be more sudden than mine, and far more permanent. When push comes to shove, you'll realize that whoever takes over for Bo will expect to inherit your services, just the way Sims expected to. The only freedom for a man in your situation's the kind I'm offering."

I took a step away from him, shading my eyes against the suddenly bright sunlight piercing the trees. I needed to be at Kaiser Permanente, the hospital where my family was being taken, to hold Carly's hand and hear my brother's account of their ordeal, help them begin the long process of healing from this trauma. But the certainty in Braxton's voice froze me.

Hard experience over the previous three years told me he was right. They *would* come.

I thought of the box of ashes still sitting in my office. Maybe Lawrence hadn't felt any braver than I did. Maybe he spent all those years as a CI as frightened as I felt now, not primarily for himself but for those he loved and couldn't protect.

My voice shook. "What do you mean, freedom? What 'freedom'?"

"The freedom to fight back," Braxton said. "That's the only one that matters. For your sake, I hope they leave you alone. But if they don't . . . call me. Don't make me come for you."

Our business for now concluded, Braxton walked back toward the house where my brother's family had been held.

I watched until he turned the corner. Then I went the other way, striding blindly down an unknown road.

ACKNOWLEDGMENTS

Thank you to everyone who made this book possible. The list begins with my wife, Sarah Moody; and our parents, whose love and support make writing possible. Leo Maxwell wouldn't exist without my agent, Gail Hochman; my publisher, Otto Penzler; and my editor, Michele Slung. I'm grateful to everyone else who worked on this book, including Allison Malecha, Sal Destro, Julia Berner-Tobin, Tom Cherwin, Gretchen Mergenthaler, Carlos Beltrán, and Deb Seager. Last but not least, thank you to my readers.

april — 5x

April